OVERHEARD CONVERSATION

By

To, Peter

John Reynolds

J R REYNOLDS

 New Generation Publishing

CHAPTER 1

Tom Brannon heard a raised voice from the stall behind him, waking him from his reverie as the words were spoken with venomous intent: 'I have told you if you so much as breath a word to anyone'—a few seconds elapsed before— 'I am warning you. You say anything and you will pay big time...'   A moment of silence followed before the person in the stall behind continued to speak again. 'Do that and I will finish it and that is a promise. Your life as you know it will end.'

The threat from the words spoken from behind him. Turned Tom's attention and could not help but eavesdropped on the conversation overheard. No response heard by Tom to the threat's, just a prolonged silence between threats emitted. Fathomed the recipient talking was either on a mobile phone or the person with him unable to respond. Assuming the former, as nobody could be silent to this level of threats emitted. Unable to turn about to see the person who uttered the threatened words, the high back of the stalls inhibiting his view. As the language and voice of intent worsened. His curiosity piqued, the need to find out the identity of the man in the stall. More to the amount of threats emitted as the man's intense words progressively worsened. Tom had no wish to reveal himself and was aided with the stalls enclosed seclusion to each stall. Unable to turn around and peek over in revealing his interest. The mirror behind the bar was also unhelpful in aiding him from where he sat with other drinkers obscuring any view. Quelling the natural curiosity in his attempts to find out further he settled back down as a period of silence ensued.

With the silence that followed, Tom calmed, held his reactions within to say anything untoward. Tom Brannon now had become disquiet to the silence, found solace in the extended silence. Began flipping a cardboard drink's coaster up off the side of the table before him. This helped redirect his thoughts from the comments he had overheard. Attempting to flip and catch the coaster in one smooth executed movement before it could land back on the table. Executing the process in one flowing movement. Successful on all but one of ten attempts tried. He moved to search out for Terri Chapman in the bar area. She had been gone for forty, forty-five minutes. Still there was no sign of her, he noted the Wetherspoon Pub filling up as he gazed around in search. Facing forward again, his mind drifted off as if in deep thought. Absently, staring at the half pint of lager left in his pint glass. Tom gripped hold of the glass with his hands absentmindedly, as if protecting the contents. A look of determination etched upon his face that said nobody would take the drink away. Tom sat waiting, his thoughts returned to the verbal rant of conversation he heard twenty minutes earlier.

Terri Chapman, appeared from nowhere moments later. Breaking into Tom's train of thoughts as she sat down across from him. Adding another freshly drawn pint of lager in front of him.

She settled down with her own drink placed on the table. 'Did you want a small chaser, a wee dram to go with that pint?' she asked as she sat down. Terri noted the serious look on Tom's face when no reply was offered in response.

Ignoring the silent response, 'So, what has you gripping your glass, in fear of someone stealing it from you?' Terri added. Terri Chapman, once married, but divorced when only thirty-seven. She changed her marital name back to her maiden name when her divorce papers came through. Taking on the managerial post at the Wetherspoon branch in Cricklewood High Street. Manager for the past six and a half years, a role she had held jointly at another branch before in South London prior to her divorce. Terri took the night off from behind the bar. To emphasise the fact, Terri herself was drinking vodka and tonic chaser with a pint of lager.

'I was unaware that I was giving off that impression. I was thinking,' Tom replied.

'What were you thinking about? You know thinking is regarded as a dangerous habit, could lead you into untold trouble if acted upon,' Terri mused.

A puzzled expression formed on Tom's face as he smiled at the comment then brushed the comment away, consigning it to the back of his mind. Instead, he ventured to enquire whether Terri had noticed anyone sitting in the booth behind him.

'No, nobody is or was sitting there. Why?' she queried.

Tom elaborated on what he remembered from the rant that he had overheard from the stall behind, of someone speaking possibly on a mobile phone. Terri sat quietly listening and at the end could offer only one piece of friendly advice. 'Don't get involved. It's probably something of nothing, a marital tiff, someone just sounding off, a drinker baiting for an argument from the recipient on the other end of the call, trouble making. You know the score when someone drinks too much and is upset over nothing but that could be only acting on trivia.'

Hoping Tom would heed her advice. Knew Tom well enough to know taking advice was not one of Tom's fortes. Terri resumed the evening trying to turn Tom's attention away from his thoughts. Redirecting them to the night ahead.

Tom's mind could not except Terri's simple response to his questionable thoughts, but knew when to stop. Closed his mind off for the sake of Terri. Making a mental note to enquire as to whom the person had been on the following day, as Terri suspected he would. Further, he feared for the recipient of the words spoken, as they came not as a friend, but more of a meaningful threat and a warning to the receiver. He could not accept Terri's advice, to ignore what he had heard, but said nothing, remaining silent.

At the end of the night, he left Terri to close the pub. Leaving, Tom decided he would follow up his own line of enquires in the morning. No clue as to where he would begin. However, when he arrived home, he found a note on his doormat telling him he had an interview early next day at 10.00am.

Waking up early, he made his way to Cricklewood Underground Station, travelling by tube into London, alighting at Charing Cross and strode down The Strand towards the Aldwych. He had not forgotten his wish to follow up on the previous night's drama, but for now, he needed to put his enquiries to the back of his mind for later.

On the same morning. Dan Prescott with Samantha were at Chessington World of Adventure. Experiencing a fun filled day. Gripping the padded restraint bar, which held him and Samantha Tambling his cousin securely in the car on the roller coaster, as it began to take the strain. Moments later reaching the utmost pinnacle of the ride, the car hovered only for a split second suspended in space, a nanosecond later continuing forward from the summit by sheer propulsion, the car plummeted down with Dan and Sam still held tight within. Speeding down at a rate of knots, the downward propulsion going into a loop de-loop, followed seconds later after several turns before slowing down and gradually to the rides conclusion, the end. Heralding screams of derision throughout the ride from other fellow riders, the excitement, euphoria and elation of the moment. Beside him, Samantha had screamed incessantly from the moment the car came down from the highest point and throughout the remaining ride. Sam shouted above the noise, stating she felt her heart beating at a fast rate of knots. Especially from the moment they came down from the highest point; the excitement and adrenaline matched the ride. Relief came over her on leaving the roller coaster behind at journey's end as her heartbeat slowly dropped. To the now calm expression held on her face, devoid of tension, laughter returning to brightening her personal outlook.

Dan's own heartbeat slowed to normality, as his own excitement came back down to earth. At forty-two, he wondered whether his heart could take all the excitement. Dan placed his arm around Sam's shoulders as they left the roller coaster behind and moved on towards the next ride already mapped out on the schedule, pointing to the signpost showing the Waterworks Factory ahead. He asked Sam as they left the roller coaster behind, 'How was that? For me, it just felt great and a pure adrenaline rush to boot.'

Without much cajoling, she said, 'You bet. Dan, I'm so glad you encouraged me to come along today, I've not had so much fun like this in a while,' Sam enthused. 'No chance of having something to eat now, is there, as I am famished.'

'Yeah, why not, could eat a whole side of beef myself,' Dan said as he guided Samantha, his cousin, six years younger than him. Turning away from the next intended ride, to the eating area. 'What would you like to eat Sam? Would you like some fast food, or would you rather go for a meal and grab a drink from the onsite pub?'

Samantha could not believe her luck. Dan was going out of his way to be kind and supportive of her. She had been depressed for a while, her breakup with Harry, her ex, had knocked her for six. Dan, her cousin, had been there for her in trying to mend her fragile esteem. Dan, not known for his compassionate side had become her rock and guiding hand ever since her parents died four years previously. Her parents were killed in a car accident involving three cars.

They both sat down at a table nearest the window. They ordered a fish and chip fare. Whilst Samantha, drank Coca-Cola. Dan had settled for a Bitter Shandy, having stated his intension to drive home. But, wishing it was a Real Ale bitter to drink during the meal. A silence fell between them, whilst the food traversed from the plate and mouth. Both plates were consumed and cleared within an hour.

Throughout the rest of the day on resuming their travel around the theme park, at one time taking in seeing the variety of animals and birds kept, Dan ensured Sam's happiness was paramount. Her infectious laughter as they went around the park meant he had succeeded in his endeavours. Having spent all day at the theme park, both headed for the exit having submitted to a fun-filled day.

Dan's mobile vibrating in his pocket interrupted his and Sam's walk back to the car. 'Hi, yes,' a silence ensued before Dan responded, 'we both, had a great day Terri,' He stopped walking, showing concern on his face with a frown. 'What's up, you sound agitated?' Dan asked, knowing from the way Terri was speaking, something was wrong. His suspicions confirmed as he let her carry on talking without interruption.

'Okay, calm down, look I am at Chessington Theme Park with Samantha. I'm going to take Sam home, then I can be over with you as soon the traffic permits. Yes, I will meet you at the pub,' Dan said as he closed the mobile up.

Dan looked up at Samantha with a wry grin on his face. 'Sorry to spoil your day, Sam. Appears Terri wants me to go over and see her. You okay if I take a rain check on that evening out we planned and I take you home and just leave?'

'Not really, but then do I have a choice. Still, I can't complain as I've had a great day,' said Samantha. 'What's Terri's problem anyway, that she cannot do without your help?'

Dan trying not to involve Samantha in Terri's problems said, 'I am not sure really. She seems agitated about something. Terri never does come straight out with her troubles, always skirts around them, but makes you feel obliged to help when asked. Besides, she does not normally ask me for help, so it must be important to involve me.'

Samantha shrugged her shoulders, knowing when Dan was not telling her the entire truth. Knew, even now Dan had held back on some unspoken words. Not wishing to involve Sam in any problems that may come from her ex's family issues. Samantha just let out a sigh, accepting Dan's not so convincing answer. The journey home was quiet throughout. Both deep in thought, Samantha in wishing Dan, would trust her more and be more forthcoming about his business affairs since he returned from America. She knew her ex- sister-in-law Terri, through her marriage to ex-husband Harry. Dan in turn was thinking on Terri's call. Not having the full story, threw up all manner of unanswered thoughts and connotations of the unknown in his mind to her problem.

Closing the car door, Samantha walked up the garden path to her front door, turned the key and entered without looking back once. Closing the door, shutting out Worlds problems.

Knowing Samantha would be okay, he, noted the time was quite early in the evening at 5.00pm, as he sped off towards Terri's home. She lived in Cricklewood, North London above a pub. If she were not in the bookmakers sorting out her predicted gambles for the day's racing, she was to be drowning her sorrows. Luck and fortune played a big part in her gambling as she won more than she lost on a bet. Other punters knew that Terri was never good or forthcoming in giving out tips or advice on gambling, as they would normally lose on the bet more likely than not, against the odds. As Terri Chapman managed the Wetherspoon Pub in Cricklewood High Street, nobody would question her. A simple life was what she strived for, but on occasion, her world could turn upside down. Dan knew Terri would never ask for his help, fact is this was the first time of asking. She always managed to sort her own problems out, even if she had to turn to using the muscle and aggression of her brothers George and Harry Tambling at times.

The drive to Cricklewood from Coulsdon became a drawn-out game of waiting in traffic due to the evening rush hour. As gas road works and traffic lights frequently turned to red held up his progress from the Northern End of the motorway down to Cricklewood. Eventually arriving at 7.30pm.

Entering the Wetherspoon pub, Dan took stock of his surroundings. It had been a while since he had last visited. Noting the pub had changed in its interior design, from his last appearance. More space provided for the diner, along the bar the usual array of pumps, of lager and bitters, more real ale for the so-called connoisseurs.

Terri ushered Dan through to the back of the pub and upstairs to her flat above. 'Thanks for coming at such short notice, Dan. I would not ask for your help if I did not need your expertise. Your experience in the army and security is what I am in need. I know you've been away abroad and only recently returned and hoped that your homecoming was for my benefit in the realm of wishful thinking, but felt I had no one else to turn to. How is Sam these days?' she asked. The way she said it, like a throwaway line, thrown into the mix.

'Sam is okay, she is fine.' he answered: ignoring his thoughts to the comment. Dan sat down with a pensive look; he knew he could not turn his back on Terri, so sat back in the armchair and waited for Terri to explain herself. She stood by a bookshelf, all manner of books sat on the shelves, more for show than for reading. Dan had never seen Terri read or even hold a book. Observing her casual wear, in denim jeans that hugged her slight figure and an off-white top with an emblazoned motive of Wetherspoons Pub imprinted on the back. He nodded to Terri acknowledging that he was ready to listen, to whatever caused her to call for help.

'Not sure where to start... an old friend of mine has gone and got herself into a right old state and ruffled a few feathers in the process with a group of villains in South London. I know what you are going to say the villains of yesteryear have long gone. The likes of the Kray Twins and the other family south of the river, the Richardson's, part of a bygone era. Splinter groups have erupted from these vacated troubled areas to form and create more problems over the lean years as minor crooks grow and prosper and fill the void. My friend's name is Penny, Penny Connor; she lives in Croydon with a flatmate who by my reckoning is not completely right in the head, a right dipstick. No sense of what goes on in her own backyard.'

'So where is this leading to, with your problem needing my services?' Dan enquired.

'If you give me a chance, I'll explain everything in a moment. It's not easy talking about someone you know and could be in trouble and does not even know it.'

'I take it this friend is the person in trouble,' Dan pushed further.

Terri looked up, 'No, it's not Penny.' Having second thoughts on whether to involve Dan in Harry's problem. Being family, felt wrong to impose Dan with a family member's error of judgement, more so when the person now sitting in front of her, had thrown her brother Harry out. Dismissing her misgivings, swayed by her friendship to Dan and not wishing to upset what relationship she had had. As she looked at Dan sitting opposite expectantly waiting for her to speak, any question of regrets she felt, dispelled with the first words she uttered.

'You just earlier, intermated Penny was the one in trouble.' Dan corrected.

'Yeah, okay it is Penny. Dan, I am not sure whether I should tell you what I am about to reveal. They concern Harry.' She commenced, stopping to allow Dan to react. When nothing was forthcoming, she continued. 'I've never come between Harry and Samantha, I'm not in any way condoning what Harry did to Sam, you know me, I hate all violence unless it's warranted. Especially when it comes to hitting women, for that there is no excuse, whatever the provocation. In Harry's defence, he has been under a lot of pressure in the last six, nine, maybe twelve months.'

'Terri, what are you talking about?' Dan had just left Sam before coming on to Terri's home. 'Harry has already gone, left two, three months ago, never seen since, from what Sam has said. Is he up to something?' he asked. Samantha's relationship with partner Harry Tambling duly suffered at the time this happened and only survived until recently, due to outside interests. Ultimately with Harry developing a drink problem over the six months prior to the split, through stress in which he became progressively violent towards Sam, unbeknown to Dan who had been working abroad until recently. On Dan's return from time spent in America, he caught Harry by chance when visiting Sam, inflicting a stream of volatile abuse at her before lashing out with a fist to her face. To which Dan reacted by aiming and connecting a fist at Harry's jaw, snapping his head back, a consequence from the punch. Harry collapsed to the floor from the blow, unconsciousness followed. When he came too, Dan physically picked him up, dragged, frogmarched and ejected Harry out through the front door informing him to go and never to return. Harry never did return, but Sam has held a fear that he would and pass vengeance on her ever since.

Harry Tambling, who at thirty-nine, was the landlord to a public house near Croydon, The Waddon. For several years, not known to Sam, he was at times involved in certain criminal activities whilst using the pub as a legitimate business, as cover to the criminal element. Over the years, his name had become synonymous and held high within the Croydon community for his contribution to charity causes. To his community his illegal activities were unknown and shielded by his own men surrounded him and whom followed him avidly without question. His reputation intact as he never knowingly involved himself in his capers or illegal activities first hand, he remained in the background, only involving himself in the preparations and organising of schemes and plans. Dan who knew of Harry's dealings, kept his cousin in the dark to this end.

'No! At least I don't think so,' Terri responded

'Then why are you bringing Harry's name into this problem,' he continued.

Terri paused: 'I was with another friend, name of Tom Brannon, last night we met up for a meal here in the Wetherspoon Pub. He overheard a phone conversation from another person sitting in the booth behind him and asked me whether I saw who was sitting there. He said it sounded like a man, that he was threatening to harm someone on the other end of his call. I told him that I had not seen anyone on my return from the lady's room.' Terri stopped talking as if reflecting or not knowing what to say next.

Dan saw the hesitancy and said, 'Well if nobody was there, why are you now hesitating, acting as if you have something to hide.'

'Because, I did see someone as I returned from the bar, the person was coming directly towards me as I was going back to my seat, I acknowledged him when we were passing each other. He was heading for the front entrance and I was heading back to my friend Tom. When Tom asked me, who may have been sitting in the next stall behind him and then stated what he had heard. I told him to say nothing and stay out of the problem,' said Terri, as if in a rush to get something off her chest.

'So, you saw this person; was he coming from this particular stall in question?'

'Dan, what I am trying to say – although not very well I may add – is that this person in the stall was Harry? Harry Tambling, my brother and your Sam's ex.' Terri stopped herself saying any more.

'You saw your brother and no words of acknowledgement or communication said between you both,' Dan asked shocked.

11

'He just said, "Hi, Sis, cannot stop, I am in a rush. Catch you later sometime soon," and then left,' Terri answered. 'I did not even know he was there at all. Never saw him arrive at the pub.'

Terri's face implied that Harry maybe about to harm to someone. Dan knew that someone could not be Sam, as he had been with her almost constantly since he virtually threw him out. 'So why did you not speak the truth to Tom Brannon.'

'Because I did not exactly see Harry coming out from the stall. I only saw him coming from that direction, heading towards the exit,' explained Terri.

'So why do you feel Harry capable of another wrong. He would have learnt from harming Sam,' said Dan. Dan knew himself what Harry was capable of doing, having known what crimes Harry had committed in the past. Knew before, he could hold his temper at bay, but now knew when his temper fired up, he would blow a gasket when riled now.

'So, go to the police, let them deal with it. Harry is not my or cousin Sam's problem anymore, and for the record I know more about Harry and that his pub is just a cover for his other rackets of dubious activity around South London. However, much he tries to keep this in the background.'

'Harry may not be your concern anymore, but I saw him earlier, miles away from his own neck of the woods. He never ventures far from his manor in Croydon unless I call for his help. He is up to something. I don't think he was here in Cricklewood for his health.'

Dan saw that Terri was working herself into a state, while trying to control her temper from flaring up. He had known Terri for as long as he could remember; when he spent most of his time in Soho while on leave from the army. Through his visits to the Marquee Club, off Piccadilly, a place where he had seen several bands play. He met Terri, befriended her, staying overnight on occasion when she lived in central London. Kept in touch with Terri, whenever he returned from working abroad, even though no permanent romance became of their relationship, Dan required and wanted no complications while serving in the forces. He had his independence and she hers, no questions asked.

'Look I will make some enquiries with the contacts I have, but I cannot promise anything, other than that I will do what I can to help.'

The relief on Terri's face as he spoke could be a positive reaction that transmitted into silent spoken words of 'thank you'. From Terri as her face softened. 'I knew you would help if asked, you're a good friend, Dan.' she said, as she embraced him around his neck, placing a peck on the cheek.

'Have you no clue as to why he was in your pub last night,' he asked.

'Nothing, too say why he was there. Just nodded, said a few words of greeting and left through the exit without another word,' she answered,

About to get up he stopped to ask: 'Is there a chance that Tom Brannon and I could meet up and repeat to me what was said in regard to the conversational transit of words he heard. Could be a clue in what was actually said, but if you would rather him left out of your affairs, I will need to follow and direct myself down another avenue of thoughts.'

Not wishing to allow any contact without her being there, Terri replied with reservation. 'After telling him not to get involved, I would hope that he could be left out of my brother's problems, but if you insist, I'd like to speak to him first before you do and explain. Okay.'

Not the reply he expected her to say. Dan said he would like to hear what Tom heard from his own mouth. He allowed Terri's wish to speak to Tom first and made no objection, so reluctantly agreed.

Suspecting that Terri was just looking out for her brother and her friendship with Tom Brannon on the back burner, for the sake of her brother's problem.

CHAPTER 2

Dan agreed to help Terri. He stayed seated in front of the bar, whilst Terri began to usher the last of her customers in the pub out. Shouting, they all had homes to go to. The bell for time rung, ten minutes earlier by one of her bar staff. Washing the glasses, cleaning the bar tops and tables from the day and night's work. Terri finally allowed the working bar staff on that night to leave through the front door, locking up again when the final member of staff left.

Sitting down together across the bar, Dan and Terri caught up with all the gossip from events in recent years. Recalled the time when they first met up in London's Piccadilly. Appraising the fun times, they had between his tours of duty within the army. Time within the army had taken its toll on Dan's sense of fairness. Before joining the army, Dan was more and more going of the rails, trouble followed him around like a plague. Drink often angry at trivial comments made. His only piece of luck was drugs never played a part in his life. The army he knew was the only place where the aggression would be channelled to good use. The experiences whilst on duty changed his view on life. Of politicians, due to the hypocrisies of politicians on defence policy. Many a time Dan had pondered what would happen if the roles could be changed around. With the politicians fighting on the frontline instead of the ordinary soldiers. Would the inadequate provision of weapons, the blinkered views to wars they create themselves in the name of peace would ever change? He concluded they would be just as bad as they were governing the country.

Dan had through the army become tolerant of his opponent's troubles, but conceded that if they did not actively go in as peacemakers, then the devastation and harm to innocent human lives in those countries would have been carnage on a massive scale.

Inviting Dan up to her flat, Dan proceeded to follow Terri upstairs to her rooms above the pub and continued where they had left off, drinking several more cans of lager together with a few measures of Scotch Whiskey, losing count of how many. Assuming all the cans strewn across the wooden flooring and the odd couple that remained on the coffee table to his left were the total drank between them. They both drank enough.

Dan woke up next morning. Declining Terri's invitation to follow her to bed, claiming that as he was too drunk to raise a token response, he would not wish to start something he could not finish.

The following morning, his back ached and his neck stiff from sleeping on the only sofa available to sleep on. A cold draft had whistled through an open window, left open during the night while he slept courtesy of Terri allowing fresh air to circulate. Dan went to the loo, as he was passing Terri's bedroom on the way back, the temptation took over to look in on Terri. She lay flat out on the bed, not leaving much for the imagination. Fast asleep and no bedding covering her, he went over and covered her with a quilt, when she rolled over under the cover deep in sleep. Leaving Terri to sleep on undisturbed, Dan returned to the sitting room. The state he was in, he felt his head about to explode and joining Terri with his neck. Was never an option.

His head left him in no mood to count the empty lager cans strewn about the floor. Just excepted he had had more than enough, not been a heavy drinker since his army days, his head reminding him of how it felt to have someone hammering away with no redress. No chance in recovering instantly. Could not move his head without wincing at the discomfort, Dan tried to turn his head to bring some movement in the stiffness to his neck, despite the pain and discomfort. When he heard, someone walk in through the lounge door, turning his head around and making a pained grimace as he recognised Terri on entrance. Could have sworn she was fast asleep and little chance of awakening.

Next thing Dan heard was Terri walking into the sitting room, 'Heard you come into the bedroom earlier. You cannot walk around quietly, made more noise than a herd of elephants.'

Dan would swear Terri had drunk as much as he, how can she be so cheerful looking and not suffer any ill effects. Her hands held between them a tray on which when placed down on the coffee table, revealed a fried breakfast. Looking up he saw Terri grinning back at him, 'You were asleep when I came in earlier. Thought you would like a good hearty breakfast inside you. Might help with that hangover,' she said as she walked away, turned and backed up to the door. A backward look, as she heard Dan murmur a response before her exit.

Dan stared, knew the last thing on his mind was a big fried breakfast. He accepted the black coffee given on Terri's return from the kitchen. 'Never thought I would get back to sleep again.' He stared down at the breakfast. 'Thanks, not sure I can face the fry up. Feel like death warmed up right now, with my head, neck and my back pulling out all the stops to remind me of where I slept.'

Terri pictured in her mind what could come next, 'Well don't throw up on the carpet; the bathroom is along the corridor or you can clean it out when you've finished.' The statement said, without humour or sympathy.

'I will just make do with this coffee and maybe another after thanks,' Dan said. Changing the subject he asked: 'Where do I find this Tom Brannon, if not in the pub?'

'I will let you know when I've spoken to him as agreed, I owe him that,' she responded.

'Would it not be better if I came with you and sat in the background, while you have your say, then you could introduce me.'

'No. Think it would be better if you were not there,' she said.

'Is there something going on between you two, or is there something else you're not telling me,' he said. Dan, felt he was missing some information, as if a secret to which he was not privy.

'No, not in the way you're surmising. Tom Brannon is a friend I have known only in recent years, his marriage had broken up, not long before I met him. Why his marriage broke down, he has never said. Although we are friends, I do not know enough about him to let him into any problems I may have.'

'What do you know about him?'

'Only that he divorced his wife four, five years back. Has said he has a son and one daughter from his marriage, he rarely sees either. They must both be in their twenties now and old enough to have moved out, or could still be living with their mother. He does not speak much about them, only that they favoured their mother more as he spent a lot of time away from home, was a workaholic or so he reckons. Never said what his line of work was, I have never pried.'

Again, Dan reluctantly agreed to wait on Terri, knowing friendship can at times hinder progress in aiding a friend. Recovering enough to know he could pursue along another line of investigation, he made his farewells leaving Terri's home. His head still throbbing despite taking Paracetamol pills to help with the headache. Hanging back for another hour drinking more coffee before setting off back to Croydon. Hoping the roads would be clearer on the drive back to his pad. Not wishing to meet anyone, wanting only the sanctuary of his home.

Friday lunchtime, unlike any other weekday lunchtime was never a good time to travel through London, even allowing for the short cuts he knew along the way, Dan found the drive back, with the hold ups mainly caused again by on-going gas and other roadwork repairs. Slowing down his progress further, were the amount of buses and volume of cars driving in from out of town and daring to think it would still be quicker than driving around on the M25 with the main Airport traffic connections at Heathrow. Traffic lights on route were another problem. Apart from passing through a green light allowing him to drive across Hammersmith Bridge, all were red. Dan never did like driving through London, but he knew not to suffer from road rage that falls prey on some motorists, just to stay calm and focus on the drive. Treat all other drivers as complete idiots who feel that they are the only drivers with access to the road.

Three hours later, arriving at Sam's home in Coulsdon, collecting a few items of clothes at his home in Purley along the way. His head now not pounding as he pulled up outside, he noticed Sam's car still parked there. *She never said she intended to take time off work today*, he thought.

As he alighted from his car and stood there, Dan looked at the bay windows top and bottom and noticed the curtains still drawn closed. He took his mobile out from his jacket pocket and rang Samantha before entering the front gate. No one answered at first, tempted to enter should something have happened. Something Dan always refrained from doing as he could always see a time when he may walk in on Sam in a compromising position, though unlikely in her current medical condition. Sam answered, pushing away Dan's line of thought. Asking whom it was, when hearing Dan's voice, she acknowledged his presence by telling him to use the key. He entered the front door. Samantha shouted down the stairs that she would be down shortly telling Dan also to switch the kettle on.

He turned his head towards her as she entered the kitchen. 'What's with the curtains still being drawn together?'

She looked to him, a frown on her face before replying that she had been up most of the night, unable to sleep. 'It happens when someone does not return home or does not inform one they will be late,' she said.

Dan shook his head side to side, 'Being your cousin does not mean you need to wait up for me. I would have stayed at my own place if I thought it would keep you up too late. You know that.'

With agreeing to help Terri and only the day before spent time with Sam, several hours had passed between their time together at the Theme Park. Seemed a long time ago now. Sam had taken a step back in her anxiety attacks. He dropped the subject saying, 'Look I'm back now, so until I give Shirley Henson, a good friend of mine a ring and see whether she can call in and stay a while, maybe a couple of nights. You sit on the sofa in the front room and drink the tea while I open up the curtains, get some sunlight into the place.'

Returning, he brought his own tea in and sat down. How to let Sam know he would be helping Terri for the next few days and would be out most of the time. His thoughts on the words to say, too open up and reveal that Harry her ex-partner, is the reason for his non-appearance at times. Dan just opened up without knowing how Sam would respond, feeling he had to explain him disappearing at times.

Content as she looked, a pained expression of depression enveloped her that grew inside her, raising the anxiety she had to another level. Twelve hours ago, Samantha was a completely different person. Someone more confident with life and the life ahead, with positive vibes abound and her self-esteem back in full. Concern found a way of reaching Dan as he tried to fathom why such a transformation should have occurred to the woman now sitting before him, from the carefree person that had emerged twenty-four hours earlier. How and why had this happened? A question he asked himself repeatedly subconsciously to himself. Inwardly he knew the answer, knowing he was at fault in revealing his immediate plans.

'Look I did intend to stay here, but why don't you stay over at my place where maybe a change of scenery will help.'

Sam agreed. Dan collected a few items of clothing from Sam's bedroom, packed a case and both then left for his home.

Shirley Henson answered, picked up the phone on the first ring. 'Hello, Shirley speaking.'

'Shirley, just the person I needed to speak to. How are you fixed to babysit for a few days?' Dan asked before she could say anything else.

'Oh! Thanks, Dan. Thanks for that. No, how are you or sorry I have not spoken to you for a while. Just fire away and expect me to drop everything at a whim. Now that you find you're in need of a baby sitter.'

Dan expected the humorous response to his call, ignoring the wisecrack he carried on and said. 'I've been busy, love. Caring for my cousin since her ex left.'

Shirley ignored the reason behind Dan's absence. 'Thought I was your girlfriend and do not say love to me. Makes the word sound irrelevant. Ever heard of the phone before now, could at least ring and let me know you are okay now and then. Or am I just the flavour of the month for a bit on the side, as and when you feel like calling or want something.'

Ignoring the rant, he continued, 'Shirley, you are all heart. That is why I love you so much and yes, maybe I do take advantage at times, but I need a favour. Will you help or not?'

Quietened down she enquired, 'What kind or favour?'

'Can you spend some time with my cousin Samantha at my pad, I have a little business to attend to, need a friend to help out, whilst I'm out and about. Sam seems to have had a relapse to an on-going problem I thought she had recovered from.'

'Must be some problem if she is that bad; what is wrong with her, you never have told me?' she asked.

'I'll tell you when I see you. Can you help me out for a few days, yeah or nay?' he answered, with a question,

'Seeing as you asked and I bare no grudge for long. How can I refuse; you are lucky I have nothing else to do at this moment? When do you want me to come over?'

'Now if you can,' he replied, 'and thanks, I'll owe you.'

No response came at first, then, she said, 'I'm on my way.' The mobile link going dead seconds later.

Placing the mobile on the worktop in the kitchen beside the doorway entrance, Dan went back into the front room. Sam had snuggled herself up on the sofa and lay there asleep. She lay there peacefully, which in Dan's mind he was thankful, thinking it maybe the best for her. He now had to find some answers to Terri's problem and find a way of speaking to Tom Brannon should Terri draw a blank.

A knock at the door meant that Shirley had arrived. A familiar female voice calling his name out confirmed his thought was correct. Dan opened the door and ushered her in to the front room where Samantha still lay asleep.

'Does she know I'm coming to stay a while?' she asked,

'Yes, I said that I would ask you over. She has been asleep ever since I rang you to help out,' Dan answered.

'Making up for last night's lack of sleep no doubt,' said Shirley adding: 'poor love,' when no remark was said to reflect her comment.

'I'm going to be out for the rest of the day, have a job of work that cannot wait or be put off. Fill you in when I find out more on what I need to know, and thanks Shirley,' Dan said putting his jacket on as he headed for the front door.

Shirley shouted out as Dan went through the door, 'Where can I contact you if your needed and what do you want me to say to your cousin when she wakes up.'

'You'll think of something. I'll phone you later,' Dan said.

Shirley need not worry about the when Sam woke up, as Sam stirred when the front door slammed behind Dan as he left. Took one look at Shirley and frowned, 'Who are you. How come you're here and where is Dan?'

'He has just left; he asked me to keep you company,' Shirley answered.

'Always in a rush these days, suppose he is running around after that Terri,' Sam said as she rose off the settee. 'Should have woken me up and told me you were coming around. I would have been better prepared to receive you. Besides, why does he feel I need company, something happened?'

'Apparently, he did tell you. Just said to keep you company while he is out there working, said he had to go somewhere and you needed the company, you seem fine to me though.'

CHAPTER 3

Dan came away from meeting old army friends. Walking out through the Warner Brothers Complex, Dan continued into the Back Road behind Burger King. The Back road often used as a shortcut was not the most appealing to walk through at night, had on occasion been occupied by one or two gipsy caravans until moved on by the police holding Council Eviction Papers. The clearance of rubbish dumped, cleared only when the Local Council felt the need to clean up its act. Refuge waste bins set to one side of the road halfway down, a token gesture to the amount of rubbish strewn across the road. Heading back towards the commercial trading estate and arriving beside the P C World Megastore and continued walking along the main road and onwards up Purley Way passed the five-ways intersection lights.

Awakening from unconsciousness. Not knowing how long she had been out. It was dark and late at night. She tried to force herself upright into a sitting position, but felt a sharp pain from a wound in her side. She relapsed into unconsciousness for a further ten minutes. On wakening focused her attentions on her surroundings. She found herself lying between two industrial waste bins. Vaguely noted the signs giving her reason to believe her whereabouts to be near a hotel. She was on her own, alone, nobody in sight. Silence broken intermittently by the traffic passing by, a car or truck racing passed at regular intervals.

As she felt around the wound she murmured aloud to herself, 'Where am I, the bastard has gone and left me for dead no doubt.' She felt cold and frightened that he could still be close by. That her assailant would come back and complete the job, ending her life. Could not remember who the attacker had been. No clue given as her assailant attacked from behind, but guessed at one name. Accepting she must have passed out. Coming too, she was in agony. Trying to sit up only made the pain worsen from the wound in her side, her hands went in search and found a sticky substance, dark in colour; she could not make out what, due to the lighting not filtering behind the large refuge bins. Logic told her it was blood, her blood. Her hands, clothing and tarmac surface around herself, now congealed. Hidden towards the rear of a Hotel, judging the building exterior, obscured from view by the two waste bins. What she took to be an alley was also access to a main road, allowing only one car to pass by in either direction. The pain eased, thinking that the wound and blood loss not as bad as she first thought. Made a slight movement to ease the discomfort she felt. Produced a sharp stab of pain. Reality of her deluded state of mind, brought about by her blood seeping again from the wound, her own fear added to by tracing another wound in her stomach.

Thoughts of dying brought back the fear she was trying to suppress. With nobody around and not knowing if anybody would come. Panicked by fear and angered by her predicament. Pain from the wounds heightening her anxiety all over again, she did not want to die, not now. Attempted to cry out, came more a whimper than a cry for help, escaped from her mouth. From the pain and blood loss, made worse for the attempt to call out. She felt faint, slumping down again for her trouble, slipping back into unconsciousness.

Without money for cabs and unfit to drive he walked home. Dan Prescott was laughing to himself, remembering a joke or two said that night, as he reached the traffic lights at the Lexus Car Showrooms in Purley Way. He was still heading towards his home, in Purley. Dan passed the Aerodrome Hotel and the parking area at the forefront and side. He glanced and noticed something move, a body lying between two large refuge containers. Dan knew someone was in trouble and from the appearance of a dress or skirt was female. Unsure whether she was alive, Dan called out, 'Hello, are you okay?'

No response came. Approaching closer, he saw first the pool of blood on the ground around the body, then looking up to the top half of the body. Found he was staring at a loosely dressed woman. Not sure, if she was dead or alive, hidden in the shadow of the refuge bins. Found a pulse on checking. Dan's mobile gave no signal, needed to go on charge. The mobile completely dead he ran into the hotel calling for help in the foyer. Telling the receptionist to call emergency services for ambulance and police. That he had found a body of a woman laying between the bins, just alive.

The police arrived first as a patrol car pulled up shortly after Dan's emergency call request for an ambulance. The officers on patrol duty assessed the situation and called in for backup. Another police car turned up within minutes, followed by an ambulance ten minutes later, the ambulance's progress hindered, held up by a commotion outside a local nightclub entrance with drinkers strewn across the pavement and onto the road. The hotel became a hive of activity to the commotion Dan had stirred up. Dan had to explain how and why he was in the vicinity repeatedly. 'I was walking past the Hotel coming up from the Warner complex, he heard someone whimper, coming from the industrial bins to the side here. Investigating came upon the woman. The Aerodrome Hotel floodlights around the property barely giving the parking area enough light, only sufficiently enough to see someone laying there in between refuge bins, to the rear of the hotel. Thought the person may have been sleeping off a bad night, but the hotel close by, rejected that idea. Came up closer to the body, seeing the blood, knew something amiss and more serious had happened and called emergencies, as I feared the worse. I noticed she was female by her dress and long hair and the chest's physical appearance. Found a pulse and then her taking in a short breath of air, only then knew she was still alive, barely. Then I raised the alarm.'

When prompted, he continued, 'spoke to the constable when the first police car showed up as I came back outside the hotel.' This he repeated three times, to three separate police officers. The flashing blue lights and sirens coming in around the back of the hotel produced a crowd at the scene, mostly people staying at the hotel, as Detective Inspector Tony Mattock arrived to find the scene cordoned off with blue tape and traffic directed to move on, driving onwards and not to stop. Before he went any further Mattock phoned in to state that he was passing and had pulled up to the scene along with DI Helen Smith, then hanging up he said, 'So what do we have here, Helen?' he said speaking to his fellow officer as he closed in on the crime scene, ignoring the crowd assembled, taking in the scene and the wounded victim.

Knowing that Mattock would have gone to speak with the person who had found the woman, to access the crime scene before he confided with Inspector Helen Smith, who questioned the constable to know what had happened on his arrival. As DI Mattock came up to her, she relayed what had happened 'Sir, we have a female, with stab wounds to her stomach and side, two wounds that we know of. There was no form of identity found on the woman. The person who found her, a Dan Prescott who you have already spoken too. He was first on the scene, walking past on his way through to his home in Purley. Came from the Warner Complex intending to walk back up Purley Way too Purley and home. Claiming he had no money to use transport. When seeing, a body lying in the bin area to the hotel. Heard a noise and found this woman slumped between these two refuge bins, pointing them out either side. When seeing the blood, informed reception, who called for emergency services. The paramedics are with the woman now, but they will tell us more about her injuries before they take her of to A & E. From the amount of blood, she is lucky to be alive.'

Mattock listening, took in the crime scene area. Confirming what he had heard from the main witness 'How did she come to be here, does she work around here or been meeting someone,' he asked

'No, Sir. Appears someone had brought her here and dumped her body between the bins assumed the victim dead or spooked before completing the job,' Detective Inspector Smith replied.

One of the paramedics came up and said that they were ready to take the woman to the nearest available hospital at St Georges, Tooting.

'How is she?' asked Mattock.

'Two nasty wounds, sedated for now. You'll know more when you check in with the hospital once they have accessed the extent of her injuries,' the paramedic said.

'Just another day at the office for you guys?' Mattock said in a way of conversation.

'Not always, some lives tragically end before we can reach them. This time we were lucky,' the paramedic remarked as he walked away.

Mattock pulled Helen to one side. 'Have someone follow the ambulance and keep me informed to her condition and ask when it's likely we can talk to the woman.'

'Yes, Sir.'

DI Helen Smith turned to go and relay the instruction when she felt Mattock touch her elbow. She looked back. 'Helen, we also need to find out her name and why she ended up here. With no ID on her, ask around here, the hotel reception, could possibly be staying here, find out if anyone knew her or recognise her from the photos taken.'

'What photographs, Sir?'

'The pictures that photographer over there is taking, if he is the press. The press knowing of this crime, on the scene already probably means someone tipped them off. If he is not then why has he been allowed to come onto the crime scene and take the pictures, either way I am sure he would rather help the police with them enquires. Would appear, almost perverted with intent if he does not.' Helen followed Mattock's finger pointing at someone on the perimeter of the crime scene taking close-up pictures of the victim.

Sergeant Price walked up to Mattock. 'I have organised a thorough search of the area for the missing knife or weapon used in the attack.

'Well done, Sergeant, at least someone is using their head. Inform me if you find anything,' Mattock said on leaving the scene behind.

CHAPTER 4

DI Helen Smith relieved the police officer who had spent the early hours, sitting outside the hospital room. Helen waited for what seemed an eternity, waiting to speak to the woman stabbed that night. Established the patient had been in a deep unconscious state all the time since admitted until thirty minutes prior to Helen's arrival.

Doctor Petra Nordic commenced her rounds of patients under her charge, shortly after Helen arrived. Notified that a woman who came in during the small hours of the night, had regain consciousness ten minutes into her round. By the time, she entered the private side room, given her condition on arrival, the woman was stable, still weak from the amount of blood loss, but with a drip attached to her lower forearm, showed an improvement. DI Smith pressed Doctor Nordic to when she could speak to the patient. The doctor shook her head at Helen insistent attitude, took umbrage and told Helen the woman needed rest and to give her some time to recover, to come back later that day, she could have five minutes then, but not to put the patient under any undue pressure. Although the patient barely awakes, she was not out of the woods yet. Helen asked whether the patient had given her name yet. The doctor said the name of her patient given was Penny Connor and lived locally.

Helen informed Mattock by mobile to the news that of the victim in stabbing that night was now awake, not sufficiently enough to be able to talk to her.

Later that day, Helen entered the side room and introducing herself, walking up beside the bed showing her police ID, to back-up her statement. Asked her to confirm her name and whether she was up to speaking to her about that nights stabbing, asking whether she knew the person who had stabbed her or give a description of her assailant.

At first, she was reluctant to speak, but encouraged by Detective Inspector Smith to the fact that she would arrange to protect her from any other attempt made by leaving a police officer outside her door, on her providing some information. Confirmed her name as Penny Connor and lived in Waddon across from the park, in a flat in Ford Close, behind the main Duppas Hill Road leading up to the flyover leading onto the Fairfield's Hall roundabout.

Penny Connor could not name her assailant as she was grabbed from behind and bundled into a waiting van, a rug thrown over her as she entered the van and hands tied behind her back, lack of light prevented her from seeing anything then. She passed out, next thing she knew, she was waking up between two big bins, with stab wounds. She tried to raise herself, but the pain that came from the knife wounds that had pierced some stomach muscle and hurt so much she passed out again. Woke up, found herself lying in a hospital ward bed.

'Do you know anybody who would do this to you, who wanted to harm you?'

Penny started to fade could not respond to any further questioning said, 'Can you leave please, I can't answer any more questions, I am too tired.'

The doctor, along with a nurse also in the room while the questioning went on came over to Helen stating she should leave to allow the patient to rest. She tried to ask one further question, but, under Dr Nordic persistence, 'Detective Inspector Smith, will you kindly leave, you can continue with the questioning, at a more convenient time, when the patient is more able to answer. The patient at present needs her rest.'

Chief Superintendent Fred Homer sat in his office when Mattock came in. 'Ah! Detective Inspector Mattock, please come in. You are dealing with the stabbing case from last night, any news. The hotel has been complaining about the bad publicity that will follow on from the incident.'

'Not much, Sir, we are still following up with enquires. DI Helen Smith is at the hospital as we speak. We have established the name of the woman as a Penny Connor, who lives on her own locally in Waddon. So far, all we have to go on is that an assailant attacked and stabbed her from behind. Attacker could have been spooked, ran away from the scene. However, the other theory is she was dumped there and left for dead. Nothing found in the hotel, a search carried out outside around the car park. Still checking the surrounding area, the trading estate, replacing the Airfield formerly Croydon Airport. No knife or weapon found yet.'

'I've a press conference to go to at noon today, about this case, seems the victim has stirred up the media since the story broke in the tabloids. I would like to know how the press were on the scene so quickly. We only knew after the woman had been found stabbed,' Chief Superintendent Homer enquired.

'One of the line of enquires we will be following up on, Sir, also the fact that a photographer being there to take pictures, ahead of the police car arriving. Almost like a publicity stunt that went terribly wrong, could have been a lot worse. We could have had a murder enquiry on our hands,' replied Mattock.

The phone rang on Chief Superintendent's desk. Before he answered he, requested Mattock keep him in the loop as to what was happening in the on-going case, waving Mattock away, so that he could answer the phone.

Mattock left wondering why the Chief had decided to get involved in the case. To his knowledge, he only needed to know when a case, had been solved. To only, enhance his profile to the media.

Still no reply to his text message to Terri Chapman to when he could speak to Tom Brannon, Dan decided to ring around the hospitals to find out where the stabbed victim he found was taken. The paramedics had taken the woman to the hospital, not revealing her destination. His first call made to the Mayday Hospital met with no response to his enquiries. The second hospital he called his luck was in, as he succeeded, the call to St Georges at Tooting, A & E Dept. When asked about her condition, they asked him whether he was a relative and who he was. Not wishing to divulge that information, he hung up. Neither the paramedics nor the Police would not reveal to me to which hospital the woman had been admitted. Only knowing someone had arrived with a stab wounds at Tooting, enough information for him to work on. He had asked to know which ward she had been place. Told, 'That information is confidential.'

Next morning Dan read the newspaper report on the previous night's events at a local hotel in Croydon. The person, a female was so far unnamed. On a whim, Dan had emailed Terri a picture of the woman to see if by chance she had known her. In Dan's mind Tom Brannon's conversation and the woman stabbed could be the consequence of the heated phone call.

Dan looked up his text messages. Terri had text to confirm that the newspaper photo was that of Penny Connor, her friend. He had text back to find out whether she had spoken to Tom Brannon. Ten minutes later his mobile rang, 'Hi, Terri,' he answered.

'What! Do you know where they have taken him?' A few seconds passed by. 'Okay, I'll see what I can find out.' Dan was confused. The police around lunchtime picked up Tom Brannon by car from his home. Why and what else has he done for the police to come knocking, he thought.

Terri, he recalled said she had known him for four to five years, but knew little about him apart from that he had parted from his wife, prior to him moving and living in Cricklewood.

Dan rang Shirley to keep in touch and find out whether Sam had known a Tom Brannon, seconds later he hung up.

He had drawn a blank, Sam knew nobody of that name. Again, the question in his head rang out. Tom Brannon is in police custody. Appears he ignored Terri's advice.

Dan claiming, he was a reporter for one of the nationals rang the police station in Croydon, asking for any news on a Tom Brannon, taken into custody in North London, and whether they could state to which police station he was likely to have been taken. Being evasive, the operator only confirmed that a Tom Brannon, taken into custody, was now helping them with their enquiries into a case they were currently involved in. 'Which police station had he been taken to?' Dan asked.

'Here at Croydon Police Station,' the operator answered.

Thanking the police officer taking the call, Dan hung up. He rang Terri and asked was it possible that Tom had been in contact with police, despite her telling Tom to say nothing.

'When I first told him to say nothing on the subject, he seemed quite positive that he would not say a word,' Terri said.

'Only way Tom Brannon could be taken in for questioning is if he had spoken to them. The police may think he is a suspect. Tom has been taken to Croydon nick for questioning,' Dan revealed.

Terri asked, 'Why does he need to go to Croydon. Tom was here at the Wetherspoon's Cricklewood branch. Tom would not have anything to hide. He must have spoken to the police here in Cricklewood. So why Croydon? All he had to do was to repeat what he had overheard from the telephone conversation. That is if he did change his mind and speak out. He has no idea who Harry is, or to that matter Penny Connor.'

Dan said, 'Look, at the moment we're as much in the dark as to Tom Brannon's life history. Until we hear from him, we will hold onto what information we have. May have been taken in for something else, we could be jumping to conclusions here,' Dan responded.

'I've known Tom Brannon long enough to trust him not to mess me around, his past, if any wrong doing has occurred, then I reckon that as far as I am concerned is history. Who is to say that someone else is not making waves on something from the past' Terri stated.

'Terri, if he has a record, the police would have that on their database. Would be reason enough to haul him in. Either that or he is their only lead to your brother's problem,' Dan answered.

'Could drop in to the cop shop and find out what if anything is going on,' Dan said. 'If you say you trust him, then it could be that he is being made the fall guy by someone who could hold a grudge against him, he could do with a friend.'

'You're asking me to phone instead. I could, but how would I have found out where he had been taken, if nobody left a message,' she countered.

Dan thought for a moment then said, 'Ring Croydon police and just say a friend of yours found out through a newspaper source, someone you knew in the reporting world, no need to give details as to who that source is. You know Tom Brannon as a friend, you heard that he had been arrested by the police and that you are just making enquires as to why he was picked up, let me know anything you have found out, go from there. Could be he was picked up for any number of reasons and no connection with the other night.'

'Yeah but Croydon, long way from Cricklewood. Okay, I will ring back as soon as I can,' Terri replied and hung up the phone.

Croydon Police Station became a hive of activity when the front desk besieged by a group of youngsters wishing to pick up a friend who had spent the night in a cell. Due to a fracas at one of the local night clubs, would have been released earlier only for him and another police officer on duty last night, the youth attacking the officer on entering his cell; attempting too foolishly escape while still in a drunken state.

The police sergeant on desk duty shook his head as he stated this fact, 'Considering where he spent the night, at his majesty's behest, downstairs in the enclosed confines of a secure cell with no possible way of escaping. It was a rather foolish act on his part, drink aside, to attack a police officer while in custody was pure stupidity. So, no he will not be out today.'

'Is he to be charged?' said one of the hapless youths.

'What do you think, son,' the sergeant replied.

While this went on, Tom Brannon escorted through the doors along with the accompanied police officers, who had picked Tom up earlier, pushing their way through to the interview rooms to the rear of the front desk.

'What's his problem, another person accused of threatening police brutality to an officer of the law?' asked the same youth inspired to speak out again.

The Sergeant responded, 'Not your business, son, he's here on police business. Unlike you who, will be arrested for blocking up the police station foyer with a wish to make trouble.

'What trouble,' the lad asked.

The Sergeant not willing to start another commotion in the foyer, just said, 'Could you all run along now and go home, if you are lucky, we may be lenient with your friend. Should the lad, behave himself and cause no further trouble we will release him tomorrow?

A call placed through to Detective Inspector Mattock from the front desk informing him that a Tom Brannon had arrived and taken through to one of the interview rooms on the ground floor. Fifteen minutes later, DI Tony Mattock came downstairs from his office and entered the interview room holding Tom Brannon. With DI Helen Smith who already remained waiting for Mattock to appear. They both sat down facing Mr Brannon, DI Helen Smith set up a tape to run and only then acknowledging Tom by saying,

'Good morning, Mr Brannon. Thank you for coming in, we need to ask you a few questions as to your whereabouts on Friday night and what you have been up to since leaving your last employment,' Helen said. Mattock took a backseat at this time in the proceedings, electing to let Helen ask the initial questions. 'Do you wish to have a representative of the legal profession with you here?' she asked.

'Why. Am I being arrested for anything?' he asked

'No, but I must warn you that anything you may say, may be called on and used against you if charged and brought to a court of law. Do you understand?'

Tom replied, 'Yes.'

'Mr Brannon, can you state your answer onto the tape yes or no that you understand your rights for the record.'

'Yes, officer.'

'Can you confirm that you are Mr Tom Brannon?'

'Yes, I am Tom Brannon.'

Helen looked to Mattock before asking Tom, 'Can you tell us where you have been in the last forty-eight hours?'

'I've been at home in Cricklewood or I've been sitting in a local bar. Can you tell me why I have been brought here?' Tom asked.

Calling Helen to one side he said, 'I take it nobody has taken the trouble to tell him why he has been brought in for questioning.'

'All in good time, Mr Brannon,' Mattock said responding to Tom Brannon's enquiry.

'Have you ever heard or do you know of a woman, name of Penny Connor?' Helen said continuing while checking her notes.

Tom looked from Helen to Mattock and back to Helen before answering, 'Heard the name mentioned in passing, but no, I do not know her or ever met her personally. But what has that to do with me?'

'You say you do not know this person, but have heard the name mentioned. Where would you have heard the name and who might have known her?' Helen continued

'Cannot remember; look, what has this all have to do with me?' Tom asked.

Mattock broke in saying, 'We have reason to believe she may have been targeted, for whatever reason, in which we are just following up enquiries in connection with a criminal act recently. We need your help in establishing your own involvement and whereabouts to our on-going enquiries. To this end, can you please answer the questions asked by my colleague?'

Tom stared back at Helen whilst listening to Mattock. 'As I have just relayed to your colleague, I do not personally know the woman.'

'Why is it that at this precise moment, I fail to believe that,' Mattock stated. His attention drawn towards the door as a message written down on a piece of notepaper handed to the police officer standing near the door. Helen took the note passed onto her by the officer. Reading the note, she in turn handed it over to Mattock. The note stated that earlier a telephone call came into the station enquiring into the stabbing, no name given as to the caller; just making an enquiry, it was from a supposed reporter for one of the National Press. Mattock looked up at Tom Brannon, a question formulated in his mind as to whether Tom Brannon had any knowledge of the call made. However, then he thought Tom had no prior knowledge of the stabbing at this stage. Mattock transferred the note in his hand, consigning the note to his jacket pocket.

Returning his gaze towards Tom he asked, 'Your residence is in Cricklewood. Is there anyone who can verify your whereabouts two nights ago, and since?'

'You can speak to a Terri Chapman, she manages the Wetherspoon Pub in the Broadway. She can verify my being there,' answered Tom.

'What line of work are you in?' asked Mattock.

'Have no work or commitments at present, still looking around. Keeping my options open so to speak.'

'Where and when did you last work?'

'Has something happened at my last employment of which I have left some three months ago, no response was forthcoming.

Not answering the question asked by Tom, Helen continued: 'Why did you feel it was time to move on, if you had nothing planned to move on to?'

'Times were changing, but my wife had left me for someone else. The climate at home required me to move out and recession played a part in my decision with work became a problem. Work was not doing that well. Took the decision to look elsewhere for a new challenge, I left amicably.' He looked back at Mattock. 'Look, if I'm being honest, due to a business merger. I knew my job was on the line and redundancy offers were made'

'Why do you think that you were made redundant?'

'Never told outright, but when you are told you are to go due to cuts in a merger. You do not always hear the truth as to the whys and wherefores of those decisions made.'

'Who had you upset enough, to be shown the door, do you bear a grudge or have an axe to grind against anyone in particular that you would harm in anger due to you leaving?' asked Mattock.

'You would have to ask my previous employers. All I know is that I was made redundant.'

Mattock was unconcerned as to whether Tom Brannon had been made redundant or not. Pondered as to whether this would be a reason to possibly attempting to kill someone. Yet divorced from his wife and now lives alone, he frequents a pub locally near home in North London. Does not conform to the theory of the single divorced are all bad and out for revenge. Maybe some just have eccentric ways.

'Do you still have the keys to the premises, to your previous employment. Apparently, you never handed them in or were asked for them on leaving?'

'Yes, not on me now, but yes, they are back at my place. I never thought to hand them back, completely forgot about them. Only discovered the keys when I had reached home, is this the reason I've been brought here to Croydon, bit over the top for reporting a conversation heard.'

'Have you been back since your leaving?'

'No, never felt the need to return. I had left. No reason for me to go back either.'

Mattock motioned Helen to follow him out of the room, walking a little way up the corridor he turned around facing Helen. Well what do you think Boss?' enquired Helen.

'Not sure yet, need to find out a little more on Tom Brannon, fill in the blanks on his background. Take a trip over to North London, Helen, and speak to this Terri Chapman, maybe she can back-up his whereabouts the night Penny Connor was stabbed. Find anybody else who could verify, while I'll speak to his former employer.'

'You think he did it, Sir?'

'Apart from his having keys to the premises, there is no proof that he has any connection with the case, so we cannot hold him. He claims not to know Penny Connor. Take him home in a car. Along with one other officer, have a sneak look around his abode. See what you can find.'

Seeing Helen coming through on her way out along with Tom Brannon, the desk sergeant tried to grab Helen's attention. His endeavours helped by a drunk seated suddenly getting up to approach the desk. Trying to avoid a collision, she just stopped in her tracks. A quick look to the desk to make sure someone was on hand to deal with this person also brought her attention to the sergeant's hand held high. A constable at the desk grappled with the drunk, while Helen took time to speak to Sergeant Price informing her that another call, this time from a Terri Chapman, asking after Tom Brannon. Enquiring, why was Tom Brannon arrested?

CHAPTER 5

Sam, happy in herself, showed no outwardly sign of needing Shirley's company, but despite the situation, both found time to make light of the circumstances that had brought them together. Each told stories of each other's lives, laughter came from all the tales told, where and how Shirley and Dan met up, life with Dan as cousins. The bond Sam had with Dan since arrival back from across the pond. The fact he came back when problems with her marriage started to go pear shape. Sam began to rely on Dan more. Any worries that had Dan concerned about Sam's condition or state of mind were dispelled, Shirley at ease and Sam laughing so much and showing no sign of stress with the light banter between them. This the first time Shirley had really spoken to Sam. Both opened up to how much Dan was integral to their lives.

Shirley said, 'Dan was more of a companion come boyfriend. He would frequently stay for weeks on end. Then he would return here to his own home. Ring her when he wished to go out up town or locally. It allowed independence. It works for us.'

Sam listened and then spoke herself when Shirley had left an opening. 'To me Dan has been my rock since the breakup from my ex. I have been depressed, slowly getting my head around the fact that Harry had taken his problems out on me. Dan showed up at the right time out of the blue from his time in the states. I must be the reason he felt he needed to go back to his home. Keep an eye on my welfare. I need to stand on my own two feet now, stop relying on Dan to be there.'

The phone rang in the hallway. Sam noticed the telephone in the front room and picked up. Sam's demeanour changed almost at once, the transformation in her facial expression was dramatic. Sam dropped the phone. Shirley picked up the phone, but, too late the caller had rung off. Sam stood transfixed. 'Who was that on the phone?' asked Shirley. Sam just stood there. 'Sam, what is the matter. Who was it on the phone?'

'It was someone asking for Dan, said that a Penny Connor involved in a stabbing the night before, had taken a turn for the worse and had been taken to theatre,' she relayed.

Shirley not sure how much Sam knew asked, 'Did you know the woman yourself?'

'In a way, yes, we met up at a health and fitness gym near here. She used to bug Harry my former husband, with her over the top criticism of his work and friends in the pub. Always made out he was up to no good.'

Wishing she had been quicker to the phone instead, Shirley risked a further reaction by asking Samantha. 'Would he ever take it upon himself to stab someone: let alone a woman.'

Samantha looked at Shirley, 'Asked me that a year ago, I would have said no, but after his recent behaviour in the last twelve months and what he did to me recently, you tell me.'

Silence ensued, both sat back in the armchairs. Music heard from outside brought their attention to a car pulling up in the driveway. A door key enter the keyhole and open the front door, but nothing happened, no sound of the door closing, nor any sound from the hallway or someone moving around. Yet the music kept playing form the car, no car doors heard opening or heard closing. Shirley rose from her seat and drawn towards the window, she drew the net curtains away from the window, noticed nobody was inside the car. Sure, she heard no sound of doors opening or closing once the car pulled up. She peered up and down the road, apart from the elderly couple who lived opposite, nobody else were in sight. Only noise was the quiet from the lack of music now terminated from inside the parked car.

Samantha came up and stood beside her, 'Who is it?'

'Not a clue, accept for Dan's car nobody,' Shirley answered.

As they both gazed out of the bay window peering first towards the front door and seeing nobody in sight either at the main house door or within the space between the car and door, then both in unison turned to look up and down the road in the opposite directions within their limited view from the window. Samantha gave out a scream as a key turn in the front door lock, not expecting the front door to open, having seen no one there seconds earlier.

Shirley called out in shock, when Samantha screamed. The scream was unexpected. Front room door opened to reveal Dan as he entered unaware that he was the reason for Samantha screaming out.

'What the hell is the matter? Why is Samantha screaming out like that?' he asked,

'Where have you been, you frightened the life out of her, frightened the life out of me when she screamed out,' Shirley replied.

'What do you mean where have I been? You knew I was going out. Now I come back to find a nervous wreck. What happened?' Dan reacted.

'I mean where did you go after you pulled up, hearing nobody at the front door coming in, we went to the window, could not see anybody around. Then suddenly without warning, out of blue, you open the front door. Scaring the hell out of Sam,' she explained.

'One of the wheelie bins had fallen over, rubbish bags were strewn all over having come out of the waste bin, all down the side of the house; went to retrieve the bags and placed them all back inside the wheelie bin in the alley. Never thought I would be scaring you both witless. Sorry.'

They all relaxed from the situation created from the scenario panned out moments earlier. Samantha and Shirley carried on talking and laughed at each other's jokes, relieved that Dan now back and waiting on them with tea. Dan stayed with the coffee, never a lover of tea.

He left the girls to their giggles of laughter. Drifting out into the garden and sat down into a wicker armchair deep in thought, the wicker chairs arranged around a garden table set up outside his patio windows. The garden a good size, not too big and not too small, that one felt cramped or confined. His neighbour Perry Selsdon, helped with the garden duties, as Dan spent much of his time away. Perry a keen gardener had an allotment locally and given he had retired several years earlier offered to maintain the garden for which Dan paid a small remuneration for his trouble.

Dan supped at his coffee. His thoughts turned to Terri confirming that Tom Brannon had returned home. Harry, he knew could have been responsible with the stabbing of Penny Connor, his motivation that Penny had been taking a swipe at his credibility and self-esteem around his pub and the local Croydon community. What Penny had on Harry. He could only guess. He concluded that with Harry's change in attitude in recent years could easily be accountable. Knew also that Harry would not get his hands dirty, had able-bodied men under his command who would stop at nothing to question any order given to do his bidding. Harry was known for his generosity in his local. Those he knew, who frequented his pub on a regular basis gave him an alibi to cover his activities in the underworld. But, he became elusive to those same people who wanted to know his stance on criminal activities. Safeguarding the Publican image he gave out.

Given Harry was in his sister's pub up in Cricklewood, Dan construed that he had found an alibi in Terri of his non-involvement. If Terri by chance had confronted Harry on his knowledge of the attack on Penny Connor, letting slip her information came from Tom Brannon listening into his telephone conversation possibly on the night of Penny's attack. That would explain how the police could have hit on Tom Brannon, making him the fall guy if Harry's plan went awry.

'Why have you come out here to the garden, our company not good enough for you now?' Shirley enquired on watching Dan. Dan unaware that Shirley had been standing there and Shirley speaking out shocked him out of his reverie.

'Sorry, was not aware of you being there. I was thinking,' he responded.

'Thinking, that can be a dangerous hobby,' Shirley said with a hint of humour.

'Ha, ha! Always was the comedienne,' he laughed.

'Is warm out there on the street. Okay if I join you, will not cramp your style will I. Make my escape now if you want me to,' continuing the comedy theme.

Dan did not say a word, just waved her through to join him pointing to a seat opposite. Samantha appeared moments later, before another word was uttered standing at the patio doors.

'Can I join or is this a private party?' she asked.

'You've perked up. You can join in if you wish. I'll let you,' he said smiling up at her.

Pulling up another seat, she sat beside Shirley. Everything stayed quiet, hushed into silence, both the women surveyed the garden. Drinking in the quiet and calm peaceful surroundings the garden exuded. The garden immaculate, all bushes and plants trimmed back now flourishing and in bloom. Grass cut to perfection, not a blade out of place.

Shirley spoke first. 'Own up, this garden is not all your handiwork is it. It looks too good for the amount of time spent here.'

'No, you are right. I have had help with the place. Next-door neighbour Perry is a keen gardener and retired, offered to look after it while I had been away. Does a good job and puts me to shame? So, I pay him to keep the garden tidy.'

A period of quite returned 'Did you do whatever you left this morning to do?'

'Yes,' said Dan

'What did Terri want that was so important you had to race off to yesterday?'

'Oh, nothing much, one of her customers needed some help.'

'Hmm, seems she only has to snap her fingers lately and you go running to her.'

'That's a bit harsh. She has only called once asking for help. That is all. Besides you said you were okay about me going, before I left you.'

'Yeah, I know. Then again, I think maybe you would have gone whether I agreed or not to her, after all she is my ex-husband's sister.'

After moments passed by, she said, 'Maybe I'm just feeling down; I know I should not be relying on you being around all the time. Perhaps I'm being selfish and I'm used to the fact that you have been around of late.'

Shirley looked at Dan and gave him a wry smile. He shrugged his shoulders and splayed his hands apart as if to say, *what else can I do?* As Sam showed signs of strain. To still not quite being herself. Either way Dan question himself whether his allowing Sam to stay here in the first place was helping. Rising from his seat, he left the patio, excusing himself and disappeared off into the house.

Shirley followed Dan shortly after, finding him packing a bag in his bedroom. 'Thinking of going somewhere?' she said seeing the bag.

'You want the honest answer. Deep down, I know Harry still is up to no good. I know Harry a lot better than Sam herself knows; Sam only knows that he runs a pub, but that Harry has his fingers in every pie of crime in this area. She is as far as I know totally in the dark. He never gets his hands dirty, but he masquerades as everybody's friend, all the time masterminding some criminal act behind the scene. Maybe, just maybe he is the one person who is still controlling Sam's current existence and her mind.' As Dan said this to Shirley standing in the bedroom doorway. Sam came up quietly behind Shirley, on making herself known to both, she turned and left leaving them to descend the staircase.

Dan looked at Shirley and Shirley looked at Dan. Realising that Sam had heard every word spoken. 'Damn, she was not meant to hear that,' he mumbled as he looked up to the heavens.

'I'll go after her,' Shirley said.

'No. I will go; I should have kept my mouth shut. Any explanation now would be better coming from me.'

CHAPTER 6

Detective Inspector Mattock stood staring out of his office window. His back felt a presence, a crawling sensation up his back. Turned about to find DI Helen Smith closing in on his office doorway, the door already open she walked straight into his office.

'Sir, I have just been looking at the notes we have for the current case and although we have no knowledge of Tom Brannon working at or near the scene in recent months. The fact that he left under a suspicious cloud; there is no evidence that precludes all the suspicion falling on him from the information we have. I would agree to your earlier assessment, saying he has no possible connection to the stabbing, apart from overhearing a heated conversation, which could have been a marital tiff. Should we speak with the woman who called in enquiring into Tom Brannon taken in to the station?'

Mattock thought for a second, 'Yes, you follow up on that lead, have you the name of the person, ask the front desk if not and I will talk to this Dan Prescott, see where that leads us.'

'I have the name of a Terri Chapman. But would you rather I come along with you to speak to Dan Prescott before I talk to Terri Chapman.'

'Helen, was that the name Tom Brannon mentioned, as being the landlord to the local pub in Cricklewood.'

'Yes, maybe it would be sensible if you came along as well, two ears being better than one as the saying goes,' mused Helen, knowing well enough another officer would be with her as backup.

Ignoring the remark Mattock said, 'Dan Prescott has a cousin, name of Sam, short for Samantha I believe. Once married to Harry Tambling, maybe still is. Became violent towards his wife Sam, progressed worse gradually until when Harry lashed out at Samantha. Then told he had a drink problem, which had escalated over the year previous. A normal problem when someone instinctively turns to drink, more so as a publican with open access. Marital fallout follows through one person hitting out at another. Dan Prescott threw Harry out of the house. This information came by talking to people in the know on the street.'

'Your informant, I take it.'

'No, I remembered an article in the press in respect of a family rift.'

'Of course, Sir. Apparently, Harry has had past issues with a Penny Connor over the years,' Helen continued.

Mattock looked up at the mention of Penny Connor. 'Harry Tambling could be the lead we have been waiting for. Yes, Helen, I think Harry Tambling is our first port of call. Then Dan Prescott, lastly Terri Tambling. Harry Tambling, Terri Tambling, are they related or just a coincidence?'

'Yes, only her name changed when she married someone from North London, her surname is now Chapman.'

'Okay I'll drive,' Helen said as they walked together, in unison out towards the car. 'How do you want to play this, Sir?'

As they drove out from the station foreground, Helen raced out narrowly missing a car by inches as they crossed the highway, over and onto the street opposite the station. Only the screeching of brakes and sounding of horns made them aware something was amiss. 'You sure that you would rather drive, Helen, roads could be a whole lot better if you were not,' Mattock said.

'I thought you were in a rush for answers, Sir,' she replied,

'No point, if we cannot reach there alive and in one piece,' he countered

'Now you are questioning my driving,' quipped Helen, as she drove onwards.

Nothing more said between them until they pulled up alongside the kerb outside The Waddon pub. A scuffle was in progress as they exited the car, the scuffle broke up, as soon as they were spotted getting out of the car. Those involved, as well as those cheering the fight on, ran off in various directions expecting a chase. Mattock signalled Helen not to bother running after those involved, motioning the pub door. As they both entered, the noise they entered hushed to a silence. Recognised for being the police, but when they ignored the sudden quietness and amble up to the bar. Service resumed as the clientele continued talking, the noise returning to where you could just about hear yourself speak.

Speaking to the barman on duty, they introduced themselves, showing his badge. Mattock then asked whether they could speak to Harry Tambling the owner, the barman informed them that Harry was away on business. When asked what business, a shrug of the shoulders was all they received for an answer. 'When he returns can you tell him to come down to the station and ask for Detective Inspector Mattock, we have some questions he may be able to answer,' Mattock said before they made their exit.

'What do you reckon, Sir?' Helen asked.

'We had no warrant to search the pub or his living accommodation, so we assume that we were told the truth. If Harry Tambling is on the premises and then does not make an appearance at the station, we assume that he has something to hide. If he is away on business, would like to know what business venture he is involved in and where.'

'Bit of a conundrum to be solved, Sir,' said Helen.

'Helen, we will play it by ear for now. Could be that events may play out in providing answers to questions yet to be answered. Let us see if Dan Prescott is more forthcoming when we speak to him. I think we will invite

Dan Prescott down to the station, may open up more in an official setting.'

Dan Prescott was more than willing to go, he seemed too willing. Mattock when entering the Croydon Police Station, took Dan straight through and up to his office where he asked another junior officer to provide some coffee or tea, whatever. Dan Prescott sat in front of Mattock's desk, while Helen sat behind Mattock, to the right. Mattock wished to convey a non-committal approach, just a cosy chat. Observing Dan's reactions to Mattocks questioning. Once tea had arrived, Dan had asked for coffee and the formalities over. The questions asked by Mattock at first centred on Dan Prescott's background, and what he did for a living now he was out of the army, then asked what he knew of Harry Tambling. On this Mattock felt Dan held back, stating only that on his return from America, found him treating Sam his cousin like a punch bag, mentally and then physically. Witnessing at first hand Harry hitting Sam made him see red, when he himself then attacked Harry Tambling and threw him out of the home. Asked whether he knew of Harry's temper before he married his cousin and if he was capable of violence, Dan never a person to talk, left Harry's criminal activities out of the police domain and kept only to Harry's recent change in attitude towards his cousin.

When Dan left the police station, Helen approached Mattock's desk. 'I felt he was holding back on certain information regarding Harry Tambling.'

Mattock, reaching for his jacket hanging on a coat stand behind his office door, 'I agree with your analysis, Helen,' leaving his own thoughts at that. He walked over to the window and as he stared out of his office window overlooking a side street, he noticed Dan leaving the building below. A car across the street made contact with Dan, words spoken, after which he opened a car door and gets into the car. Mattock frowned, calling Helen back into the office, beckoning her to look out of the same window. 'Dan Prescott has just got into that car across the road. Now the only people who knew of him coming into the station for questioning, were the three of us. Dan Prescott never made any calls from here, neither did he have a mobile phone on him and nobody else has made a call out of this office, yet we have a car parked outside waiting for him to come out and he willingly gets into that said car as a passenger and drives off.'

Helen watched on as the car sped away turning left into the flowing traffic, 'Did you take note of the license plate number?'

'Here,' he said as he wrote it down on paper having already made a mental note. 'Get a check on the number, find out to whom the car is registered, to an individual, a hire company, or is a company car. Looking the state and condition of the car, a Ford Focus year 09, I suspect it's the latter.'

'Sir, could he have just flagged down the car knowing the person driving by?'

'Helen, the car was already waiting out there, long before Dan Prescott came out of the station. I stood here waiting for Dan Prescott to emerge to see in which direction he would leave. The occupants of that Focus knew he was here. The question is who?'

'You suspect more than one occupant.'

'Yes, as he enters the rear seats of the car, which would suggest that, someone else occupied the passenger seat beside the driver. If not two people, possibly three including the driver,' Mattock concluded.

Dan left the police station refusing any lift back to his abode wishing to follow up on his list of enquiries. Stepping down into the street his eyes drawn to a car waiting across the road and Mitch Sanders, someone he knew hailing him across the road, who sat in the driver's seat. Knew he worked for Harry Tambling. Inquisitive, he ventured over to the car after Mitch motioned to him.

As he approached, he bent forward to see who occupied the passenger seat at the front of the car. George not an unknown to Dan directly, his reputation alone made other people wince at his sight. Generally known as Tiny a nickname given when in his youth, due to his size, if ever referred to as tiny, you would not expect to find a person with a build and frame to match.

Mitch spoke saying, 'Dan, the boss wishes to speak with you and told to wait, expect you to come out of the cop shop.'

'Harry knew I was here, how?' Dan asked. 'And why should I come this minute?'

'I am just the driver and messenger boy; you know what the boss is like.'

'Mitch, you should pick your friends more carefully. Does not improve your street credibility, when your only purpose in life is to be errand boy.'

'Just get in or I'll have to ask Tiny here to help you.'

'Hello, Tiny, no offence, just wondered why Mitch had brought the gentle giant along,' Dan replied in response knowing he was goading Tiny, as he started to get into the back of the car. Dan met Tiny on occasion over the years and each time. Tiny reacted to the taunt. The first three times on meeting, Tiny overpowered Dan with his pure size and added weight, but, over the intervening years since. Dan had learnt to overcome Tiny and his extra weight and height, by using the skills learnt whilst in the army. Dan could not help himself by throwing Tiny a throw away comment, 'Fancy your chances do you.'

'Easy, Tiny, he is winding you up. Don't take the bait,' Mitch said to calm the situation down, not knowing the reason behind Dan's remarks.

By the silence that Tiny gave out, but saw the annoyance and reserved thinking that restrained Tiny from exerting his presence over Dan. Dan became aware that these latest defeats, at the hands of himself. Had not been conveyed to Harry his boss or Mitch.

Their eyes met across the car's divide. Each now knowing where they stood as Dan now knew he had the advantage. That advantage Dan would use at liberty, but Dan knew his strength and muscle at some point in the future, he could use. So, would cultivate a friendship with Tiny, rather than make him an enemy.

Journey's end was outside The Waddon as they drew up alongside the kerb. Tiny had promptly stepped out of the car the moment Mitch had turned off the car engine. Dan and Mitch close behind as they entered The Waddon moments later. Tiny had already run into the pub and was swallowed up by the noise that erupted as the pub door opened. The noise level expounded again as both Mitch and Dan entered. Music blaring from the duke box, deafening the eardrums be the sheer volume. As in most pubs you enter, everybody inside turns to see who dares to enter their manor.

Harry sat in his usual spot, sitting at the far end near a staircase leading up to the rooms above. Too Harry's office and living accommodation. Tiny stood behind Harry confirming Dan Prescott arrival.

As Mitch and Dan, made their way around the bar to the back, a path opened up as the customers allowed them to come closer to Harry who had stopped talking to several drinkers seated at the bar. Dan was then steered to seats, at the rear of The Waddon. Mitch returned to the bar, ordering a pint for himself, before he sat down at the table himself. Harry jovial and playing the happy publican more for his customers than for Dan, beckoned for Dan to sit on the bench seating to the rear. Mitch sat beside Dan whilst on the other side Tiny hovered and then sat in the chair in the corner. Harry sat opposite in a benched seat to himself. He moved his down towards Dan and said in a whispered voice so that those at the table present could only hear. 'Dan Prescott, been a long time. Kept to my word and left Sam alone. You are possibly wondering why I had you picked up. I heard from my sources that you had an invitation to our police station. Thought that you may need help in some way and I know we have had our differences. But also, heard you were also at the scene of a stabbing several nights back, not far from here.'

Dan stared back across the table at Harry, then looked either side of him, Mitch one side and Tiny the other. 'Am I meant to be intimidated by these two goons either side of me and you looking menacingly with a smug-like face. I do not know your source, although I could hazard a guess. What intrigues me is what problem you feel I have that coincides with my being at a crime scene and with the police, you're either worried I may say something or could you be responsible for the stabbing that night.'

A scowl etched on Harry's face, hinted to the latter, the scowl was brief as the smile returned, followed by false laughter, Dan sensed this was to compensate for Harry's confused customers looking on nearby.

The pair Harry had been speaking to on their arrival, appeared to be angst at Harry's change in character, but refrained from saying anything. Glancing at each other, they conveyed a silent message of wariness to this side of Harry. This was the first time they had seen someone remotely challenge Harry Tambling, by someone they had only twice seen before in previous visits. On those occasions, Harry and Dan had been on friendly terms. Dan and Harry now appeared to have issues that went against friendship that could harm any business transaction they had with Harry.

Harry's stance and manner changed tack, 'Dan, look I've no quarrel with you, just trying to be friends for old time's sake. I heard you were in the nick and I sought to offer some help should you need it. A mutual friend said you were witness to a stabbing I know you would be incapable of doing yourself, not knowing the full facts. When the police come calling on you again, thought to offer help.'

Dan tried to soften his response. 'If I need your help, I would not ask for it. Your kind of helping hand would be more trouble than it is worth. I think I would like to leave now.' Dan went to move, but when Mitch beside him, did not move. He looked over at Harry. 'That okay with you?'

Harry stared back, the scowl returning with contempt for Dan. Moments later, he said to Mitch, 'Let him go.'

Once outside The Waddon, Dan looked for transport back to his home. No bus route directly back to his pad, started to walk hoping to flag down a cab or taxi. His wish granted on seeing a taxi coming around the bend from Croydon Centre, off the High Street.

A commotion had erupted at the hospital when Penny Connor found lying dead in the side- room hospital bed she occupied. Security and hospital staff were in pandemonium as to how. Nobody saw anybody go into or come out of the room. What made matters worse was hospital surveillance CCTV cameras failed to pick up, on the comings and goings, due to a malfunction with the camera positioned outside the room.

Helen standing at the wall chart, looking over the information collated to the knife attack. Received the call stating that the hospital phoned saying that Penny Connor had been attacked at St George's. On alerting Mattock, they both arrived at St George's to find that Penny Connor had died, to the cause of death. Someone had injected a fatal substance into the drip feed going into her arm. The hospital were still trying to ascertain to what was injected into her. Mattock asked to see the CCTV video camera overlooking the room, only the answer was not what he expected or wanted. The camera would show up nothing, they had no footage available.

The hospital refused to take blame for the death of Penny Connor, due to the lack of nursing staff working, claiming that they could not have someone constantly in the room twenty-four-seven.

Mattock left the hospital fuming, leaving Helen to talk to the hospital staff. His temper in check on his feelings and the spoken word towards the inept running of a hospital to the safety and protection of its patients in allowing all and sundry to walk in and out unchecked. Now he had to explain why a victim of a crime, came to die whilst in her hospital bed to his Chief of Police.

Chief Super Intendant Homer was in a meeting with several of his officers when Mattock showed his face at the door, having already telephoned ahead on the events at the hospital. Homer had arranged the meeting in response, to determine why Penny Connor came to die and the information accrued until Penny Connor's sudden death. As Mattock entered the room, all eyes turned as one. Homer looked up from his desk and encouraged Mattock to come forward and tell everyone in the room what the latest situation was in respect of the case now that Penny Connor had died. Mattock not having had time to go to his own office commenced by telling all present that the information so far was now to be treated as a murder investigation. The fact that the CCTV had not been able to help witness who Penny Connor's assailant was, they only had enough information to work in which to ascertain who the likely culprits were.

One, Harry Tambling who had a run in with Penny Connor over a period, issues that could harm his integrity. We only know that Harry Tambling held in high esteem by the community, recently known to have a violent streak.

Two, Tom Brannon who was a former boss of the firm for which he was last working with, up until he was made redundant. Possibly sacked. His relationship with the deceased is unknown, but as she was bad mouthing Harry Tambling, then she may have had issues with men in general. Was she instrumental in his leaving, his wife had left him, with him moving to North London. Could be that she was the reason for the break up; these are just two of the questions that now we have no answers to.

'Sir, I would like to bring in Tom Brannon for further questioning, also Harry Tambling and one other, Dan Prescott, whose cousin is Harry Tambling's ex-partner and wife.

'Been said of late that Harry Tambling has had a drink problem in the last year, which ended up with him hitting the shit out of his wife, not a nice person to know if Tambling has continued with his lashing out at women through drink. We have it that because of Harry. Hitting out at Samantha Tambling on one occasion. Which Dan Prescott witnessed at first hand on returning from the Americas, Harry subsequently thrown out of the family home, taking a beating from Dan Prescott in the process. Penny Connor as a friend of Samantha is another connection to all three.'

CHAPTER 7

Amidst the early morning mist, Dan sat on a bench. This is where Dan Prescott came to think, he found sanctuary on these playing fields at the top of Purley Way. Apart from the odd car passing by, the peace and quiet early in the morning gave him all the time required to let his mind work its way through the last few days' events.

Only on this occasion he was not alone, Mattock had been passing when seeing Dan Prescott, recognised by the coat he wore. An Army and Navy combat outfit. He pulled over to the kerb, and watched. Observing and waiting to see if anybody else was to turn up. Half an hour elapsed and still Dan Prescott sat alone, no newspaper to hand to read, or mobile used during that time. Mattock drove down to the entrance, parked behind the clubhouse/changing rooms and walked on to the recreation fields in question and found Dan sitting on the same bench on the roadside off the playing field fifty metres from the entrance/exit gates.

Dan noticed Mattock as he walked up beside the playing field towards him; he closed his eyes at the sight. He thought to himself, *Can a man go nowhere for a quiet piece of me time. What can Mattock possibly want now?*

'Dan Prescott, saw you as I drove by and could not wonder why a man would wish to be on his own at this early hour of the morning without a dog. Stopped and thought maybe you were meeting someone,' said Mattock,

'No, I come here on occasion for the peace and quiet, and to think,' responded Dan

'How is your cousin, I understand she has had emotional problems of late. Samantha, is that her name?' Mattock asked.

'Yes, she is okay, has her days, some up and some down, as and when. Recently had more ups.'

'So, if you are here to think, I'm now wondering what your thoughts are on this morning.'

Dan mused to himself for a few moments before he spoke up, 'The price of freedom, why do other troubles follow you around like adhesive.' He stopped, as if reflecting what he had just said before he continued, 'The price of freedom is seeing a family member come alive with a long-wished dream for peace. Being more open and less secretive to whatever trouble and woes ails you. Most troubles are not of your own making, but of what others perceive and contribute in falsely accusing you of misdemeanours and in fabrications of lies, that are pure fiction by the perpetrators of false information. What troubles do you think are causing me problems?'

Mattock took stock of the words spoken by Dan, 'I'm not sure where you are coming from, but if this is about the stabbing of Penny Connor or whether Harry Tambling is still the cause of your cousin's current mental state, then maybe you should tell me what you know of Harry Tambling and if there is any connection to the Penny Connor stabbing.'

Dan opened slightly to Mattock and fed him some insight into Harry's relationship with Penny Connor. 'I can only say that Penny Connor's bad relationship to Harry goes way back. Penny who has been friends with Samantha since they were both at school together, when Harry came on the scene he was to become the friend who broke up that friendship. Penny could not cope with the intimacy growing between Sam and Harry. Jealous of not being part of Sam's life, it is possible. Harry Tambling did not help the situation by the constant put-downs. Myself, I was off the scene living a life in the army, later the SAS. My being away; left the field open for Harry to get closer to Sam, eventually leading to marriage. At that time, I had no reason to be Harry's enemy.

'When leaving the army, I decided to go state side and travel around. Six years later after travelling all over the States and down in South America, I arrive to see Harry on this one occasion hitting six bells out of Sam. I took exception and exacted my piece of justice on him, told him not to come back into Sam's life. Harry may have had troubles, which in turn turned to drink. That does not mean you can hit a woman about, especially when it is my cousin, family, taking the knocks. Harry has not come back into Sam's life, but that has not stopped her being paranoid on what had happened and that he is still constantly playing with her mind. Have not seen any sign that he is posing a threat.'

Mattock said nothing, weighing up what Dan had said. On the one hand, he saw no reason to think Dan was involved with the death of Penny Connor the day before. On the other hand, he saw Dan getting into a car on leaving the police station after their talk. So, begged, the question?

Dan made the first move to leave, getting up from the bench. As he passed Mattock by, Mattock asked the question. 'Dan Prescott, you were seen getting into a car outside the police station yesterday, after our talk. Who knew you were at the police station yesterday?'

'Why do you ask?'

'Curiosity, of who could possibly have known of you being at the police station. When not having made any phone call yourself, at the station or on your mobile on your way out?' Mattock explained.

'Harry Tambling's men were passing, and offered a lift in the car. At first, I was reluctant to get in, but they made a valid point in their persuading me otherwise.'

Mattock knew Dan had lied to the car had been just passing, having seen Dan get into a parked car across the road on leaving the station after they allowed him to leave after questioning, but let it go for now. 'What did Harry have to say when you saw him?'

'I'm not sure I can answer that, as not much had been conveyed in conversation with him,' replied Dan.

Mattock bowed his head as if the conversation between them had elapsed. Dan continued to walk away when Mattock called out. 'Mr Prescott, at this moment in time, I have no evidence to suspect you of any wrong doing. That is not to say that there is no evidence. If you are holding any information back, I can assure you that we will find out. Be warned that you are not completely in the clear. I will be watching you.'

Dan continued to walk, as he continued his walk out of the park he said over his shoulder, 'I'm sure you will. Have a good day, Detective Inspector Mattock.'

Dan never looked back as he made his exit towards Purley, leaving Mattock looking on.

Throughout the rest of the morning before businessmen and shop employees commenced another working day. The trains and buses full to the brim with passengers caught up in the early rush hour along with the cars, trucks and coaches that made up the frantic race to reach work, the business trips or fun trips to historical sites of interests and throw into that mix, taxis for the indulgent few. Mattock's stop to talk with Dan Prescott; allowed the traffic to build up. Mattock now found himself, entrenched within the rush hour traffic. He phoned ahead to inform whomever was on duty that he would be in late due to the volume of traffic holding him up. Not able to provide an estimated time of arrival nor not wishing to announce himself by using the siren, Mattock frowned and could not believe the utter contempt other road users had for each other. The anger and raised vocal abuse said behind closed car doors. Mattock found the sounding of horns and impatience started to affect him, when the abuse was aimed at him.

Leaving the playing fields, he eyed the Aerodrome hotel as he drove by. He took a left turn at the traffic lights, just as they changed from green down to red.

Parking up in the Aerodrome Hotel carpark. Mattock enter the foyer and walked up to the receptionist, showing his ID, requested to look at the guest register. The receptionist stated she would need to speak to the manager. Mattock noticed the receptionist, Susan the name given on a badge on her the lapel, had a tattoo on her ankle, a butterfly. She opened the door to an office to the rear left of the reception area. Seconds later the manager, a Mr Hopkins stepped out. Asked to see Mattock's ID Card. Mattock explained he wished to ascertain who had been booked in on the night of the stabbing of Penny Connor.

Reluctantly the manager allowed Mattock into his office, directing Mattock to a computer console and the only two chairs available. Both sitting, the manager proceeded to access the Computer, several screens flashed by before the monitor revealed a list of people booked in on the previous weekend in question.

Mattock came away from the hotel with a copy of the information he had asked for, most of the information acquired, discarded and destroyed. The manager confirmed the incident had created a lot of unwanted publicity, but Mattock stated that the investigation was now a murder enquiry.

By the time, he arrived at the station he was vexed enough to scowl at the desk sergeant when asked to take some post upstairs with him. Him thinking, *What am I, the office boy?*

Helen came into Mattock's office late that morning having spent the night with several friends at a local bar in Croydon. 'Morning, Sir, you're early.' Seeing the mood on Mattock's face, she refrained from saying anything else. Allowing Mattock to stew on his own with the soured look on the face, along with any problems festering on his mind, she walked out into the main office. Grabbed the mail accumulated in her inbox. Three letters in total. As soon as she had sat down, the phone on her desk rang. It was the desk sergeant downstairs. She put the phone down and made her way down to the desk sergeant on duty, where she was handed an envelope handed in that morning. The envelope with her name hand written was from the hospital. Inside she found a note with the medical results from the coroner and mortuary labs findings. They confirmed that a poison injected into the duct of the feed drip that fed into her body sustaining her life, ultimately ended her life.

'Think you need to see this note with med results handed in at the desk.' Handing the note to Mattock, as he read, Helen took in the implications in that they were now dealing with a murder investigation as he put the note aside. 'Right, I will go over all the information we have in this case, find out anything we may have missed. Helen, you talk again to the hospital. Ask around as to whether anybody had seen anything untoward, whatever, someone could have remembered seeing somebody that at the time of questioning previously did not remember or could not remember.

'In the meantime, I have been given a list, a copy of guests staying at the Aerodrome Hotel, which I picked up this morning, can have the list checked to find out whether anybody had or has a connection with the deceased. Could be our killer could be among the guest list.'

Mattock failed to inform Helen of his meeting with Dan Prescott earlier, of the information to who picked up Dan Prescott outside the station and where he had been taken subsequently shortly after. His mind returned to the meeting he knew he was due to have with his boss, Homer. He had to relay to him, to date made no further progress in the case. The only difference between his last appointment with Homer and the one he expected to have shortly was that the victim, Penny Connor was now deceased and now a murder investigation.

The meeting if it was a meeting, short and sweet. Over before it had started. The tabloids had already broken the news to Homer on Penny Connor's demise. Mattock's face and lack of humour, gave out the message of someone given verbal diarrhoea from a superior.

The morning did not get any better. When a call from the outside main investigators room. A constable not on the case relayed that Tom Brannon telephoned in stating he had received a printed message, highlighted by a florescent felt tip marker pen; received that morning through his letterbox. Tom's own name hand written on the envelope. The typed message stated in bold capital print – THE TRUTH WILL OUT IN THE END, nothing else.

Two hours later Mattock held the note in his hand. *What is this note meant to mean, any idea? Any clue as to who would send you this and why?*

He was speaking to Tom Brannon, who shook his head side to side and shrugged, saying only, 'I thought I had no enemies till this arrived. Apart from my ex, who I have not seen in several years, only this business with the phone call I had overheard.'

'I would suggest that you know something. You are holding back on information. Maybe you know this person and not telling. We are now investigating a murder enquiry into the death of Penny Connor, who died yesterday whilst in hospital recovering from stab wounds. Do you know this woman? The woman stabbed in Croydon a few nights ago, shortly after your supposed abusive caller made his call. Penny Connor, known to Harry Tambling, who in turn is related to your local landlady Terri Chapman, could he have been the mystery caller in the booth behind you the other night?'

'What are you trying to insinuate, Detective Inspector Mattock? That Terri knew her own brother was the person I overheard on the phone. When I enquired as to whom the person was, sitting in the stall behind me. She replied nobody. I have only met Terri's brother once and I did not see him that night. Surely, she would have admitted her brother Harry was there that night, which would explain why she inferred it was domestic trouble and not to interfere,' said Tom, realising now why Terri would not reveal the truth if protecting her brother from a criminal act.

To nobody and without thinking, Mattock spoke his thoughts aloud: 'Yes, precisely, but we have no conclusive proof that he was there or that he was involved theoretically in organising the stabbing of Penny Connor in Croydon. This would let you off the hook. However, this is all supposition only. Still does not explain, you are receiving this note and why.'

Tom Brannon spoke up for himself again, 'Besides, how would he know I had listened to his conversation, unless someone who knew him, told him. Terri.'

Mattock left with the printed note, stating that he would be back to talk with Tom again later. Not wishing to drive back to Croydon and return, Mattock phoned the Croydon police station for someone to relay a photocopy of Harry Tambling's photo to the nearby nick.

The note he would hand over to forensics to trace fingerprints and DNA if possible.

CHAPTER 8

Penny Connor's death hit the tabloids. The fact she had died whilst in hospital, did nothing to the security issues surrounding hospitals in general. Too many deaths now reported in various hospitals up and down the country in general, because of the understaffing of nurses and doctors. Now for a member of the public to just walk in unseen or unmonitored due to CCTV cameras not working. The tabloids were having a field day. Bringing again the plight to public concerns to security.

The headline news had already done the rounds on the TV news media coverage during the night before. Terri Chapman stared down at the headline printed across her newspaper:

Female PENNY CONNOR IS FOUND DEAD in HOSPITAL WARD

Her mind was in panic mode, but a sense of relief also. *Now the truth will stay unanswered as to who initially stabbed her*, she thought. The police probing had affected her, suspecting her brother in the first place, the fact that Penny Connor had caused her brother Harry more trouble than he had ever knew about, emanating from the past. Long before Harry met Samantha. Reading the findings in the reports increased and heightened her nerves.

Dan Prescott read the papers. He found himself wishing he had not been involved with Terri Chapman and Tom Brannon who today he had still never met. He knew he should have insisted; fact is he intended to find Tom Brannon, agreement or no agreement. Their meeting was overdue from the outset. DI Mattock was bumbling along as if he had all the time in the world, suspecting all and sundry, but getting nowhere fast. The last three words – GETTING NOWHERE FAST - he could aimed at himself right now, *Enough of this moping around waiting, now its action*. Stirred, by the feeling that his own hands were tied behind his back and without the ability to proceed further for too long. The decision to move forward was made easy. Not wishing to provoke unwanted excuses to why he needed to move cautiously. Now Penny Connor had died. He felt Tom Brannon may have walked into a minefield that was about to turn on its head. His thoughts turned to Sam. Knew that Sam's welfare safer in his home than her own. Sam's own past connections to Penny may as a former friend not excluded her from any trouble ahead. Harry knew of her friendship to Penny Connor. Knowing Harry had no knowledge of where he lived. Gave Dan peace of mind along with Shirley's helping hand.

Harry, appeared to be the obvious suspect, his previously known involvement with Penny Connor, meant he had held back when speaking to DI Mattock on news of his known knowledge of how Harry was involved in Penny's life. With his constant war of words latterly with Penny Connor. Later his marriage to Samantha, which had Dan, not witnessed first-hand on his return the America's. That Harry was now capable of hitting woman unprovoked. This still rankled Dan, to the extent the unwanted help he had agreed to with Terri in respect of her brother went further than he would admit. Knew deep down he was only helping to aid Tom Brannon, whom he had still to meet. Penny's regular taunting of Harry in public in recent years would have unhinged the sadistic side of his character. Left dormant over the years. Having hit out at Sam, he knew Harry could go off the rails again, triggered off by Penny's rants. That Tom had been in the pub in Cricklewood. Could mean if questioned into the Penny Connors' stabbing and Harry found out, find Tom taking the rap. Now he thought, knowing the only way Harry would find out would be through Terri. Could he trust Terri to keep quiet on the night, a night later Penny Connor stabbed in Croydon, Harry arranging for the crime to be committed in his mind as he ranted over into his mobile phone with Tom listening on in the stall behind him; Terri was Harry's sister. Whose back was she more likely to cover if push came to shove in this scenario; question answered itself, Harry.

In Cricklewood a phone rang, 'Hello, Tom speaking.'

Nobody answered to Tom's response. Everything was just silent, then he could hear someone breathing heavily, but nobody uttered a word. Patience was never one of Tom's virtues, his patience wearing thin at somebody telephoning him and not carrying the conversation forward by keeping quiet. Tom said, 'Hello.' Again, still no response, then the caller hung up. Leaving Tom bewildered, holding a dead silent phone line.

He tried ringing 1471 for his penance all he heard was the time of the caller, but the caller had withheld his or her number.

Tom sat down reclining back into his armchair facing a television with a Freeview box placed underneath the TV cabinet on which the TV sat. His mind had already discarded the caller on the telephone as a crank. He had spent the morning scouring the local newspapers looking through the job ads, with no luck in work jumping out from the pages to pursue. His enthusiasm for finding work jarred, by the lack of work available. He turned on the TV, after flicking through the channels, found nothing of interest, so turned the TV off.

Laying his head back in the armchair, he closed his eyes, drifting off to sleep minutes later. Half an hour later Tom woke up with a start, 'Huh, what's that? I would swear I heard something,' he said, half-asleep he was about to drift off to sleep again when he heard the telephone ring. Knew the ringtone sounding off probably the sound he heard waking him up moments earlier. In his bid to pick up the telephone before the next ring, Tom dropped the phone, losing his balance as he stretched across boxes of work brought home, but never rehoused elsewhere inside the flat. By the time, Tom reached out for the phone, the phone stopped ringing. Tom decided if the call was important, they would telephone again.

Fully awake, up and about, Tom looked pensively at the phone willing it to ring before he moved away and left. The bell on his door sounded, on opening the door, a stranger stood about to sound the bell again, Tom not saying a thing, waiting for the stranger to speak out.

'I am here by request of an acquaintance of ours, a Terri Chapman. Do not suppose she has spoken of me, has she? Name is Dan, Dan Prescott.'

'No, not said a word. So, what can I do for you?'

'That depends on what information you can provide, I am here as I said, because of something Terri wished for me to consider. To be honest, the fact Terri has not spoken to you puts me in a quandary. How well do you know Terri Chapman?' he ventured.

'More than I know you at this point, you're making life difficult by standing on the doorstep. Instead of standing out there, you had better come in and explain yourself and why you are here,' said Tom.

Dan at first ignored the attempted comical remark from Tom, said as he walked in pass Tom and into the indicated room by way of a hand movement hinting at the first room on the right. Tom followed up Dan from behind, beckoned at an armchair for Dan to sit down in with Tom sitting in the only other armchair in the room. Dan noticed Tom was like him in not being very materialistic, a lack of furniture and only a TV and Freeview box, also a small coffee table with one maybe two newspapers, one on top of the other laying on top.

Tom, watching Dan, broke the silence, 'Well now you are in, perhaps a coffee or tea before you tell me why you are here, or maybe something a little stronger. I am afraid I have only beer or lager to offer in that respect. Terri did not tell me she was intending to come here this morning, or was that just a ruse to see me.'

Dan said, 'Coffee, yes coffee will do.'

Five minutes passed before Tom returned holding two cups, one he prompted for Dan to take. The heat given out by the hot coffee, willing for Dan to take the cup. Leaving almost instantly and returning with sugar and a spoon. 'I do not have sugar,' responded Dan when offered the sugar bowl.

'Apparently, you overhead someone she knew ranting to another person, three nights ago, from a stall or booth behind you in a local pub. Terri asked me to find out whether a certain known person she knew was in trouble and confirm what you claimed you heard,' Dan said

'Terri claimed that she did not see anybody sitting behind me. Are you saying she lied to me?'

'Yes and no. She recognised the person who came from that stall's direction, but as there are stalls further down from where you sat, could not be precise in saying that this person was in fact sitting in the booth behind you.'

'So, why not just say that?'

'Terri can be very protective in the way she holds back on information, I understand you were told to let the matter drop and forget about the conversation, pass it off as a domestic dispute.'

'Yeah, that's right,' Tom replied. 'So, who was Terri protecting, me or the other person.'

Dan replied, 'Both, presumably. Terri did not want your involvement in what mess the other person may be getting into, although that could be too late now.'

Evaluating the snippet of news just given to him, Tom found himself saying, 'My guess would be the other person. Would I be right?'

Dan did not need to think on this subject, 'Sorry, but knowing Terri and the other person involved, I would say your intuition and summation is spot on.'

'What would you do in my place?' Tom asked.

'If you had any idea on whom you had overheard and were thinking of helping the other person on the line, I would say unless you knew who the receiver was. Do as Terri suggested' stay clear and carry on with your life. I have a suspicion that that was furthest from your intention. I reckon you have already involved the police. In which case I would tell you to be very careful on what you do next. Take the warning at face value if you wish, but watch your back.'

Dan went to leave, then hesitated and said, 'I have my own reasons for helping, besides my knowing the person you are up against. Terri has asked me to keep quiet until she had spoken to you concerning this person. I am having trouble thinking whether she will inform you. If as I suspect that is the case, I will override her wish for silence when next we meet. Until I contact you again. I mean what I say, that is the watch your back part.' With that, Dan left Tom thinking on, as he walked out through the front door, back out onto the road.

A blue Ford Focus sat beside the kerb forty metres up from Tom's home watching the coming and going of Dan Prescott. Both Tom and Dan were blissfully unaware of the car and occupants. The driver Tiny and his partner Mitch occupied the passenger seat. Instructions given whilst they sat waiting for Dan to emerge from Tom Brannon's home, was one of them to follow Dan Prescott, whilst the other remained watching Tom Brannon's place and follow Tom Brannon should they not leave together.

Mitch nominated by Tiny to follow Dan, by insisting he would remain in the car. Mitch found his tracking skills were laid bare, finding Dan standing over the car he no doubt had arrived in. Parked around the corner from Tom's home. Only a hundred metres from where Tiny and he had parked unsighted. Racing back to where Tiny still sat in their car. He tripped up and ended sprawled across the pavement.

A police officer had been watching Tom's house standing well back inside a garden hidden by the high hedge surrounding the garden, in the driveway. Noticed the car Mitch and his partner sat in, phoned into his local police station to the situation. Mattock enforced the need for backup, for the police officer now watching over Tom's property. Standing back and just keep an eye on proceedings as they unfolded. Informing his own station, that backup was required as he described the scene before him.

Mitch noticed the police as he ran passed and stumbled tripping up over a slightly raised paving stone, the officer concealed behind the garden hedge. Mitch looked from the police constable to the parked car, any attempt to catch the attention of Tiny thwarted. The copper looked at his stumble, a smile at his clumsy footwork stopped any form of eye contact happening. Mitch gave a wry smile as he prised himself off the footpath. Gave an upward shrug of his shoulders, while opening his hands outstretched to emphasise without words he was a klutz, a clumsy idiot.

The officer's smile enhanced back. 'Always happens when you have two left feet and do not look where you are going. What were you running away from anyway?'

'Not running away, officer, just remembered I had to be somewhere else,' Mitch said.

'Where would that be, Sir?' the police officer enquired.

'Where would what be?'

'Where you had to be, that was so important you had to run back.'

Thinking quickly, Mitch said, 'Had to meet someone at the Wetherspoons pub in the High Street. Five minutes ago,'

The officer stared back at Mitch, 'Not from around here are you, Sir?'

'What makes you think that?'

'If you were, you would have known that to get to the High Street you would be running in the direction you were headed initially, not hightailing back this way.'

Twenty minutes had passed since Mitch took off to follow Dan Prescott. Tom Brannon remained inside his home. Tiny knew from the experience that the only way to initiate some decisive action or response from someone like Tom Brannon was to set the ball rolling by provoking a response. As he got out of the car, he suffered a bout of cramp in his calf. As his calf seized, tightened up, trying to straighten his leg made it ten times worse, his need to walk it off to relieve the stiffening pain shooting up his calf. Once out from the car, he cursed as he saw Mitch hovering down the road, talking to someone hidden behind a high hedgerow surrounding a garden, a driveway. *Why now? What is he playing at?* Tiny thought. *Meant to be trailing Dan Prescott, don't tell me the numbskull has been caught out already*. He closed the car door. Intending to stretch out and walk around on his feet, while at the same time find out who Mitch's companion was. Pulled up, stopping suddenly on seeing the police uniform. He approached from the opposite side of the road.

Mitch attempted to walk back to the car. Tiny ducked down behind a four-wheeled drive car parked close to the kerb. Watching Mitch, questioned by the officer. Also, noticed another officer coming up the rear, behind Mitch. Not able to hear what was said and could not approach any nearer without revealing himself. Cramp in his leg calf having subsided, Tiny retraced his steps back to the car, keeping low.

Once back in the car, pulled out from the kerb and drove slowly down the road towards Mitch, pulled up to a halt as he wound down the driver's car window. 'Mitch, there you are. Sorry, officer, is there a problem?'

The officer looked over to Tiny sitting behind the wheel, and then took note of the car, a Ford Focus. Facing the way from which Tiny had driven. Then said, 'Maybe there is, maybe there is not, depends on what you were doing parked back there, back up on the left. Been watching you for the past hour, you were there when I arrived and only now do you come looking for your friend. Your mate, Mitch is it?' When no one responded to the question he continued: 'He alighted from your vehicle not half an hour since, I'm guessing following that fella coming from the house over there. Judging by the fact he came running back this way, he was coming back to your vehicle and not as he has stated, getting himself lost, tracing the whereabouts of a certain pub in the High Street, which is in the opposite direction to the one this Mitch came running.'

The other police officer noted earlier, came up from behind Tiny inside the Ford Focus, leaning into the open window and took the car keys from the ignition. 'Good afternoon, Sir. I think that both you and your friend should come down to the station and answer a few questions as to what you both are doing watching that property, and why we find your friend following a man to his car coming away from the said property. Someone will return you to your vehicle later. Our police car is waiting a little way up there on right. Can I ask you to get out of the car please, Sir?'

Tiny reluctantly got out of the car. When Tiny looked at Mitch as he walked away from the car, the stare told Mitch that he would be getting grief later when they sorted their current problem out. Seeing the officer was by himself, he chanced to assault the officer and run off before he could cry for help. The officer second-guessed his intention and calmly stated that backup was already on its way. Any intention to make a break was futile. Distant sirens heard to highlight the fact.

CHAPTER 9

Tom arranged a meeting for that evening with Terri, Tom said nothing of Dan Prescott's visit that morning. The unexpected cancellation by Terri, however, seemed more than a coincidence, almost appeared that Terri had knowledge and knew of his meeting with Dan that day. Mind games were not one of Tom's favourite pastimes or hidden talents. That aside, it did not detract from him thinking that someone could be playing games. Terri had not mentioned her brother's appearance and Dan held to his promise to Terri in not revealing the occupant in the stall. The not knowing niggled at Tom's brainbox, wishing he had prised that information from Dan. He allowed Dan to hold onto that snippet of news. Rueing the missed chance, Dan had left a number to contact him. Now with that meeting arranged cancelled, pondered as he peered down at his mobile. The police had not confirmed or denied, but suspected Harry Tambling, brother of Terri being the person sitting behind him that night. Maybe he already had the information to Terri and Dan's little secret.

The Aerodrome Hotel guest list comprised of two sheets. DI Helen Smith had scanned the list several times. She had already spoken to fourteen guests staying the night Penny Connor was stabbed and to no avail, everyone so far could vouch they had no connection to Penny Connor. Most had stayed over following a wedding reception held that night including the bride and groom staying in the honeymoon suite. The remainder, no name stuck out as a known criminal. Helen all but gave up on finding any link amongst the guests. She had checked all the guests' names against criminal records ever recorded, with no result. Her resolute waning when checking the vehicle licence plate numbers, against those reported stolen in the past month. Again, nothing came up, the DVLA had the spare number plates found in the car boot, car registered to an elderly couple Mr and Mrs Armstrong, but the trail ended when records showed this couple had died eighteen months previously, involved in a car accident, both died instantly at the scene. Then Helen as a last option, an afterthought, traced back a further two months with the second set of license plates screwed on the vehicle. What came up, she found two stolen cars reported within a week of one another. Two cars were parked in the car park on two separate nights one after the other. The first a Renault Clio parked on the Friday night, then later a Citroen, parked in the car park on the same night as the stabbing. The details did not match the number plate to the car on either. Both had bogus numbers. Sending a couple of officers around to the addresses given to the receptionist, revealed bogus non-existent addresses. Room 10 on the night prior to stabbing a Friday night, Mr James Holder, booked in only for the one night. On the Saturday room 10 yet again booked out to a Mr & Mrs Kevin Stubbs. Coincidence or just down to luck that the same room: should be booked on consecutive nights. Why use stolen cars to drive around in and park where a crime would be committed.

Helen used her mobile to contact Mattock, 'Sir, I have gone over the guest list staying at the Aerodrome Hotel. At first had no success in linking anybody to the crime. Then processed car registration numbers, against any stolen cars reported in the last month around London. Came up with nothing but when going back a further two months, the two license plate numbers to both stolen cars parked at the hotel were to be found involved in two separate reported incidences. Two guests booked into the hotel, booked in on different nights, Friday and Saturday. Weekend of the stabbing, both booked in the exact same room, addresses given by guests non-existent, each car's registration numbers not matching the vehicles parked but to the two cars stolen within the last two months.'

The chances of stolen cars used so openly Helen thought strange in the light of a criminal act, taking place, concerning attempted murder at the time. Mattock then spoke as if he had been reading her mind. 'Why use stolen cars at a social function like a wedding unless they were not part of the wedding entourage. Put a trace on finding the whereabouts of these cars, could be some footage or sightings of them on CCTV traffic cameras, revealing their movement since leaving the hotel. Also, the CCTV cameras to the hotel see if we can recognise who or whom the cars belong to when driven away on the following days. Could be they belong to the same person covering his own tail. Same receptionist may not have worked duties on both days.'

Helen responded, 'Have that as my next job, Sir. Thought I would get you up to speed with my progress and findings.'

'What are you after, brownie points? You work well as part of this team. You have no need for flattery. Your mind does not switch off when given any job, just focus on the now. Praise will come after, or not.'

Helen smiled at non-committal accolade and responded, 'Nice to be told, also appreciated.'

Mattock answered her response saying, 'Just do a good job; do not let your head swell too big. By fishing for complements all the time, we may not get any work out of you.'

'Just when I thought you cared, you go and spoil it.' Helen laughed, turning off her mobile before Mattock could respond back.

Next call was to the hotel, asking whether she could look at the tapes from their CCTV cameras to the car park. Followed by calls to traffic control to see if any footage showing the movements of two cars, providing them with registration number and makes of car from the hotel.

Mattock replaced the telephone back in its cradle. He Stretched out his legs to relieve the stiffness of cramp he felt in his calves. His office resembled a crime scene in its self, with paper strewn everywhere across his desk and floor regarding the present case in hand. Along with other unsolved cases. Nestling in the "In and Out" trays, further cases neatly tied up in files, solved or unsolved. The Penny Connor Case, Mattock thought was moving along in one area, but still no nearer finding the killer. The fact Helen had come up with possible links to guests, nothing concrete, pointing at the stabbing on the night. The hospital's failure to provide footage of the visitors coming and going into St Georges Hospital gave a clear indication for an accident waiting to happen in their regard to lapsed security arrangements so far.

The phone rang. 'On my way.' Placing the telephone back, he made his way to the exit. In his haste to leave pushed the exit door into another officer coming into the main office, Coffee spilt everywhere. Frustrated, Mattock could only say, 'Shit, I cannot be dealing with this right now.' Leaving the officer looking in his wake, as Mattock walked off down the corridor and down the staircase with no sign of a backward glance.

Helen and Mattock were watching the CCTV video tapes back again, showed clearly two individuals walking away from the hotel and getting into the Renault, leaving the forecourt by the exit, into Purley Way heading north towards five-ways Waddon, Croydon or London.

Nothing on tape videoed of the stabbing, as the camera pans around the parking and surroundings to the refuge bins, all it revealed, was the arriving and departures of clients and guests that frequented the hotel and its facilities. Mattock stared down at the screen alongside Helen. The two men seen driving away in the suspect vehicle, clearly showed that one was white and the other black. Both wore hoods over their faces, but the white man had a tattoo on his forearm, just could not make out the unclear markings or pattern. The blurred print appeared to be that of a mystical nature, a dragon holding a shield before it. 'Can we get a closer picture of the tattoo, maybe a bit clearer, can't be many tattoos of that nature about. Ask around the Tattooists Shops and see if anybody has a record of making these markings on someone,' Mattock said to Helen.

'Due to the unclear faded markings, the tattoo could have been done a while back, which would suggest we are looking at an older man, than the impression of a young man wearing a hood given out,' Helen added to the equation.

'It's the only clue we have to go on right now. Have you had any joy with Traffic Control and their cameras showing up anything? Cannot believe they do not have CCTV cameras operating around the back of the hotel.'

Helen replied saying, 'Said they are still trawling the CCTV link up for the cameras in this area. I will run it pass them again now. Must have been able to track the cameras tapes down by now.'

'You carry on with that; I will go back to the station. See if I can start the ball rolling in having someone tracking down the tattooists around Croydon. Find anybody who would remember having etched this design on someone. The receptionist at the hotel, Susan, I noticed had a tattoo on her ankle. Could start by asking her where she had hers done. Be discrete when talking to her.'

A cause for concern reached Mattock's ears upon his return to his office, sitting behind his desk sat Chief Superintendent Homer, shuffling through the paperwork on Mattock's desk. Mattock forewarned that the Super was there. He tried to act surprised as he entered, as he pulled up. 'Morning Super, anything wrong or get lost on your way to your office.'

Homer looked up at Mattock. 'Do not waste your time trying the funny stuff on me Mattock, it does not wash. What news have we on the Penny Connor, found any answers yet.' Mattock went to reply, but Homer stepped in before he could say anything. 'From what I can see from the notes on the desk which is a mess, a wonder you can find anything that corresponds with the case. So, what have we got, I'm getting it in the neck from above in the Government.'

Government, why are they getting involved? Mattock thought. 'Sir, why the involvement of Number Ten, I have the feeling that someone is pulling strings to hide something. Everywhere I go I am hitting a roadblock. The hospital fail to record data in CCTV cameras, the hotel just happen to have CCTV of the parking area at front and side, but not where a stabbing occurs around the refuge bins. The CCTV picks up two men driving away from the hotel in a car with number plates stolen from a car reported about three months back. Before that CCTV footage revealed that one of the two men's arm had a faded tattoo. Seen getting into the dodgy car on camera and driving off. Everything conspires against us at the moment,' Mattock said as a way of speaking of his frustrations to the Penny Connor case. He concluded by informing Homer to not worrying about the state of the paperwork, he was aware of everything to do with the case, as he has it all stored in his head, each in its own compartment. Everything was in hand. He would tell the Super when he had more to go on.

Homer, tensed to speak out and remind Mattock who he was speaking to, 'The fact you have all relevant details in your mind is bye or leave, if anything happened to you whilst the murder enquires went on, nobody would have a clue what stage the case was in. Sort out the paperwork. What is that saying? Someone with a tidy desk is someone with a tidy mind.'

Ignoring his superior as Homer walked from his office and dropping the notes he had acquired back onto the desk. Mattock picked up the telephone and arranged for a police constable, along with one of his own officers to go around every Tattooists in Croydon. He did not hold out much luck in his quest.

As he picked through the notes, he came across one referring to another case. Looking at the photo, he asked himself why the photo had found its way into the spread of photos on his desk. The picture was that of Martin Mandrell. What drew Mattock to the picture he could not say, except he felt there was a missing link; something. The man in the photo was trying to tell him something and he was missing the point. Martin Mandrell was a villain, well known for a robbery that hit the headlines back in the seventies. He had taken part in the heist of a jewellery firm in Hatton Gardens. A loose note with a paperclip at the top of the page was sitting where the photo lay; Martin Mandrel's name appeared at the top, lifting it up off the table Mattock began to read the brief history of Mandrell. The missing link between Mandrell and Connor glared out at him, they were father and daughter. Mattock called out from his office, Helen who had just walked into the detective's room walked in, 'What's up, boss?'

Can someone find out where a Martin Mandrell is? Last I heard, he was doing a stretch in Parkhurst Prison. Seems he has a daughter, in Penny Connor.

'How so, Sir?' asked Helen.

Mattock pushed both the note transcript and the photo across the table towards Helen. 'Father and daughter, never knew he had family, let alone a daughter. This concludes that Penny Connor had been married at one time.'

Helen said, 'Then how is it this piece of information has not come to light before?'

'Good question, Helen. This photo was not on my desk this morning,' Mattock said as he went to his office door. He noticed Phillip Moore, one of the other DI on duty that day. 'Phillip, you were here this morning. What time did you get in?'

'About nine, why do you ask?' he enquired.

'Has anybody been into my office before I turned in this morning?'

'Not to my knowledge.' With that, Phillip just shrugged, splaying his hands apart.

Walking back into his office, Mattock stood over his desk. Shaking his head side to side, he looked over at

Helen who had remained seated throughout saying, 'I am sure that Phillip is on a different planet to everybody else. If the Queen walked in with all her entourage, he would not notice a thing. Someone must have dropped him on his head when born.'

Helen said, 'Shush, Sir, walls have ears.'

Mattock stared at Helen, glanced back at Phillip Moore. 'Yeah well, pity they did not add any ears to his head. Probably not heard anything, stoned deaf.' Helen stifled a snigger.

Making their way from Mattock's office, Helen took the pro-offered photo of Martin Mandrell from Mattock's hand. Helen offered to take the photo along to records and try to find anything more on Mandrell. Mattock said he would find out where Penny Connor's estranged husband could be holding out. Leaving Helen whilst agreeing to meet up later, he walked from the police station to a nearby café, bought a latte to go and drove off to his home, stopping halfway to drink his coffee, away from the station, stopping at the playing fields where he had spoken to Dan Prescott. Later, drove home to an empty house, completely forgetting he arranged with his wife to meet up at her parents for a meal arranged several weeks earlier. Mattock collapsed into an armchair, he was asleep as soon as his head hit the backrest.

Two hours later, rested and fed on what he could salvage from the fridge in a matter of twenty minutes. Tin of tuna, a jar of opened mayonnaise, an onion and bread from the breadbin, making do with a sandwich he felt he was taking a prompted healthy option apart from the mayonnaise. Mattock was back on the road driving and heading back towards the office. His mind refreshed could not stop thinking about his case, the feeling that he was getting the run-around by certain conflicting information. One hand his information telling him that Samantha Tambling, Harry Tambling, Terri Chapman and possibly Dan Prescott had known Penny Connor. On the other hand, some-how we find Tom Brannon mentioned in a statement, that he had overheard someone threatened in a phone conversation. We have assumed he has led us to assume that he is the caller that he made the provocative onslaught to a female, by process of elimination that nobody could confirm that he did not make the call. Why is he assumed to be the guilty party, based purely on him prefabricating this storyline.

CHAPTER 10

The Waddon Public House, as usual stopped still as Dan entered, resuming only when those present recognised who enter, the small talk recommenced as every group of drinkers carried on, from the quiet and silence back to a hub of noise descended back on all those in the pub. This happened whoever came through the door with no exception. Familiarity breeds contentment. Harry Tambling sat at the end of the bar talking to the same two people Dan had seen the last time he had entered.

He looked at the pair closer, he had not taken much notice on the previous occasion, but this time, he took notice of one. The Asian as someone he had seen on several other occasions, not in The Waddon. Dan could not place the name or where, his mind searched, but came up blank. Pushing the problem to the back of his mind, knowing it would surface again as to who and where later.

Harry sat with not a care in the world. Never looked up when Dan entered. Only Dan approaching sought his attention and demeanour change to one suspicious of a foe coming in arriving to cause trouble. 'Why are you here? If trouble is what you want, I can give you plenty, former brother-in-law or not.'

'That is the greeting you most want when you come through them doors, a feeling of welcome,' Dan said as he surveyed the bar and promptly sat down beside the Asian and his partner providing a barrier between Harry and himself. Turning to the Asian, 'I bet he does not talk to you like that. Bet he lays out the red carpet for you. What do you say?' Dan turned to the barmen and asked for a pint of his usual returning his gaze onto Harry. 'Good morning to you. I would buy you a drink, but I would not like to let good money go to waste.'

The barman eyed Harry before he pulled the pint, setting it before Dan. 'So why are you here?' Harry asked.

'Came to have a quiet word with you, but you appear to be busy. So, I thought I would just have a peaceful pint until you were free or is now not convenient,' Dan said in response.

Hearing no answer, Dan picked up the pint and sought a place on a seat, away from the bar, back to near the entrance to the pub. Sitting down he pulled out a notepad he had obtained that morning and commenced to write down a few notes. All the while Harry ignored his clients and watched him going through the motions as he sat down. Harry returned his attention to the Asian and his friend.

Dan had made a mental note of the faces, the Asian and his partner. As no names provided as introduction by either, or communicated to him by Harry. He made a written note before he read a newspaper left on a nearby seat by the previous owner. Harry, he knew was being a complete ass. Knew Harry had been trying not to show interest on his sitting there. Failing miserably as Harry could not stop watching him every time Dan moved to the bar or turning the newspaper from page to page. On the odd occasion, the Asian would glance in his direction following Harry's eyes.

Speaking to several local drinkers' he knew from previous visits; all knew of Harry's relationship going sour and ending in divorce. None knew of Dan's involvement in the breakup or the reason. Refusing to put his sister, Samantha's, family troubles into the public domain. Whether Harry had spoken up to carry favour in his pub, he could not pick-up on from the word of mouth said.

Tom Brannon's problems had instilled Dan's interest back into Harry's business affairs. Dan was beginning to suspect Harry's involvement in Penny Connor's death. Current and recent family histrionics aided that suspicion further. Tiny and Mitch entered The Waddon just as Dan ordered his second pint, on his return to his seat Tiny stepped in front of Dan. 'Does the boss know you're here?'

'What do you think? Dan responded with amusement, 'That question beggar's belief that you even thought to ask.' As he continued without another word pushing Tiny to one side as he carried onto his seat.

The locals went out of their way to allow Tiny and Mitch to pass through around the bar to where Harry sat with his companions. A few words whispered passed between Harry and Tiny, before they sat down in seats behind Harry.

Shortly after the Asian and his partner were beckoned to come and join them. Deep in discussion. Dan tried to eavesdrop, to make out what was being said, wishing he could be nearer. Never one to be able to lip-read. He could only guess at what was spoken, catching only the occasional word.

He heard a rush of wind pass by as the pub door open. Dan eyes followed everybody else in turning his head towards the door to see who came in. Simultaneously, everyone turned back and continue with whatever had preoccupied them previously. Ted, a local cab driver had come in through the door. Looking around the bar he and Harry's eyes met. Ted acknowledged Harry that his cab stood outside awaiting his fare, promptly leaving out of the same door. Harry and the Asian shook hands before the Asian and his partner made their departure from The Waddon Public House. The Asian determined avoidance of eye contact with Dan as they left.

Moments later saw Tiny and Mitch follow through the same doors together with Harry. Harry's departure brought a level of talk to interest in his leaving, but subsided on the door closing behind. Dan stood up and made his own exit. Standing outside, he looked in both directions. Saw Harry's car in the distance heading towards the five ways crossroads, Purley Way. Dan's own car parked in the opposite direction in Epsom Road alongside the railway track, before Duppas Hill Road going up towards Croydon

Flyover. His eyes turned and saw that the car in which Harry departed in turn right into Purley Way. The cab in which the Asian departed, nowhere in sight.

Dan still outside the pub's entrance walked towards his own car. Seconds later a police car pulled into the kerb alongside Dan. The window slid down revealing the face of DI Mattock looking up at him. 'If I had known that you were here, Mr Prescott, I would have arrived earlier, but I see that you are leaving. Can we offer you a lift?'

'We are not going in the same direction Detective Inspector.'

'Why not tell us where you were headed and maybe we can have a chat along the way. You have met DI Smith I assume. Hopefully, you will come willingly.'

'This lift you offer is not out of the kindness of your heart Detective Inspector,' Dan interjected.

DI Mattock smiled back at Dan. 'I had hoped you would help with our on-going enquiries into the death of Penny Connor. The fact that you are here just makes our job easier in that we can offer some assistance while you answer a few more questions. We can all go on inside the pub here, but I am sure you would rather not be seen, to be helping us with our inquiries.'

'You have a perceptive mind, Detective Inspector, but just getting into your car would if anyone was looking give that impression.'

'I'm just making a formal request. If you would like we could arrest you on suspicion of possibly a drink driving offence and take you down the station.'

'How would that stick if I'm not driving?' Dan said, happy to go along with this banter.

'You are now going to tell me that your car is not at this moment parked in Epsom Road. That would be diverting the course of justice by lying. We can go on all night with this Mr Prescott, but with us continuing with this charade, the more likely it is someone will alight from that pub.'

Dan smiled as he got into the police car, conceding he was losing the mind games for now. 'You win. If you please, home James'

'You appear to have a sense of humour Mr Prescott. Can assure you murder is not something to laugh about, when you could conceivably be one of the suspects for the murder.'

'If I was, then you would have arrested me long before now I suspect, Detective Inspector.'

'Then why worry to who may see you helping the police with their enquiries?'

'Who said I was worried?'

'Then why are we not talking inside the Waddon openly, when I see that you clearly wish to be somewhere else,' Mattock conveyed.

'Detective Inspector, it is a dangerous world out there as you well know. Talking to or with the cops carries its own problems, as it sends out mixed messages to those in the criminal world.'

Setting off from the kerb, the driver drove into a U-turn, driving back towards Purley Way. Turning left at the lights and on up towards Purley, Seeing the Aerodrome Hotel on the right as they drove passed prompted DI Mattock to ask Dan Prescott if he knew anything or heard anything about the attack on Penny Connor through his circle of friends. Not receiving any answer, he repeated his question again, to which Dan turned saying, 'I heard you the first time.'

'Then why don't you answer when questioned the first time, instead of remaining like a dummy unable to speak,' Mattock replied.

'I was thinking up what to say in response also thinking as to whether I should help you, may find myself a target.'

'You do not seem the kind of person who would let a problem get in the way of helping others. Can you say that your cousin would be safer, without help to safeguard her life should she be threatened in the event of your finding yourself in danger?'

'I grant you that Samantha's health and happiness is my prime concern. If I knew problems would arise from her marriage, no way would I have absconded to America. You may question my involvement in Harry, but I have known Harry along time and long known of his involvement with crime and only in the last year has he become a problem. He may act the big man, but I believe he has gotten himself into something which potentially will drag him down and destroy his standing around here.'

Mattock mulled over Dan's words. 'What theories do you have that give you concerns of his impending danger. Do you know who is behind the death of Penny Connor?'

'Like you, Detective Inspector, all I have is an instinct for finding the truth. I do not know of who is behind Harry and pushing his buttons. Only faces that keep cropping up whenever I have been to the Waddon Pub recently. Information that I have has not established to be fact yet. In answer to your question, do I know who killed Penny Connor, the answer is no,' Dan said.

Mattock thought of pressing Dan Prescott into telling him what he knew, 'I trust you know what you are doing, but if you should find anything, you will as I have said before, let us know and not go in guns blazing, or I will have you brought in for preventing the police in our own investigations by concealing evidence.'

'Message received. If I gave information of my own theories, would you be able to reciprocate in kind.'

Mattock knew if he was to give out information to Dan Prescott, he could compromise his own investigations. 'Could be a problem there, if you were acting without telling us why you would need the information required. Withholding any information connected with the case would jeopardise your position in that I could ultimately lead to you charged as an accessary to the murder of Penny Connor. We would need to work together with no transparency, co-operate with one another should the information established prove of importance in our investigation. If we do work alongside each other. I do not wish to be made a fool off. Do I make myself understood?'

Dan knew he could undermine the Detective Inspector at any time, 'Understood.'

A meeting of minds had taken place, with both parties suspicious of each other, wary of divulging, too much, too soon, of information leaking out. Mattock knew he was co-operating with someone he knew little about prior to the murder enquiry. Likewise, Dan not known to divulge information to the police, normally worked alone without police help due to the time given between theory and action hindered by red tape amongst other problems.

Mattock dropped off Dan outside his home, as Dan alighted from the police car he turned to Mattock asking, 'Is it possible to have a look at some mug shots of known villains on record?'

'Why the request, have you someone in mind we should know about?' asked Mattock.

'Have seen recently several people of Asian origin who have been cropping up in The Waddon, getting too cosy with Harry lately. Just curious as to whether they're known elsewhere throughout the criminal scene in this part of London.'

'Why not check out that possibility now, Mr Prescott. Could be a vital piece of information we need ourselves. Maybe we can be of use to each other after all,' Mattock said, informing the driver to return to the station.

Mattock rung ahead to have microfiche with mug shots of known villains on file, on arriving he made Dan sit down and go through the microfilms available, while he sat alongside Dan to spot check any faces that Dan picked up on. Helen made herself available to run checks on any faces pointed out by Dan. He described each of the pair. One was Asian of slim build, shaven with piercing grey, green eyes that stared right through you. Short cropped hair and left ear that looked as if it half chewed. The other also of Asian ascent, same height, but slightly bigger, only visible marking was a scar made from a knife wound just to the right under the jawline. Several hours passed by, with no match to his description of faces on the microfilm, also mug shots to those not placed on microfilm and still in archive photo albums. 'Sorry I wasted your time, Detective Inspector,' said Dan.

'Was worth taking a look through the records, does not help, but eliminates those we have,' Mattock replied. 'You said you have seen these people a lot recently at The Waddon. When was the last time you noticed their appearance?'

'Just before you turned up at The Waddon today. The Asians, together with Harry and his own men drove off in the direction of Roundshaw, Wallington.'

'From the descriptions, you have given of the two, we can check around and see if anybody knows them,' Mattock stated.

Dan concerned that any police involvement this early may scare them off said, 'Can you hold off approaching these two as I would not wish to spook them.'

'If they are up to anything criminal that is not for you to say how or when we proceed, we the police will act as and when I or we deem a need for action to be taken. You on the other hand will do as you are told, if you intend to play a part without our knowledge, I could deem your participation as an act of assisting the criminal activity, by interfering.'

Staring straight ahead, Dan focused on the facts he knew. Not completely accepting that the police would act swiftly when called upon, when it came to action the police were known to drag their heals, due to orders from high above or red tape. Rising, he made to go. Looked at Mattock, smiled at him, 'We will see.'

As he walked out of Mattock's office without another word, Mattock shouting at him as he left, 'Dan Prescott, do not do anything rash that jeopardises our efforts. I will hold you accountable for any action you take without our knowledge.'

At the end on the corridor, Dan shrugged his shoulders as he descended the stairs, 'We'll see,' was his final comment to himself, as he alighted from the police station back out on the street. He made his own way home.

CHAPTER 11

Sam felt constricted with her reliance on Shirley. Her health had taken a turn for the better, but Shirley still treated her as an invalid, capable of breaking down at any time. Always cleaning up after her, after every meal provided, even sending her up to bed too rest. Whether Sam was tired or not, nor wishing to rest, found this constant over caring obsession towards her too much of a constraint. Dan not being there, she could not find the words to argue her case in telling Shirley that she wished to be alone. When Dan asked Shirley to help and stay behind, she welcomed having someone around, now wished for her life back and for Shirley to go. The mobile rang. Shirley picked up and answered seconds later, when asked who it was, the reply always the same, someone trying to sell something.

Dan had remained in contact through Shirley's mobile. Never made direct contact through the house phone. Shirley spoke to him for ten, fifteen minutes before she passed her mobile to Samantha, 'Dan asked if he can speak with you.'

Samantha took the phone into the next room, returning minutes later. Handing the mobile back to Shirley saying 'Does he ever keep you in the dark. I just asked, what he was up to, he replied nothing much, when I said he was being evasive as usual, he just said will speak to you later, go over everything when you are better. When asked if I am okay, I am better I answered, for which he said, I will let Shirley be the judge of that. Have to go, catch you later,' he then hung up.

Samantha clearly ruffled by Dan not saying anything. 'So, what's your prognosis on my condition, what have you been saying about me, Shirley? I thought you were a friend, seems like your keeping tabs on me for his benefit, that why you are still here, make me out to be a mental case. What is he up to, Shirley? Why does he keep me in the dark, but can openly talk over his problems with you, or am I right in assuming the talk is all about me?'

'It's not like that, he told me not to reveal why he is out all the time and keeping hush-hush. He does not tell me everything either. Just tells me to stay and look after you.'

'Well, I'm fine. Feel a whole lot better, so thanks. You can go now. I need my space back, to be on my own. Think it is time for you to go home now.'

Shirley making no move to go anywhere said, 'Not sure Dan would have me leave just yet for a while. Asked me to stay until he came back home. Look after you and keep you company.'

Miffed at the constantly having to justify that she was well enough to make her own decisions in life and not reliant on others making her choices for her without any consultation. 'So, he is not content to making me feel like an invalid. You are now to be my jailer. Make sure I do not leave.'

A key in the lock turning, took them both by surprise. Dan came in through the door, back heeling the door closed behind him. 'Well that's the welcome I like to see, my two best girls in the whole world greeting me at the door.'

Samantha and Shirley both looked at each other at the same time. Surprise and suspicion gripped their faces as he had only just hung up on them both. Shirley glancing down at her mobile still held in her hand. Samantha held spellbound to the fact she was tearing into Shirley, to the theory of Shirley talking behind her back about her health.

Both girls staring back at him, mouths open. Dan stood wondering what he had done wrong with a bemused look. Not wishing to stand in the doorway, he continued into the kitchen where he laid down a take-away on the kitchen worktop surface. 'Thought a Chinese meal would do for a change, my treat. I could have rung ahead but the mobiles dead. Hope I have picked out what everyone is likely it eats? So, what have you two been up to today?'

'You have only just spoken to us,' cried out Shirley. 'What do you mean your mobile's dead, only minutes ago, you have been talking to us both on my mobile?'

'You can't have, my phone is off. Here, check if you do not believe me,' reaching out, offering to give his mobile over towards Shirley.

Shirley took the phone from Dan, promptly checked the phone and found no sign of life. Looking at her own mobile, checked the last call to come through on her mobile and frowned, unknown number recorded. Sam looking over Shirley's shoulder had seen the same on both mobiles. Sam responded first by asking Dan where he had just come prior to entering the house.

In the meantime, Shirley not convinced plugged the electrical lead into Dan's phone to recharge his mobile.

'Why?' he asked.

'Just answer the question, Dan, please. Stop answering a question with another question,' Sam stated with a slight irritated edge to her voice. 'You could after all have taken the call out prior to entering here.'

'Okay. I have just been dropped off from the cop shop by the police, been helping them with some enquires,' Dan answered. 'So why the interest in where I have come from?'

Sam looked at Shirley and Shirley back at Sam. Dan accessed the look on the women's faces. 'Has a call come through from someone on your mobile?'

'Yes, but the call appears to have not come from yourself. You have not another phone on you?' A shake of Dan's head the response. 'Then someone, we thought was you, just telephoned us portraying to be you, sounding like you, and we both fell for the person's voice as he spoke to the both of us.'

Dan took the mobile from Shirley's hand and promptly checked for himself. 'I do not know of anyone who can mimic my voice; you are sure it sounded like me?'

'What do you take me for, Dan?' asked Shirley. 'If I can't recognise your voice, then it is more that certain that Samantha would have picked up on it not being yours.'

'Well, what did he say?' he enquired.

Shirley unconvinced that Dan had not been on the mobile to them, looked down at Dan's mobile recharging.

'Nothing, just asked how we were. That is what so strange, why ask and talk about everyday things. He even knew about how Sam has been lately. I will say one thing for the caller. He was good at his impersonating of you.'

Dan, none the wiser, spoke to DI Mattock on the mobile whilst it charged. Explained the situation that occurred whilst he was ferried home just moments ago, and what transpired when walking through the front door.

'We are on my way back? said Mattock, making the sign conveying to DI Smith to turn around and go back before the phone went blank.

They turned up ten minutes later, pulling up outside Dan's home. Within half an hour, notes had been written down of all the information that had transpired, prior to and after Dan Prescott's arrival. Both Sam and Shirley stating over and again, repeating every tiny detail.

Mattock stated he would if needed request an officer to remain on the premises should the caller phone in again. Dan declined the offer as Sam said she would like her space back and was insistent that she would be okay.

Mattock and DI Smith made their way out of the door, as they stepped over the doorframe. Mattock could not help but see marks in the doorframe near the lock, faint scratch markings. He pointed these out to Dan Prescott 'What are these marks here near the lock, has anybody tried to get into your home?'

Dan leaned over to the left Mattock's body and felt the markings on the doorframe, 'First time I have seen them. Cannot say whether anybody has tried to force, if the night light was off could be key marks due to trying to find the lock, there is nothing missing to my knowledge. Sam, has anyone tried to force entry through this front door?' Dan asked.

'Not since we have been here,' Sam replied,

Mattock continued out through the door, 'Have another check, see if anything is missing. Could be something, could be nothing.'

Shirley picked up Dan's mobile which had been recharging for the best part of an hour and a half. Picked up and checked it herself. Dan's insistence in that he had not made any call. Deflated when the mobile last calls confirmed Dan's statement, when no calls registered on Dan's mobile, made since earlier that day.

'The women have been here for two, three days. Staying over, would be surprised if anyone had been trying to get in and them not hearing a sound,' Dan said playing down the implications to the message Mattock was trying to put over.

DI Helen Smith already in the car, waited as Mattock slowly walked back down the garden path, entering the front nearside passenger door to the police car. Helen had elected to drive back to the station. While Mattock made notes to their visit into his notebook.

'Helen I'm not sure I know how I feel to the calls, whether connected to the case or whether this is a separate problem unconnected or whether we are being manipulated,' Mattock said.

DI Smith and Mattock spoke again of the fact that Harry Tambling's was once married to Samantha Tambling. Due to his aggressive attitude through drink and work related problems. Then hear that his drinking is non-existent after the fallout. Which begs the answer as to why, and what made Harry aggressive towards Samantha, if not the drink, something he has found so easy to give up following the break-up. A ruse to get out of the marriage he could easily have walked away from without the violence. Appears now to have involved himself in criminal activity of which we only have the word of Dan Prescott. Harry has no criminal record, no one has been able to pin any crime to his name despite the people he associates with as being well-known criminals, who have records as long as your arm. One of which is Tiny, a minor petty crook and until recent years has been in and out of prison for petty local crimes almost all his adult life. The Asian person Harry apparently has connections with, we need to establish where this person has come from, and to what he is up to that involves Harry Tambling. If he was working in the background for a number of years, why get his hands dirty now.' Arriving back at the station, they went back over all the files again checking for anything that they could have missed, while rechecking Dan Prescott's information on Harry Tambling.

Mattock spoke with Sergeant Price, requesting if he could spare any of his officers. Asked him to speak with the local telephone companies and obtain recent phone records on Shirley and Samantha's mobiles contacts and incoming calls, within the last month or two. 'Helen,' he called out whilst replacing the office phone down on the desk sergeant. 'Have someone organise a search of Samantha Tambling's home for possible bugs or other devices, to confirm whether the house was clean, devoid of any spying equipment, as to whom maybe spying on her if found.'

Helen was perusing over the notes and photos of the crime scene, combing through to find any possibility of that missing factor into either Penny Connor's death and Samantha and Harry's marital problems including the violent acts of aggression from Harry on Samantha. Other than that Harry's name cropped up in both lines of enquiries. Is Harry a victim of a witch-hunt, Harry with a person of Asian descent does not constitute to wrongdoing?

At that precise moment, her train of thoughts interrupted when Mattock walked back into the room, stating the arrangements he had made arranged through the desk sergeant and with another colleague to check out the mobile companies.

He walked into the room holding two cups of coffee, 'Time for refreshments I thought. What do you say to that?'

Helen mocked shock on her face. 'That is a first, are you feeling okay?'

CHAPTER 12

The dark tales told, circulating about Samantha's life at the hands of Harry Tambling. That followed by Dan Prescott throwing out Harry Tambling from their family home, on catching him in the act of hitting Samantha. The reasons given for his dependency on drink and filling a void in his life were sketchy. He never told anyone the reason he turned to drink, he only knew that it brought a sense of relief to the problems that thwart him.

Samantha spent the weeks following Harry's departure, behind closed doors. For six weeks, she would not go out and face neighbours, friends or family alike. The markings on her face were only now starting to fade. Mental scars would remain for several months longer. Dan did his best to compensate for Samantha's mood swings. Through the months following, Dan took it upon himself to nurse his cousin's esteem back into the outside world. She confined herself within her home. To his mind for too long, stopping her from becoming a hermit imprisoned in her home. The thought that Harry would reappear into her life always a danger that always played a part on Samantha's mind. One reason that Dan stayed around was also to monitor Harry's movements in around the local area. So far, Harry had distanced himself, not even bothered to telephone Samantha to arrange for collection of his belongings. His office desk still locked, remaining unopened in the study. Dan often wished to break the lock, but Samantha insisted that she did not want anyone or anybody to rummage through the locked desk draws.

Harry had the only key and not wishing to worry Samantha even though he suspected the contents could reveal Harry's movements. Dan kept his own distance.

Dan appeared at dawn, knocking on the door of his own home. Samantha answered enquiring what had happened to Dan's own key. 'In my pocket, did not wish to walk in on you and Shirley and create another surprised outburst from either of you.'

'Only twice has that happened. Are we that scary, beside what do you expect us to do when you are out there trying to spook us.'

'When was the last time I spooked anyone recently. You tell me you are okay. Then when I come into my own home, you react by jumping out of your skin at the first time of opening the front door. That is not the reaction of someone, who is not of a jittery disposition and reasonably sane actions.'

Samantha shook her head in defiance, not believing the words coming from Dan's mouth. She turned to Shirley and said, 'Lives on a different planet at times, does not live in the real world. Making assumptions on what does not affect him personally. Probably thinks what has happened in the last few days has been magnified to frustrate his logical self-assured mind.'

Sam and Shirley stood watching from the sides as Dan went through to the kitchen and made himself tea and taking his tea with him into the garden. Ignoring the fact, he had asked no one else. Decided not to comment further on their wisecracks. Both miffed by the way Dan just waltzed in ignoring the comments made by them both. Instead wrote away on a notepad, looking up every now and then deep in concentration, oblivious to their presence.

Diagrams, drawings sketched with notes at various points around the sketched outlines. Shirley not one for being in the dark, came up and stood behind Dan watching as Dan wrote away. Only when Dan had stopped did she ask what was on her mind. 'What is this all about, you are not normally one for writing down notes and drawing diagrams. This anything to do with the problem you seem not to be sharing with us?'

'Trying to put down in writing the people who have become wrapped up in this case, because Tom Brannon has started a chain of events involving the death of Penny Connor, someone Sam knew a while back and known by her ex.'

'So why, are you actively involved yourself, has this to do with Terri Tambling in North London?' Shirley asked.

'In a roundabout way, yes it does,' Dan answered. 'I've been trying to keep the problem from Sam as her ex seems to hold all the answers to why she feels threatened by him returning home. Only the police have somehow gotten their knickers in a twist and think that I am not being up front with them about Harry Tambling.'

'What gives them reason to think that? I mean you are helping your friend Terri. That is what we have been led to believe,' Stated Shirley

'That was how it started out, just that. Harry's involvement has been highlighted, in that is if what Tom Brannon has overheard in listening into a phone conversation, could possibly be connect with the death of Penny Connor. Police infer that he is under investigation along those lines, based on information they have received of which I am not privy to. The fact I know Harry Tambling implements me due to Terri having brought me into watch over and find out whether Harry is in trouble. However, what has me thinking is whomever you or Samantha thought you were speaking with on the telephone call yesterday. Someone has mimicked my voice, which you both said was the clear-cut work of someone who definitely knows me inside out.'

Shirley listened with a backwards glance to where she knew Samantha stood, behind her at the doorway, slightly hidden. 'I think you need to speak with Sam, put her mind at rest. She is a lot stronger now than you give her credit. I agree had this been last week, any talk would be too much for her to take in. Your presence has held and dispersed any fears she may have had. Do you have any clue to who could or would impersonate you?'

Dan put the notepad and pen down, drank the tea, continuing to look ahead with a pensive look upon his face. Shirley sat down opposite looking at him, with a flickering movement of her eyes implying that someone else was behind him. Turning confirmed his suspicions. Samantha came forward appraising the situation, now that Dan knew she had been listening to his comments. What she did not know was what else Dan refrained from telling her. Sitting alongside to the left of Shirley, adjacent to Dan, she motioned Dan to carry on talking. Accessing his options if any, decided to bring Sam up to date on what was happening as much as he knew. From receiving the phone call from Terri at the theme park, to why he thought he had to help Terri Chapman out. The police involvement in him, his position with Harry and the police, Shirley's presence and what was her own part in Harry's troubles if any.

After a moments reflection, Dan said, 'Sam I was asked to keep quite by Terri to Harry's current problem with Tom Brannon. In respect of yourself I decided not to add pressure to your own problems.' said Dan, more to himself, 'maybe that was a mistake on my part, I can't say.'

Dan remained silent whilst looking up at Samantha before he carried on. 'When Terri phoned on my mobile at the theme park,' he began, 'I had no idea why Terri called at the time. You know I have known Terri a long time now despite her relationship with Harry, we go back years and as we grew up together later in our teens we got closer, we were more like brother and sister at first with no romantic desires. As soon as the teenage years grew to an end, we had grown apart with my wish to join the army. This made Terri make her feelings different and wanted us to get closer, fear of losing me. I would not commit to the married life, had already set my mind on joining up for the army. We only saw each other when I was on leave. However, apart from that, romance would take a backward step as my army life came first as I never knew when I would be sent away to fight, or take up a cause against another country. You sign up for the army and you have no choice in the matter. The army has priority over anything else in your life.'

Dan stopped talking on his past relationship with Terri and focused on the initial phone call he received. 'Terri never asked for help, always sorted out by her brothers if trouble came knocking. Well, when Terri phoned, I knew something was up for her to ask for my help. Never has asked for my help in the past, so agreed without question. At the time, I did not think the problem would involve your ex, Harry. Anyhow, Terri was concerned about a conversation heard by one of her customers. Turns out your Harry, is the person a Tom Brannon had overheard speaking on the phone. Not one for mixing words, your Harry basically, threatened someone over the phone.'

Samantha asked, 'So why not just say that when I enquired what Terri wanted you for at the time of asking. Now I have just heard you mention that Harry has spent a double life of crime outside the pub. Is he in trouble, and why am I the last person who is told, was I that much of a threat to him.'

Dan replied, 'You would need to ask Harry that, all I know, is he wanted to keep you out of any backlash about his other life. I have known him to have a criminal life outside the pub. Small stuff, but his involvement with Penny Connor was to be his undoing. From the look on your face, you know who I am talking about, whether he is involved in her death and suspicions seem to indicate this.'

'So, why do you feel the police suspect you if Harry is responsible?' asked Sam.

'Because I found Penny Connor the night she was stabbed at the Aerodrome Hotel. I was the one who asked for the police and an ambulance to be called. I was the one that "surprise, surprise", knows Harry Tambling who happened to be the person using threatening language to another who happened to get herself stabbed outside a hotel around Croydon and left for dead. Only redeeming feature is that Penny Connor was alive the last time I saw her, seen going off in an ambulance to hospital. I had no idea who the woman was when I found her, only found out recently and that you had known her. Evidently someone decided she was a threat and went in to finish the job at the hospital, under the watchful eyes of every worker working in hospital and CCTV cameras.'

'That's just coincidence and if you are now working and helping the police in their pursuit of those involved, surely you are in the clear,' said Samantha.

'Maybe you are right,' was all Dan said.

Shirley sat their throughout while Sam and Dan spoke, listening to the two-way conversation, speaking up she interrupted, 'Does either one of you know who would be trying to play mind games with us by impersonating you, Dan, over the phone.'

Dan answered, 'Anyone could basically sound like another if you are not concentrating, by throwing in the odd word or phrase that you expect that person to say. For you to fall for this you would have to know the person, or a mimic. To my mind that leaves family and friends only. Who, I have no idea, but if you were mucking around, playing a joke on another, you would possibly laugh about it at some point throughout your speaking to that person and reveal the prank almost immediately.'

'Would you play a prank like that on someone,' Sam interrupted.

'Never thought about that personally,' Dan replied.

CHAPTER 13

The newspapers ran a story the following day. A drug swoop had taken place that night at a warehouse in South London, where a haul of category 'A' drugs has been found on the premises, with a street value of six million pounds. The owners of the warehouse in question are of Asian ascent believed to be the Hou-Lin Hoi family, known by police working in drugs for the past months. A cartel that had been under suspicion in the last six months, had moved in trying with some success to infiltrate the gangland world of South London.

During investigations throughout the last six months, a South London man, seen on a number of occasions going into the warehouse, had not been seen since the night of the raid. So far, nobody had come forward or been arrested in connection to these investigations. Astonishment had been echoed that the CCTV footage of the premises had failed to give clear pictures to those frequently seen in or around the warehouse. The lack of information accrued, was insufficient to prosecute those actively involved. The Asian owner's non-committal claim that they were unaware of any criminal goings on at their warehouse with the absence of CCTV footage, were unable to recognise those involved.

DI Mattock placed the newspaper onto the desk before him. A discussion of the night's events was circulating around the table. Try as he may, could not get a word in as recriminations and accusations flew all around. Nobody was taking responsibility for the one blot on the investigations.

The Warehouse are owned by Asians with an unknown white person had been seen in and around the warehouse on more than one occasion. Too Mattock, there was a possible link with the Asians seen at The Waddon being the same and in cahoots with Harry Tambling from Dan Prescott's information given. Harry Tambling being the white person involved on camera. Only the unclear picture held on CCTV, leads to the unconfirmed result for a conviction.

Several miles away Dan Prescott reached the same conclusion. Discarding the tabloid paper onto the table while Sam and Shirley sat opposite and looked on. 'If Harry is involved, will be the first time he has got his hands dirty,' Dan said as the paper landed.

'Why drugs? Is that his thing now?' Samantha replied.

Dan could not think of one reason not to suspect Harry into supplying drugs. What hold have the Asians on Harry that he would join forces and deal in drugs, *how deep has he gone?* Would this be the reason that changed his character that inevitably ruined his marriage to Samantha, turning him violent in his treatment towards Samantha? *Is he taking drugs, how involved in the trafficking of drugs is he?*

Believing now, that he knew nothing about what Harry was capable of, his time travelling around America for five or six years; never to stay in one place for more than two weeks at any one time. Losing touch with family, friends and Sam alike back home, only to suddenly come back and find Sam his only remaining living relative in turmoil. Could not believe that Sam's parents having died in a car accident? Would bring about the change in Harry. Deeming it a necessity to given his criminal activities an upward boost.

'Never known Harry to take drugs, was always like me in that the thought of trying drugs or using drugs never entered his head,' said Dan,

Sam thought before saying, 'So why did you automatically think that Harry was the white man in the newspaper report.'

'I never thought that I would see the day Harry would strike out in anger only to find him strike out at you. So, find it possible that Harry could have changed his views on drug dealing,' Dan answered. 'You two will be okay, I need to take a walk. Clear the cobwebs from my mind.'

'What are you going to do?' asked Shirley.

'Not sure yet, Terri asked at the outset to keep an eye on Harry. Maybe I need to talk to Harry outright.'

'Do you have to do everything Terri asks?' Sam said sarcastically.

'Not really, but...' said Dan, leaving Sam and Shirley as he walked back through the house closing the front door behind him as he left, without completing his reply.

The sun was out, making one of its rare appearances at this time of year. A flock of birds erupted from behind nearby trees on the playing fields in Purley Way, spooked by who knows what. Dan sat with a coffee bought earlier. Dan was watching the birds as they erupted from the trees not thinking of why they took off so suddenly.

A voice from behind him spoke: 'Knew I would find you here, was told you had gone for a walk when I called in at your home. They could not say where you had been going, so took a guess.'

'Very susceptible of you, Detective Inspector Mattock,' Dan replied, recognising the voice as he turned to confirm his assumption.

'I take it you have read the papers this morning.'

'Yes, I take it your referring to the drugs haul found by yourselves,' Dan inferred.

Mattock sat down alongside Dan. 'Have spoken to your sister whilst there. You assumed the same answer as I, as to the identity of who the white guy maybe, with his connection to Asian clientele in his pub?'

'We appear to be on the same page on that score, but to confirm our suspicion. Are the Asians, mentioned in the report the same two I met up with at The Waddon and who own the warehouse premises the same people. Could then be possible proof of Harry's involvement in his being the white man you speak off, I still find that hard to believe, knowing Harry never had shown an interest in drugs before,' Dan said, following the line of talk.

Mattock to acknowledge Dan's question on the Hoi family being the same Asian party, Mattock had no answer to give, no photograph of the Hoi owners found to substantiate their involvement. However, information established that the Hoi family were the current owners of the premises were involved in the drug trade, as nobody had seen pictures of the Hoi family. Following a tip off to the drug haul, the police had hoped to catch those involved. Someone else must have tipped them off as they had left the premises prior to the raid. Only a search found the drugs. Mattock was not about to reveal the information acquired, to the tabloids nor Dan Prescott.

'There is nothing I can add to that already covered by the media,' said Mattock.

'Not giving much away, Detective Inspector Mattock. I wonder why you stopped for a chat, if your only here to pass the time of day. If the police were keeping an eye on a certain Asian family, then surely your experts would be more productive in acquiring proof after six months of spying into their affairs. Why are these people still on the street? Cannot believe you, have no photographic evidence with access to CCTV everywhere readily on hand if needed. I also reckon that if a white man is on CCTV, then Harry would have already been arrested, locked up in one of your finest cells.'

Mattock sat saying nothing. A siren heard, followed by the sight of a police car with flashing blue lights racing down alongside the playing fields, then disappearing in minutes down Purley Way and out of sight towards the five ways intersection. 'You think you have it all worked out, then something happens to change your own perspectives on a case. So, you are not of the opinion that Harry is our man?'

'I have not said that. But, considering there is a possibility that Harry is innocent and not arrested yet, then no. Is that the reason you are here, you are having doubts also or am I wrong?' stated Dan.

Another police car raced by, driven in the same direction as the previous, flashing blue lights with no siren blazing. Looking up Dan said, 'Looks like business as usual.'

Mattock rose from the bench, stood with a pensive look upon his face, before departing, he said, 'Our paths will meet again soon no doubt. Let me know if you hear anything,' Mattock said as he walked away.

Dan remained seated on the bench in a reflective mood. Pondered on Mattocks pally approach, like, they were best of pals now, looking on at a football match in progress across the playing fields on an adjoining pitch. He looked on as two players disputed a referee's decision having blown on his whistle for a foul. He continued watching the football match for a further ten minutes before deciding to leave. Deciding a talk with Harry was his next port of call.

Dan found his intended talk with Harry put on hold. As the build-up of traffic going in his intended direction escalating all the way down the length of Purley Way. Intending to find a local bus going in the direction of Waddon. Now observing the traffic, his plans hampered. Thoughts of walking the length of Purley Way harboured a long-walk. Thoughts of retracing his steps back home knew was another option available. Waiting for a bus going homewards just as daunting, he stood waiting beside the bus stop for fifteen, twenty minutes, still no bus in sight. The traffic going back towards the five-way intersection with Stafford Road, Purley Way crossroads, appeared moving at a snail's pace. A white van he had seen earlier had moved forward no more than ten metres in the time Dan had stood waiting. No feedback as to the delay, coming from the odd car driving passed from the Waddon Way traffic lights. The drivers preoccupied with driving home or elsewhere and traffic starting to build up away from Croydon.

Giving up the ghost in waiting, Dan commenced walking down to Waddon, changing his mind on going home. He commenced walking towards Waddon. Ignoring the traffic as he bypassed the scene with the ease that walking gave on this occasion. Eying the Hotel as he passed. A scene of normality now given from The Aerodrome Hotel to two nights previous, the crime scene. You would think no crime had taken place. Conveyed just business as usual.

Closing in on the Stafford Road, Purley Way crossroads, Dan saw police cars on each corner blue lights still flashing. Mattock came into sight adjacent to him across the traffic lights, talking with other officers. Detective Inspector Helen Smith came from behind a tree as Dan came nearer to the crossing. They both smiled on recognition, 'Mr Prescott, what are you down here for?' Helen asked.

'Might ask you the same question, Detective, saw your boss earlier. Interesting chat we had, your boss Detective Inspector Mattock and me, on the playing fields up the road,' Dan said.

Helen came closer, stopping anyone passing by from coming between them. 'He has not said a word to me yet. Anything interesting he would wish to talk about?'

'Oh! The main story in the newspapers this morning, I am sure he will inform you later. What's the problem here then, blue lights flashing every which way are racing around everywhere, all convening here at these traffic lights have you enough officers and police cars here?'

'Not sure I can tell you, still investigating information that has come to light,' said Helen.

Mattock came across from the other side of the junction. Dan said, 'Never thought we would meet up this quick again. Only some of the drivers on the way down are slightly agitated at finding themselves still caught in this traffic hold-up situation with nobody giving a reason why.'

Helen took the bait and proceeded in asking two police officers to talk with the drivers held up. Try if possible to turn some around and diverted them down away out from Purley Way. Direct them around back, left at the Toyota forecourt and over the mini roundabout down Queensway through the Industrial Estate and down onto Stafford Road if going to Wallington and to Plough Lane for Beddington and south through to Mitcham.

Ignoring the remarks scorned on their inability to not being able to organise a piss up in a brewery by one driver, who frustrated at the hold-up felt obliged to say his piece vocally. Mattock told Dan why they were in this situation. 'Two men caught out trying to highjack a car at the lights, having assaulted the driver and his passenger after they had failed in pulling the driver from the car. A police car passing seeing the incident went in pursuit as they ran on seeing the police car, fleeing away down Stafford Road towards the Waddon Pub. The driver drove off only to stall the car halfway across the crossroads. By which time drivers coming down and up Purley Way tried to go around the car bringing all the traffic to a halt in all directions. We have managed to clear the centre of the crossroads and removed the stalled car across to the garage.'

As Dan stared over to the garage, Mattock interrupted him as he nudged for Dan attention, 'Then the best is saved for last, we find the driver had just come from Croydon and found a stash of drugs under the seat whilst checking the car over. The driver and his passenger have been taken down to the police station in Stafford Road, Wallington, for questioning.'

Dan spoke his thoughts out aloud, 'Why are you telling me all this information, surely this for the police to know, not me.

'Appears that the driver is known to be a frequent visitor at The Waddon. Would seem Harry Tambling is into the drug scene. Whatever doubts you had on Harry, has more or less been confirmed,' Mattock said, 'just need to find the evidence on him. Added to his possible involvement in the murder of Penny Connor and he is toast.'

A smile crossed Mattock's face to the prospect of solving another case with an added bonus to boot.

The mobile in DI Smith's hand vibrated as her phone rang. She walked off to one side. Shortly returning as the call ended, 'Appears we have caught one of the hijackers; the other ran off into Waddon Ponds, only be a matter of time before we apprehend him.'

Plans in speaking to Harry evaporated as soon as Harry's name was mentioned. Dan felt this summed up his day, no progress in his own endeavours in helping Terri to keep Harry out of trouble. Harry Tambling was doing everything to dig his hole deeper. This was not like the Harry of old. He seemed to be under the control of another person. Could this be the Asians doing, then the question is what if anything, they have on him. What was it that Penny Connor knew ending in her death.

Word came that the other hijacker had been found, arrested both taken to the Stafford Road police station to be charged with the attempted hijacking of a car. Despite their not knowing that their crime had helped secure a drug find.

CHAPTER 14

Normality returned to the roads, with traffic flowing in all directions allowing for traffic light signal changes. Dan left the scene an hour earlier. Not wishing to stay around to what could transpire. He paid for another coffee, bought from a nearby café, no intension of hanging around, he accepted an offer of a lift into Croydon from Mattock with one of the traffic cops returning to Croydon and for Dan to be dropped off, outside the Whitgift Centre.

Once out of the car, Dan telephoned Terri, informing her of the latest developments. Terri's fiery temper as he brought her up to date took time to quell. Threatening to come across London now as they spoke, he calmed Terri down sufficiently to stop her making things worse for her brother.

Dan was now in Croydon Shopping Centre. To distance himself from Harry's mounting problems. Having stayed in the shopping centre for an hour. He returned home.

Someone was pounding his fist on Dan's front door. Awakened from his sleep, he felt alert at once. His bedside clock, showing 6.20am. Whoever was bashing the door was insistent. Dan head now alert, knew that he needed to answer the door. He cursed, 'Who the hell is that? He cursed out loud. Who was knocking at his door this time of morning, Alighting from his room he saw both Sam and Shirley in their respective bedroom doorways. Both looked bleary eyed, their faces asking the same question. He answered before they could form the question verbally. 'I'll find out as soon as I open the door and not before,' he grumbled, 'go back to bed both of you.'

Shirley spoke back before Dan took a step down the stairs. 'With all that noise, how do you suppose we can do that now we are wide awake, no we are coming down with you.'

Continuing his own descent down the stairs all he could say was, 'Suite yourselves.'

He opened the front door. He found himself pushed to one side as police officers invited themselves in, with Mattock following up in the rear ahead of DI Helen Smith. 'What the hell is going on, barging your way in at this unearthly hour. Has there been a murder or something?' Dan Prescott queried.

Mattock having walked passed Dan, turned and said. 'You could say that, where were you or where did you go when dropped off at the Whitgift Centre yesterday?'

Dan recovered from the unexpected intrusion, the two women stood on the staircase watching the commotion that was playing out in front of them confused and panicking at the same time. Then Dan realised what Mattock had just said. 'What, where, whose been murdered and why are you thinking I would know about any murder. I've been here all night, ask the girls.'

Mattock stared up at Samantha and Shirley, returning his gaze to Dan. 'That is not what I asked you. I think you had better put some cloths on and come down to the station with us. We can talk on the way, as you seem to have an alibi for tonight, which the women can verify to Helen here, while we go. I will reveal all on the way. I need to know what you were up to from the time you we dropped you off in Croydon to when you arrived home.'

Dan stood his ground. 'No, you tell me first who has been murdered, the girls will find out sooner or later.

Mattock watched the faces of the women, dithering whether to reveal anything. Knowing Dan was forcing his hand to reveal all. 'A body was found floating in Waddon Pond early this evening. It was Tom Brannon.'

Shock and confusion showed on Dan's face. Sam and Shirley only knew the deceased from Dan speaking of him in the last few days. 'I'll get dressed, but I'll need to go upstairs get some clothes. Be as quick as I can. Okay.

Yeah. Sorry that is not getting me dressed.' Several minutes passed before Dan came back down the stairs. Beckoned Mattock back outside the front door.

Neighbours stood outside in doorways up and down in the street, remarked. 'Appears you have created, something for the gossips here, Detective Inspector Mattock.'

'Well, soon as we were told that Tom Brannon had been found dead. There being only three people connected to him. Yourself and Terri Chapman who had answered her phone and her brother Harry, who we are still holding at the Stafford Road police station. Someone has gone around to see Terri Chapman from the local police station in Cricklewood. As you were still at liberty until you arrived here last night, we need to establish at what time you arrived home. Hence our arrival at your home. If the women confirm you were home all night, you may be able to shed some light on who may have reason to kill, and knew of Tom Brannon and why he was over this side of the Thames.'

A web of conceit was unfolding before Dan. He found himself unexpectedly feeling he was finding himself drawn into Harry Tambling's world. He knew nothing of why Tom Brannon had found himself faced down in a local pond. Only reason for his being back in South London would be that his wife and daughters lived in the south. Still coming to terms with the news of Tom Brannon's death, Dan could not conceal the concerned look from his face to Mattock who stood watching over him, noting every expression Dan's face gave as he sought to find a reason behind this latest criminal act.

Dan shrugged his shoulders in not knowing any response to the questions that Mattock had asked. He only knew Tom from his meeting just days ago, 'Detective Inspector Mattock, if I knew why Tom's life was ended, to which I have not an answer this minute. Harry had a reason, even Terri if she were that concerned with Harry. I have told you all that I know. Tom's ex-wife and daughters still live south of London, could be a reason for Tom's coming south of the Thames,' Dan concluded.

The hijacking incident; Tom's death could have been arranged by Harry prior to his arrest to take the heat of himself. He would be in police custody when the body of Tom Brannon was found. These thoughts came at will. Dan searching for a reason an explanation, clasping at straws of the possibilities. The mechanics of Dan's mind trawled through the possible equations and answers to the criminal acts unfolding. Drugs found in the hijacked car, seemed reckless if caught in possession. The hijacking conspired to pervert the cause of justice, underlying the fact that Harry was capable of creating criminal acts as a cover to enhance his good standing within the community and carry the air of innocence.

All this he knew was pure conjecture, nothing proven. By helping Harry Tambling's sister Terri, was he helping in digging his own grave. Nothing in turn provided a reason behind the recent phone calls to Sam and Shirley from someone purporting to be him.

Mattock observed Dan's hands moving simultaneously with his thoughts. Mattock asked Dan the question foremost in his own mind. Said as if he was interacting with Dan's thoughts. 'What do you make of Tom Brannon's death, together with the hijacking attempt this morning?'

'What do I make of Tom Brannon's death?' Dan said, repeating Mattock's question. 'I think it is unfortunate that he found himself caught up in something not of his own doing, but would question why he would concern himself with another's problem, only to become a victim resulting in his own death. But what was he doing in Croydon?'

Mattock empathised with Dan's comments. 'If he had not acted on his conscience, he might possibly be still alive. Would his death inevitably has brought his killer to stand trial or had someone deflected their crimes onto another to take the blame.'

'Sounds like you already have your killer in mind. If I am still your suspect on Penny Connor, you already know I am not the man in the frame. Nevertheless, if you are thinking Harry Tambling, then he has concocted the near perfect alibi if guilty. Your job has just been made that little bit harder to nail him. Someone asked me to watch his back, to that purpose he placed himself in your hands for possible involvement in drug dealing, at the same time provided his alibi if attributed to the death of Tom Brannon, with him locked up in one of your cells. I failed in not keeping him out of jail, but in him being locked up, there is a possibility he is innocent and made my job easier.'

'Prescott, your experience in the army or SAS in the world of warfare, makes you a loose cannon waiting to explode. With the atrocities in human life you have seen, could have influenced your mental status being question in civilian life. We hear of the trauma that veterans suffer in seeing their friends killed in action and then when leaving find it hard to adjust and fit back into normal life. With families and normal everyday arguments that does not entail having to retaliate with the use of firearms or any sort of weapons. You may be helping Terri Tambling and her concerns for her brother. That does not help him stay on the right side of the law. If he is of the opinion that he is above law in thinking he can run roughshod in South London, killing, robbing, to supply drugs on the streets. Then it is my duty to catch him, lock him up and if I need to, throw away the key if I feel he is posing a danger to the law-abiding citizens of Croydon and South London by his actions.'

When Dan looked up from the table back at Mattock, Mattock had already walked out through the door into the street, leaving Dan to consider who else might be a threat to his cousin and Shirley.

The girls, Samantha and Shirley stayed behind. DI Helen Smith summoned to go back to the station left. Allowing them to remain in Dan's home. Samantha remained seated as Shirley excused herself. Tom Brannon until recently was unknown to neither of them. Only through Dan's involvement with helping Terri Tambling, had Tom Brannon been in trouble by his interference.

Dan sat in the armchair opposite Sam. 'I feel responsible for Tom's death, if I had not met up with him.' His mood was pensive, and the news of Tom's death had been unexpected. 'Terri claims that she is a friend to Tom Brannon.' Harry was arrested, but not for Tom's death.

Mattock was telling him to back off, not in so many words. No mistaking the underlying hint was there. Dan never did take advice, something he held in common with Tom Brannon. Always saw any advice given as a prompt to instil the impetus to carry on regardless, as a positive, not a negative. To fight on, he after all was the only one who could curb trouble from heading towards his cousin. With Harry in a police cell for the moment and Tom now mysteriously put out of the way. Dan had a reason now to play his part, to ending these crimes, which allows someone to think he can end life at will without recompense. A shadow was now casting itself across the map of Croydon. The police appeared to know something, which meant that DI Mattock has not been truthful in all his words spoken. The Hou-Lin Hoi family maybe connected with the drugs raid, which confirmed their involvement in drugs, working its way around London from their warehouse base.

'Shirley, can you telephone BT and ask for an itemised bill over the last two weeks, or if you know someone in BT to give us a list of callers to this number in the same period.'

'Why would you need... ah to find out, whose been sending those calls,' said Sam, realising the necessity.

'Exactly, whilst you are finding out that information, I need to speak to one or two people so I will see you both later,' Dan said as he left the house.

Progress was slow, Tiny and Mitch had not been seen for several days. The likelihood of their involvement in recent activities appeared prominent. The Waddon Pub quiet as expected with Harry not around. Harry's position was looking hopeful, hired a good lawyer and the bar staff given assurances that their jobs were safe. Harry's ex Samantha was not likely to return and work behind the bar at any time soon. The police left nothing unturned in Harry's office. The Hoi-sin family had not been seen either, not since Harry's arrest. His legal representative informed the staff that Harry would be back amidst them soon. The police had no evidence to warrant keeping him locked up. Dan tried to establish where he would possibly find Tiny and Mitch. Nobody appeared to have seen them for days.

Reassuringly the police had been unsuccessful in finding their whereabouts also. Appeared to Dan, Mattock had reached the same conclusion. Knowing that both were still at large brought some comfort to Dan hoping he would find them both first.

He knew one or two places he knew they frequented. Trying the Dukes Head first, told nothing seen of the pair for a few months. Possibly not since Christmas last. Having drawn a blank there, he drove into Croydon trying for success at The George, a Wetherspoon Pub in George Street, another favoured haunt. Dan drew a blank again. Receiving less help in that the bar staff seemed not willing to help or give advice to where Dan could find them both. On leaving, the Wetherspoon Pub Dan noticed the Hou-Lin Hoi family drinking in a corner, away from the public gaze. Dithered as to whether he should start asking questions, thinking if he was to make progress at all, he needed answers to Harry's involvement with the Hou-Lin Hoi family. Deciding that if answers not forthcoming then he would extract what information he could whilst here.

Dan introduced himself, 'I believe we were introduced to one another by Harry, Harry Tambling, in his pub The Waddon?' The look between them, revealed how guarded these Asians were. They played dumb. Not giving any sign of recognition.

There was a third member who arrived from the bar carrying a tray of drinks. He looked suspiciously at Dan, wondering whether he had come back at an inappropriate time as he laid the tray down on the table. Then seeing his colleagues had not said anything, he introduced himself, but not revealing his name. 'Can I help you?' he asked. 'I have a feeling that my friends do not wish to speak with you.'

'As I said to your colleagues, I think you all have a mutual interest in a friend of mine, a Harry Tambling,' Dan stated.

The name sparked a reaction from the newcomer. 'What is this Harry Tambling to you, my friend?' he asked.

Dan responded by saying, 'He happens to be my cousin's ex-husband. These two I have met before, but, appear to be playing dumb or should I say denying they know me by their silence.'

'Maybe you are mistaken, friend. Maybe these two are not whom you think they are?'

Dan agitated by the word 'friend' coming from the stranger. 'First, I am not your friend; second, I do not make mistakes when recognising people I have met and been introduced to.'

'Plainly I am in the wrong by implying that I am your friend,' he said still not providing a name. 'But it appears my friends do not wish to converse with you, so maybe it would be preferable that you go elsewhere.'

Not wishing to be ignored nor spoken to as if an insignificant other. Dan left them no doubt that he would meet up with them again. Not wishing to cause a scene, he backed up and left, not before saying: 'I will leave for now, but we will be having words again soon. That is a promise.'

'Are you threatening my friends?' the newcomer asked.

Dan stared at the newcomer. 'I do not threaten anybody; I am merely stating a fact.' Dan did not stay to carry on the banter. He left without another word spoken. Dan cursed himself for not finding the information he required. In answer to a previous question, to their involvement in the underworld of crime, crystal clear to himself that they clearly were.

Leaving the Wetherspoons, Dan entered a café across the road, ordered a coffee and sat waiting from the Asians to alight from the pub. Dan drank two cups of coffee before they set foot outside the pub. Having already paid for his coffee, he left and decided to follow the two he had known. Deciding to follow them at a discrete distance, to ascertain where these people lived and what line of business they worked in.

With few people out on the street getting closer without being seen would have been difficult. Very Few doorways had room to hide should the need arise. Luck played a part when the name Chang was revealed in a short outspoken outburst of an argument. Following them was proved short lived as one of the pair hailed a taxi passing from the opposite direction. It turned in a tight circle before coming beside the kerb. No other taxi in sight and no cab firm it seemed nearby, knowing obtaining a mini cab would take too long to follow the one departing.

Dan returned to the Wetherspoon pub, he saw the barman that had possible served the third Asian. Coming to the bar, Dan called the barman over. 'The group of Asians that were drinking in the corner, can you tell me whether they are regular customers here?'

The barman freely gave an answer, showing no restraint from giving out information openly. 'Yeah, they have been here before, same day, roughly same time. Like a drink. Same guy comes up and orders each time.'

Dan receiving more information than he expected pushed further. 'Well, eh, do you have a name?'

'Yeah. Kevin,' the barman said.

'Kevin, do you by any chance know their names as I need to talk with them, especially the one who was paying for the drinks?' asked Dan.

'The guy buying the drinks, his name is Chang,' confirming what Dan had heard out in the street a while back. 'The other two are Chan and Li, normally here with another guy, name of Harry. Runs a pub nearby I think.'

'Do you know where I could find these three, if not in here?' Dan probed.

'Not sure about Chan or Li, but Chang he has a restaurant down in South Croydon. Been there myself, serves some good food and one of the better Chinese restaurants, around here.'

'Thanks, Kevin, been a big help.' Dan tossed him a tenner. 'Thanks for the info.' *I should have talked to the barman before, save me hanging around waiting*, he thought.

Leaving, Dan headed back to The Waddon. Find out more on Harry's situation, without asking Mattock or Wallington Police Station, which may bring unwanted attention back to him? A call to his mobile curbed his enthusiasm in this direction. The call came from Shirley. She had information in respect of callers to the home. Shirley provided with a list from a friend at the local BT Telephone Exchange of recent callers in the last month.

Dan told Shirley to meet up with him on the corner of Croydon High Street, near West Croydon Train Station.

.

CHAPTER 15

DI Helen Smith had just received news concerning the man with a tattoo leaving the hotel in Purley Way. Expecting Mattock to be at his desk she opened the door to his office and found the room was empty, Mattock nowhere around. An old trench coat on the hat stand and only item of clothing that remained in the office emphasising that Mattock was not in. Only once had she seen Mattock wear this coat in all the time Helen had worked with him. As he preferred the reefer jacket. Helen closed the door behind her, turning the off the light switch left on.

The outer open planned investigation office. As on many occasions the outer office could be barren of personnel. On this occasion two PC's were writing out reports on recent cases brought to conclusion. Due to every other officer busy on whatever crime case given, new cases came up every day. Helen asked whether each had they seen Mattock. Both shook their heads. Which left the undermanned workforce hard pressed to troll through to a conclusion, more so if the cases were domestic disputes. Which could have manifested from drunken bouts off heated words, some ending in tragic circumstances.

Helen tried her phone again, again Mattock did not pick up. Had no idea where Mattock was to be found. Tried his home phone as well as his mobile again. The police station in Wallington had seen nothing of Mattock either with Harry Tambling still held in a cell.

Peering out from the fourth-floor window down towards the rear car park. Mattock's car still parked in one of the bays, meant Mattock was still inside the station somewhere. The main investigation office door opened with Inspector Alan Tatchell entering. A newly made up Detective brought in. Had been brought in three weeks earlier. Helen thought Alan was green around the collar when helping to investigate on cases, but then Helen thought all new Detectives new to this station were slow in mingle with ongoing investigative crime work before she would conceive that had earned their stripes.

'Alan, have you seen Mattock in your travels around the building?'

'Not really, heard someone say he had been called to the Chief Supers office earlier,' Alan answered.

'Thanks,' she responded, thinking to herself, *Why didn't I think of that before?* knowing the answer to that would invariably be Chief Super Homer going to Mattock's office.

'Alan, what case are you caught up in?' asked Helen.

'The Tom Brannon murder case on Waddon Pond,' he replied.

Helen could not help but speak out at why he worked on that case, when it would be part of Mattock and her case. 'Why put you on a case we are working on ourselves. Waste of your time I'd say.'

'Your boss seems to differ from your views. Homer asked me to work for him, help you both out,' DC Tatchell replied.

Helen caught off guard, tried not to act agitated by this additional change in personnel. 'Sure, we had it covered. So, what have you come up with in your search for answers?'

'From what I've been told, this guy lived in North London. Worked in Croydon when made redundant having worked there for a number of years and appeared to be highly thought of by the staff. Had trouble in his love life, now divorced from his wife and has two youngsters from the marriage. Reason for him moving to North London, travel took its toll and gave reason for him to take redundancy. Youngsters live with his wife, but his relationship with his wife has gone south since the divorce.

Wife appears to be a bit of a control freak. I'd say he had a lucky escape.'

Brannon's wife, she and Mattock had not considered. DI Alan Tatchell seemed to have helped in the case after all, reviewing her thoughts on Alan. Helen's mind could not yet grasp the idea that Tom Brannon's wife was connected with his murder. They supposedly did not communicate with one another; she had the affection of both sons, who probably take her side in any argument or dispute. If he became friendly towards another female, was she likely to provoke trouble to alienate him from every having another affair because of her inability to reason that her jealousy had destroyed her own marriage. Having no control affected her reasoning to the point of wanting control of his life still. The thought of Tom helping another could bring on its own implications of him having an affair with Terri Chapman. His wife not a forgiving person retaliates by spreading malicious gossip detrimental to the person Tom Brannon really was. Helen knew this was all conjecture, nothing proven. Helen's own mind wandering of into a fantasy world of half-truths.

'So, what do you know of his wife?' asked Helen.

Alan remained silent pondering as to why Inspector Helen Smith kept asking questions about Tom Brannon's married life. Was she testing him? Did she genuinely not know anything about Tom Brannon's family life? 'I know as much about Tom Brannon's ex-wife and family as you do.' Holding back what his accrued knowledge found out and views attained on the case.

Sensing his attitude changing slightly towards her question, Helen told herself to be more contrite in the way she dealt with fellow officers, 'Seems I may have stepped on someone's toes. I am just trying to find out whether you have seen or heard more than we had learnt, I mean, Mattock and me. Tom Brannon's murder caught us unawares. Seems personal, but must admit, had not considered his wife to be connected. Not sure Mattock has done right in bringing in help and thought of the wife's implication a possibly,' said Helen. 'I am not used to Mattock allowing another to join our, what I thought, exclusive club. Well seeing as we are to be working together on this case,' Helen smiled and said, 'welcome aboard. Still think that the wife has no bearing on Tom Brannon's murder.'

DI Mattock stormed in through door into the main investigation room for the Detectives. Remained disgruntled as he continued along the aisle to his own office. Stopping short of his office only to inform Helen that she had no time spare to consort with another officer when they had a murder, two murders to unravel and get results. Then slammed the door shut behind him as he entered. A brief period of silence ensued when Helen heard her name yelled out. 'Helen, we have two murders to solve. The Super wants results and now.'

Both DC Alan Tatchell and DI Helen Smith looked from one to the other. 'Is he always that grouchy,' asked Tatchell.

'Only when he has been in talks with Chief Super, has that effect on him. I had better focus on what I came to speak to him about,' Helen said as she closed the opened Mattock's office door.

Mattock a scowl on his face as Helen walked into his office. Motioned Helen to sit, while he perused over the notes now stuck to a notice board fixed to the wall. This was Mattock's case notes and photos to the crime scene attached to the Penny Connor and now Tom Brannon murders. Someone had cleared his desk, transferred his tapestry of information from the table to this wall chart.

Standing there for several minutes in silence, his demeanour calming down as the seconds counted down in this moment of quiet. 'Our Chief has decided to bring in another officer to our delight, seems we are not getting the results quick enough for his lordship upstairs. Thought another pair of hands would help. Apparently has been acquainting himself with the case this past two days, without my knowledge. This accounts for my desk notes now being on this wall.'

Helen stayed quiet, waiting for the dry cryptic remark of wit to follow. None forthcoming a surprise to Helen's knowledge of Mattock's subtle ways of word repartee. Submitting that no retort was coming she felt it the right time to reveal the news she originally came to give over. 'Sir, appears we have a tattoo parlour stating they had done a tattoo to the design from the description we gave out.'

Mattock asked, 'You have spoken with this tattooist and what did you find out as a result.'

'Seems this design, has been etched on two people. One of which was only recently. The other had been several years back, on a guy named Gary Parsons who had come up from the coast for the day,' Helen answered.

'A few years ago, cannot have much trade if he remembers a client from a few years back. Has this guy been there again since?'

'Apparently so, Tony,' Helen answered using Mattock's Christian name.

Mattock looked up quizzically at Helen using the name, but said nothing. He noticed a shadow of someone standing near the doorway. Mattock had seen him earlier talking with Helen when he first entered the outer room, he said. 'Yes. Can we help you?' looking up at the Detective Constable.

'Detective Inspector Mattock,' he enquired tentatively. 'I am Detective Constable Tatchell. I believe you already know about me.'

'Detective Constable Tatchell, Tatchell, that name rings a bell; you were speaking with DI Smith here earlier. TATCHELL, you are the one who has been snooping around my office. Moving things around and making this montage on the wall. Not used to leaving things as they are, are you, where I could find what I was looking for. Instead, you create this nightmare of a jigsaw puzzle.

When I wish to have the room decorated, I will bring in the professionals.'

'Yes, Sir, eh no, Sir. I mean, I was only trying to help put things in some order. Make it easier to seem,' Tatchell muttered.

'Well don't in future; I like to have everything where I can see them in front of me. Not plastered over a wall.' Mattock wanted to say something else, but thought to stay quiet. Seeing Tatchell still standing around the doorway, Mattock changed his mind and said, 'Are you going to come in or are you content in making the place look untidy by standing around in the doorway.'

Helen mused, this was her boss back, as she thought and smiled. 'I took it, that you had already been introduced, Sir. DC Tatchell is our new little helper.'

'I know that, Helen,' looking up at Tatchell, 'good, Tatchell, seems you have brought some humour into Helen's life. So, what if anything, can you add to the mix that we have overlooked in on this case.'

'Sir, I thought that maybe a connection with Tom Brannon's relationship to his ex-wife could be clue to his death,' Tatchell said.

'You think we are looking for two killers, one for each case. If you had already divorced your husband and he had the good sense to move away from any possible unhappy relationship should he rub shoulders with his ex-wife or vice versa. An encounter would lead to his ex-wife doing something as drastic as to murder him. To what aim? It was the wife who had played away in the first place that ended their marriage. What could be the motive behind her killing her ex several years down the line, Tom Brannon did not strike me the kind of man that would have any angst against her to give her reason to commit murder.'

Tatchell came into the office ready to back his corner. 'Take it from another angle, Sir, if the wife had suspected Tom Brannon of being unfaithful, before commit adultery herself. How do we know if she would not have a grievance herself against him, the ex leaves and he distances himself from harm's way by moving to North London, in his case Cricklewood, she remains in the south together with the two sons, which is nothing extraordinary given the courts generally give custody of siblings over to the mother? Except that their children are a lot older, old enough to move out on their own into the world, possibly hang on to everything their mother says. Knowing they on a good thing and hang around.'

Mattock stood up and walked over to the crime board. He knew that they still had no idea to who Tom Brannon's wife was. He looked to Tatchell. 'Have we a name for the ex-wife, you appear to be one-step ahead of us on that and to the fact he has two adult children.'

Tatchell pulled out a notepad from his inside jacket pocket. Rifled through a few pages before finding the page he was looking for. 'Her names Tina, Tina Brannon, so far she has not returned to her surname prior to her marriage. Thirty-nine years of age, the two sons, David and Edward, ages twenty and eighteen respectively. Living near Ashtead, Epsom,' looking over at Mattock when finished telling of his information.

'Helen,' said Mattock turning his head. 'Seeing as our man in the know, knows the names. Go with him and find out what you can about Tina and the young adults. It is possible she has not heard the news yet, tread carefully. Watch her reaction to the news. Well, Tatchell, let us put your knowledge of them to the test.'

'You, Detective Constable Tatchell, can find out what the relationship to the father was like with his siblings, a good relation or miffed by the divorce and living with mother,' said Mattock, gently ushered them both out through his office door with a wave of his hands.

As Helen Smith and Alan Tatchell left his office, he looked down onto his office desk, free of paper. Pressing down on his desk with his hands placed on the desk as he sat down. Then his eyes peered up at the crime board. 'At the moment, I do not buy it. However, what is it they say.

Never say never there could be some truth in what Tatchell has said.'

Mattock left his office. There was a tattooist and his client he needed to speak to.

CHAPTER 16

Dan waited on the corner of the High Street. Rain continued to fall. The shop doorways filled with pedestrians avoiding the worst of the rainfall. Dan had no other place to hide other than the train station forecourt. Shoppers hindered by only these two shops as those escaping from the rain sought shelter from these doorways. Leaving little room as shoppers and customers fought to get in or out through the entrances. Regretting his decision to meet Shirley on this corner. Dan stayed outside, allowing the rain to take its toll on his situation.

An hour had passed and still no sign of Shirley. Dan's patience tested by one or two shoppers who in a rush raced through with their umbrella up, oblivious to anybody standing in their way. With their heads looking down appeared to want to walk through Dan, remarking that he was blocking the pavement to prevent and divert their passage through to the High Street, his only way to avoid a kick in the shin, was his timely side step from contact.

A police siren signalled a timely reminder of his need to turn his hand to redirecting his thoughts to the present and his reason for standing on a High Street corner. At that precise moment, Dan saw Shirley strolling along towards him, undeterred by the hustle and bustle of the lunchtime trade heading to and from Croydon High Street to West Croydon Station. Dan relieved at sighting her, crossed into the High Street and sidestepped her gliding his arm to interlock with hers, turning Shirley around and heading back into the High Street.

Stunned and taken into a spin and arm held within a firm grip, Shirley taken aback by Dan's sudden presence and redirection in one swift movement. Shirley found herself escorted towards a café, restaurant set towards the end of the main High Street stores that fulfilled a part in a shopper's life. 'Took your time coming. I thought I was going to end up in a fully-grown argument with one of those avid shoppers. You know. The ones who feel they have more rights to be in a shopping centre because of the amount of time they spend in pursuit of the perfect bargain, but end up spending all their money on clothes they know they are not going to use at any time soon. The husband's or boyfriend's nightmare if you are the money maker in life.'

Two women turned around and looked in his direction when hearing his rant. Dan held their gaze, noting amongst the groups of diners that they were not alone, sitting towards the rear sat Tiny and a few others Dan was not acquainted with. Dan's entrance brought their attention to Tiny and his group. A smile emerged between them on first sight, Dan cursed to himself hoping to talk openly with Shirley. Observing Tiny cut short there being an open discussion between Shirley and Dan, containing the talk to just friendly banter. Thoughts of having coffee with few customers on the premises made it difficult for Dan to open up and hinted to Shirley that they may have a better chance of talking in Starbucks further up the High Street. Rising they left without ordering.

Shirley miffed at all the secrecy about their meeting up together reluctantly went along with Dan's wishes. Unbeknown by the problem Dan had, Shirley resisted challenging Dan not having been acquainted with Dan's friends.

Finding a place to sit in a corner of Starbucks. Having to be content to sit behind a small barrier, fronted by an array of coffee beans for sale in packets ready to go. Dan went up and paid for two coffees. Placing them on the table. Dan took Sam's mobile phone from Shirley. 'Sam knows you have taken her mobile and handed it to me.' Shirley just gave a curt nod of her head. Commenced checking over the logged calls over the past few days. Staring down at a list of names and numbers that had called. Dan took his time, none of the names jumped out. None that he knew personally would wish harm to Samantha. Three calls shown as not providing a telephone number from the caller. These calls, the only calls that could coincide with the calls made by whoever was impersonating him. Each call came at roughly the same time each day. Dan gave the mobile back to Shirley, agreeing that Sam should also see the list from his landline phone, should it jog his memory of who could have been calling them. Dan voiced concerns as to how this mimic would know Samantha's mobile no. Had to be someone she knew.

Dan omitted to say anything of his meetings with DI Mattock in the past two days. Deeming them to be of insignificant importance to talk about. Dan did not feel the need for the girls to know.

Dan and Shirley parted company each going their separate ways, Shirley returning home. Dan continuing to track down information re: Harry held in a police cell and how Tom Brannon came to be in Croydon, faced down in Waddon Pond.

By retracing his tracks. Returned to where he last saw Tiny in the cafe. Found not to his surprise to Tiny having departed. According to the waitress, he and his friends left not long after his own departure with Shirley. Dan noticed the two Asian people sat down where he and Shirley sat earlier. Sitting opposite each other, deep in conversation. Dan frowned not expecting to see any other reason for them being there, only that one looked up at the second before Dan went to leave again repeating his previous visit in not making an order. Outside in the street he observed the Asian who watched Dan leaving. He appeared to be holding and talking over a photograph of someone placed between them both. The other person picked up the photo, putting it into his inside jacket pocket. They stood to go asking the café owner and pointing to where he and Shirley had been sitting earlier. Only then did Dan recognise the Asian sitting with his back before, as Chang, the Asian he had spoken to at the pub.

He thought, *Someone upstairs is looking down on me, a chance to find out who and what he does just opened up for me*. Taking the mobile out from his pocket, Dan took several snapshots for his own benefit of both. Wishing he had thought to do this earlier in the Wetherspoon bar.

Dan picked up a free copy of the Standard newspaper before setting off for The Waddon pub. Checking the time he started off, at a pace, quickly walking the distance. Ten minutes later, he stood outside The Waddon. Movement from an upstairs window, as a net curtain drawn across the window, revealed that someone had been watching Dan as he stood outside. Dan stared up at the window again for several more seconds. No sign of life given as to who pulled back. Made him mindful, trouble could ensue should he venture inside The Waddon. Ever since Harry had been taken into police custody, Dan knew his talking to the police and driven away from outside the pub days earlier. Suspicion would have fallen on him to grassing Harry up.

Inside the talk, still concerned Harry. Unanswered questions as to why he was in a police cell. All anyone knew was that a dead body found in Waddon pond, which all had said that Harry could not have committed and had been inside the pub on the night of the murder. That Harry a suspect and held for another crime. The pub door opening brought on a sudden hush as Dan walked in. The silence was deafening. Dan left the door to close behind him, taking in the stares, before he stated that Harry's arrest had nothing to do with him.

Slowly the noise of talking became the norm again, escalating to the volume set prior to him entering. He thought he saw someone leaning over the turn in the staircase at the end of the bar, but the person had evaporated when Dan looked again.

The barmaid on duty, Sally, poured out the pint requested by Dan placing it on the spills tray on the bar.

As she took the money for payment, Dan enquired whether anyone was upstairs in the office. The reply was a negative response, hearing the question the other barman, Toby answered for Sally. 'Nobody upstairs: Not since Harry's arrest.'

'Then who is getting twitchy, moving the curtains in the upstairs room over the entrance,' Dan asked.

'Probably was the breeze, through the window, being open,' Toby said,

'I would agree if the window was open,' said Dan.

'Then it was your imagination as nobody is upstairs,' Toby said with a sarcastic retort.

Taking his pint Dan, left the bar and sat at the table vacated, by the pub's main door. Found a daily paper left on the seat to the next table. Saw the headlines, stating that the landlord of a pub in Croydon taken into custody on suspicion of drug dealing. Looked back to the staircase at the end of the bar, took a quick look towards the barmaid Sally and barman Toby, noted that they were pre-occupied. All Dan needed to the chance in going up the stairs, before the bar staff noticed. Dan on the upstairs landing softly approached the door to the room overlooking the front door. Quietly, he turned the door handle and quickly entered. Closing the door and confronted with Terri Chapman lying on the bed. A silence followed as they both stared at one another.

'Well, you are the one person I did not expect to see. Then again you are family, why would you not be here.' stated Dan.

'What are you doing up here, who let you up?' asked Terri.

'Saw the curtain move from outside, enquired as to who was up here and was told nobody. You know me, do not like being lied to when I know different,' Dan replied.

The door opened as Toby came in. 'Sorry, Terri, told him nobody was up here. Shall I remove him and take him back downstairs.'

Dan gave Toby a look, a look that said you could try. Terri just raised her hand. 'Leave it, he is here now, okay, Toby, you can return to the bar downstairs.'

Toby left as Dan asked, 'Why the secrecy. You have a problem with me being here. You're the one who wanted my help with your brother.'

'Not at the expense of him being arrested.'

'He is capable of doing that on his own, if involved in drug dealing, as the police suspect.'

'Why would they suspect him of that, never been involved in drugs in his life, you know that yourself.'

'Until recently I would agree, but he has tied himself up with the Hoi Sin family, I am sure that is not because they have taken to drinking in his establishment socially.'

Terri mulled over what Dan had said, 'You know this for a fact.'

'Police say they have CCTV supporting that fact, he has been seen around the warehouse that has recently been set alight. Yes, and from the look on your face he obviously has not told you that.'

'Okay, he has screwed up this time.'

'It would appear so, Terri,' Dan said. Terri could see that Dan was holding out on something as he said that, the wording almost gave Terri hope.

'What do you mean appears so?' she asked

'Have you any idea how Tom Brannon came to die? Was Harry aware of Brannon being close by when he died?'

Terri stood up facing Dan. 'For a second there, I thought you had given me hope that they had the wrong person, but you are telling me now that Harry had something to do with Tom Brannon's death, maybe even killed him himself. Harry is innocent of that crime. He was in a police cell at the time.' Terri continued after a few seconds, 'Just as he was innocent where Penny Connor's death is concerned.'

When she spoke, he watched the smirk appear on Terri's face. Dan could not help thinking that he was made a fool by her wish for him to help. Over the past few days, Terri's attitude towards him had changed. Gone was the concern for Tom Brannon. The way Tom's death easily brushed aside. Penny's demise dismissed almost in the same fashion, Harry in police custody had helped quell the stories that of Penny Conner's death attributed to Harry's involvement. With Harry held by the police at the time of Tom Brannon's death, this put the question of him responsible and cause of two deaths out of the picture.

This change in attitude from Terri. Was he wrong in getting involved from the outset, was he to be the fall-guy for the two murders as revenge for kicking Harry out of Samantha and his marriage, then Harry was about to get a rude awakening as Dan's alibi was also set in stone on both occasions.

'Terri, I think you will find Harry has enough on his plate to worry about with the Drugs, with a capital D. If your wish for him not to be colluding to murder as well, then I wish him luck. But don't go celebrating just yet,' Dan said, walking from the room, leaving Terri to stew in whatever role she had elected to play in lately.

Dan when reaching the door could not go without asking the one question on his mind, 'Did you have a role in Tom Brannon's death?'

Terri's response came almost as quick as his question left Dan's lips, 'No.'

Said not with conviction, but softly spoken, said quickly to give doubt as to question her denial, Dan's responded, 'You don't sound too sure?

'Off course I never had anything to do with Brannon's death.' Terri said more forcefully. Raising her voice and staring back at Dan coldly.

Dan refrained from talking to anybody as he left the pub. Toby the barman noticed Dan leaving the pub and was ascending the stairs as Dan looked back into the bar on leaving through the pub doors.

At this point, Dan remembered he had left his car in Epsom Road from his previous visit. With the car parked on a yellow line. Dan was not surprised that a parking ticket awaited him, affixed to the windscreen under the right windscreen wiper. To compound the fact found the wheels clamped too. A telephone number the only clue as to the firm that had clamped the car. Only when phoning the firm did his luck take a further dive, when it was established, that firm had associations with Harry Tambling as a partner.

Dan reluctantly placed a call through to DI Mattock explaining the predicament he found his car in, with DI Mattock not available to answer his call due to his attending to a matter they were not at liberty to divulge. Dan left no option other than to leave his car in Epsom Road.

He had faith in Mattock and the police in general tracing the killers of Penny Connor or Tom Brannon. Having no police training himself, only that of life in the SAS and its secret missions. All his sense of fair justice for right and wrong had come from personal experience of slights perceived by others. His time with knowing, Harry and Terri helped Dan understand how they worked. Since his return from the USA, Harry had changed from those days, being more involved and taking chances where before he stayed in the background and let others take the rap for anything that went array? Terri the sister had also come along way. It appeared friends used, to change the course of justice away from blame and playing into Harry's hands in the world of crime and conceit.

Samantha married Harry not knowing the world Harry walked in, two sides of the coin, a phrase Dan would say as being Harry. One side that showed an honest caring side, the other coincided with the criminal world. Each kept apart. Until Samantha's parents had passed away, all had been okay in Harry's world. Dan questioned his logic, to why Harry's demeanour would change, to become reliant on drink to solve his problems. Too such as, he became violent at the slightest comment, his change in personality and behaviour towards his wife, Dan's cousin,

Samantha. Was it a coincidence that Samantha's parents died and Harry's problems started up at the same moment in time, or were Harry and Terri playing him for a fool, as retribution for Dan hitting out at Harry, Dan effectively ending Samantha marriage at the hands of the senseless violence, meted out, by Harry towards her.

His own involvement and knowledge of Harry's ultra-ego past, placing him one-step ahead of the police.

Dan felt the presence of someone behind him. Before he could react, he was hit from behind. Dan collapsed to the pavement. His last conscious thoughts before he lost consciousness, was that of two pairs of hands lifting him up from the ground. Then blank.

CHAPTER 17

Mattock, found the Tattooist the unfriendliest of people he had ever met. His attitude was beyond comprehension. Co-operation became trying to the point where he had to read out the riot act to the fact he could quite easily obtain a search warrant from the courts to search his premises while an officer stood watch, whilst obtaining the warrant to ensure that nothing moved or taken away from his shop. Reluctantly, he allowed Mattock to wander around his establishment. As Mattock position another Officer to watch for any object moved by the Tattooist or his assistant. Mattock while searching knew he had pushed his luck in forcing the issue in searching the premises. Asked various questions appertaining to the design of tattoo etched onto the person in connection to Penny Connor's death, Gary Parsons. All the time he questioned Fred Carver, the tattooist. Mattock turned over several items Mattock found strange to find in a tattoo parlour. They were objects and items of a satanic nature. Mystical Books of satanic verse, a crucifix, behind a door to a back room a chalked design on the floor to which Mattock had only seen in a film or programmes on the TV screen appertaining to the darker arts.

Questioned about the magical books and the floor design, only answered by a glib outline and insight into what Fred Carver's life entailed. Reluctant to air his views and thoughts on what he saw, Mattock left unconvinced about the answers given on Gary Parsons, or to the records kept of his practice. Gary Parsons known home address was all Mattock took from the tattooist. Mattock made a mental note, to have someone look into Carver's world of mystic fantasy.

Back at Police HQ, he found DI Helen Smith and DC Tatchell deep in conversation about Tom Brannon's ex-wife and her life since their marriage split. They both agreed that she had moved out to Ashtead to distance herself from Tom Brannon while he worked in Croydon. Their relationship since the breakup strained due to her reluctance to allow her kids to move in with their father.

Helen stated, 'The two young adults David and Edward, neither had any grouse about their father, but due to the animosity between the two parents refrained from seeing their father too often, allowing Tina the mother to influence them in not staying with the father. Both appeared cut-up about the death of their father. Edward, the youngest had reacted to the news worse than David had. It transpires that Edward was a lot closer to his father than he let on to his mother's annoyance, as far as father and son relationships go.'

DI Tatchell jumped in saying, 'Tina is a designer. Makes a living decorating homes, also in refurbishing and outlook and she is highly regarded in her field. Not reflected upon if looking at her abode.'

Helen taking umbrage to Tatchell butting in re-established her position in the debate when she continued her statement. 'When informed of her former husband's death she showed no remorse or for her own kid's feelings on hearing the news. Could not tell, whether she was that concerned. Her face showed no sign of anguish or relief. Just a blank and motionless look stared right back at you.'

Mattock reflecting what he had heard, 'On the evidence you have surmounted, would you say that she could be held to account for Tom Brannon and his death?'

'We have no conclusive evidence to confirm or deny her involvement to that end,' Helen answered.

'Right, go and write up your reports on what you have found out to date. Also, make a note of any evidence we have and put this information up on our wall chart,' Mattock added.

'Before you both disappear, I've spoken to the tattooist a Fred Carver about Gary Parsons. We will need to pull him in for questioning as his description and the tattoo confirms him to be our man at the scene of Penny Connor's attempted murder. This, however, does not confirm his role in Penny Connor's eventual death at the hospital.'

Both left Mattock's office, each egging the other to write up the report. Both reluctant in the unwanted but necessary chore asked. Helen stopped sharply on hearing her name called out, turning around found Mattock coming up close behind. 'Helen, you met with this tattooist Fred Carver. What did you make of him?'

'I did not exactly meet him, was just informed by another officer of his having tattooed a man named Gary Parsons with the design we were making enquiries about. Why, is there a problem?'

'No, was going to ask your opinion of Fred Carver, the tattooist himself. As you have never met him, you can't answer,' Mattock answered.

Returning to his office Mattock rang the Chief, but told his presence was elsewhere. Playing host to a dinner organised by the local Croydon Council committee, to connect with the local businesses in helping to contain crime in their own set-ups and security.

Two hours passed when Helen walked into Mattock's office, stopped in her tracks when confronted with her boss asleep. His fingers hovered over the remote control to his computer control board. His hand never strayed from this position. Helen thought about waking him up, but remembered another case when Mattock mocked her in front of the Super, now thought to redeem this by amusing herself. Gripping hold of her handbag from underneath her own desk outside in the main office, she sought after the make-up bag from within. Mattock did not stir, he sat with his head against his chair backrest, leaning to one side. The opportunity presented the perfect position, whilst

Helen supplied masked details adding the make-up to his face. A pair of glasses outlined onto his face along with moustache and beard stubble. On completion, she beckoned several other officers in the detective's main office to see her handiwork. Quickly dispersing when sign of Mattock imminent in waking up from his nap. Helen decided to disappear out of sight. The odd snigger heard from the outer office heard, Mattock when aroused took it someone had said an amusing comment resulting in another laughing. Unknown to himself he had no idea that he was the butt of the office joke. Mattock left his office, walking through the main office he continued going out into the corridor leading onto the staircase beyond. An eruption of laughter followed him as the main office door closed behind him. Undeterred by the laughter on his exit, Mattock continued down the corridor bringing about more sniggers while passing by one or two constables on the staircase on his way down to his car. The Sergeant on the desk, called out. 'You should have gone to Specsavers, Sir; you might see better with real glasses on.' This statement brought about another bout of sniggers. Stopping in his tracks, Mattock enquired what the sergeant was talking about, whereupon the Desk Sergeant on duty merely stated: 'You may wish to take a look in a mirror, try the washroom. Somebody is having some fun at your expense, Sir.'

Seeing the slightly obscured reflection of his face, on a glass fronted advertising board situated behind the desk counter, his hand automatically went up to his face. 'Shit, I'll have their guts for garters when I catch hold of who's responsible for this.' He searched out the men's washroom in the foyer. Entering with more laughter coming from those in the foyer, the noise of laughter ending as the toilet door closed behind him. Fifteen minutes after he entered, he came back out, face completely clear of the make-up that once appeared on his face.

Retracing his steps back to his office, he re-entered back through the outer office to a plethora of laughter, saying: 'Very funny and who is responsible?' The officers remained quiet, as everybody in the office closed ranks in returning their attention back to their work.

Just one fellow officer spoke up, 'That would be telling, Sir.' Mattock had no idea as to the speaker, as all heads remained faced down focused back to their case assignments.

DC Tatchell whistled his way into the main detective's office and waylaid by quiet murmurs of laughter being self-controlled to no effect. Pulled to one side, Alan Tatchell was let in on the joke circulating, as to what had transpired with Helen in the last hour, in two minds as whether to venture into the cauldron of Mattock's office or not. The written report in hand gave him little choice but to enter. Mattock's mood was none the worse hearing the office door opening, as Tatchell entered.

Placing the written report notes on Mattock's desk, he asked whether Mattock was okay, as the office appeared quieter than the norm. Mattock peered up at Tatchell, 'You trying to be funny. Make yourself useful, go bring in this Gary Parsons into the station and take someone with you. Where is Helen, thought you were working on these together?' he said pointing towards the report notes.

'I think she is in hiding, Sir.'

'What! Why?'

'She was putting her make-up on. I think,' Tatchell said, not sure as to whether he gave away one too many hints.

Mattock frowned, shook his head, seemingly not taking the hint to his own recent amusing episode. Tatchell did not push the point across, remaining silent. 'Right, I'll fetch Gary Parsons in for questioning then,' Tatchell said as he left the office.

Tatchell found Helen as he walked from the police station. They both smiled as they passed each other. Stopping he commented, 'Mattock is not a happy bunny. Your sense of fun is all over the office, he has been asking for the culprit.'

Helen turned to reply while still walking back into the station. 'Maybe I did go too far, then again maybe not.' Helen stopped and asked where he was going.

'Calling on Gary Parsons, to bring in for questioning.'

Helen stalled from her intention to go into the station. 'Need someone to go with you?'

'Yeah, saves getting someone else from the station. Think you may have to face Mattock at some point though,' Tatchell answered. 'I have also informed someone in Brighton nick that we are on our way down to this address.'

One hour passed before Smith and Tatchell turned up outside the home of Gary Parsons in Highdown Road, Hove. Getting out of the car, they both noticed the door to his home was wide open. DI Tatchell walked up the front steps and through the front door first closely followed by DI Smith. Crossing the threshold all was quiet. 'Hello! Is anyone here?' silence greeted his question, 'Gary Parsons are you here, this is the police.' Still no reply.

DI Tatchell took the downstairs after both checked the front room to the house. 'Watch out for anything?' Tatchell said as he took to going forward towards the kitchen area at the rear of the house. Helen just nodded, not saying a word, taking the stairs to the upper rooms. Seeing blood on the kitchen floor, Tatchell called out to Helen, 'Down here.' Seconds later Helen stood behind Tatchell, both looking down at the blood, but no body.

'What do you make of this?' seeing the amount of blood on the tiled floor.

'Whoever the blood belongs to, comes from more than scratch,' Tatchell responded as he phoned into Mattock the scene they encountered on arrival. Helen meanwhile contacted the local police station informing them likewise of where and what they had found.

Mattock was on his feet and out of his office door. 'Stay where you are. I'm on my way. Try not to touch anything. You sure there is no body in the house? Keep me informed when the local plod turn up.'

Smith and Tatchell continued searching around the rest of the house, could not tell if anything was missing or out of place, found no one. The upstairs rooms were completely tidy, beds made, nothing to say someone had stayed the night. No weapon visible with blood stains. The utility room at the rear of the kitchen was clear also. All that blood confined to the kitchen, the fact that the front door was wide open on entering. Helen found out where the nearest hospital was and confirmed that they had not seen or spoken to anyone by the name of Gary Parsons.

Within ten minutes, the local police arrived and likewise checked out all around the three- bedroomed terraced property. A crime scene investigator came through the front door ten minutes later. Informed that they had only the blood to go on and all else found in order to their knowledge. No rooms ransacked. Confirming nothing had been touched. With no body, until tests on the blood could be analysed, they could not confirm whether the blood came from Gary Parsons or another source. The investigator opened the large chest freezer in the utility room, found nothing but frozen food stock. Ninety minutes passed before Mattock showed himself, another hour passed before the crime scene investigator left having taken blood samples and finger prints in each room. Leaving only the local police and Mattock talking over what remained of the crime scene. While DI Smith and DC Tatchell turned over the contents of every draw and cupboard in the house tracing anything that would incriminate Gary Parsons in Penny Connor or Tom Brannon's murder enquiries. Mattock found whilst searching the outside Garden Shed more artefacts. That could only be attributed to the black arts, which with what Mattock found lying around in the Tattooist's parlour would mean that both Parsons and Carvers where equal exponents.

A mobile call came through to Mattock as they were leaving. Mattock had already received notification via the local police as to the blood. The blood confirmed as human, on searching the medical records did not match that of a Gary Parsons. Another problem that Mattock did not anticipate in their enquires to answers. The blood in the kitchen remained for now a mystery, but with time would reveal who it had belonged to if still alive.

'Let's go. We need to go back on home territory. Another problem has turned up,' Mattock said as he got into the car DC Tatchell and DI Smith had arrived in. He had sent back home earlier to Croydon Police Station his own transport down. People were falling down a lot in this case, which started out just being a routine knifing investigation. On the drive back to London, Mattock brought his other Detectives, Smith and Tatchell, up to date with the phone call received prior to them leaving and heading home.

'Dan Prescott. Has found himself guilty and in the frame for Tom Brannon's death. This has entailed an attack upon himself, appears someone has claimed that he witnessed his involvement but by whom. I am not too sure about this claim,' after avoiding a traffic incident involving two cars weaving in and out of traffic. The incident had DI Tatchell calling in a nearby police station to report the traffic violation proving the vehicle licence plate numbers. Mattock then continued with his theory on Dan Prescott, 'Prescott has a way of obtaining information, which could get under the skin of an enemy. The last time I spoke to him he said that with Harry Tambling in police custody, this would exonerate Harry from any crime that followed shortly after, providing an alibi, which could if logic ruled in any court give reason to suspect he was also innocent of criminal acts accused of previously, for example Penny Connor.' arriving at traffic lights, Mattock refrained saying more until leaving the lights as they changed back to green, allowing him to drive ahead again, he continued with his theory, 'if by chance he

148

had, then Dan's preconception that by organising a criminal act which entailed him picked up for another small criminal offence beforehand. Therefore, his being in our custody, could and would possibly exonerate him from any murder he suspected of doing previously. Could be Harry Tambling was trying to frame another, Dan Prescott a likely candidate, seeing the friction between them both. If Dan Prescott suspected as much beforehand, would, given his nature to play maverick, try, and turn the odds back on Harry, made the fool. This in turn would make himself a target for any antagonist wishing Dan Prescott harm.' Mattock train of thoughts silenced him for a few moments. 'Am I making sense with my theory you two? Not receiving a reply Mattock continued on, 'Dan also stated that Terri Chapman, the sister, would do almost anything to help her brother, even if it meant her friendship to Dan Prescott was exchanged by framing Dan to get her brother off the hook.'

DI Smith had kept quiet in the rear of the car while Mattock drove. Mattock was doing most of the talking on throughout the journey back to Croydon, while Tatchell grunted an agreement of sorts occasionally. Although quiet, Helen listened intently to all what Mattock said. Her thoughts turned to the drugs found in the car, which led to Harry's arrest.

'Sir, if he was picked up suspected of drug running. Having Tom Brannon killed a consequence of Harry's arrest for a drugs related crime would inadvertently help him back out of lockup as it diverted and attach blame to Dan Prescott. As a prime suspect and influence us the police in freeing Harry out onto the streets of Croydon,' she said speaking up. Resuming her summation of thought, she continued: 'By Harry Tambling knowing Dan, would be called upon by his sister Terri to help, he would turn this to his own advantage by framing Dan Prescott for the murder of Tom Brannon while himself under police custody. Dan Prescott thinking that Harry and Terri

Chapman were in co-hoots together in framing him Dan Prescott.'

Mattock listening added, 'That's if Terri has been staying at The Waddon Hotel and not still in Cricklewood.'

'Only one way to finding out, would be to pay a visit to The Waddon. If she has come south to cover Harry's interests, would explain to why Dan Prescott is regarded as a threat and you already know Dan is innocent, with you providing that perfect alibi in meeting up with Dan Prescott earlier. Unless Dan has said anything, how would Terri know that? Dan Prescott to me keeps everything close to his chest, in that he never lets on unless he wants something in return,' Helen said.

The drive back from Brighton went swiftly, returning to Croydon Police Station in just over the hour. Apart from the minor traffic incident. The miles eaten up with the help of roads unnaturally clear of traffic. Checking in on Harry Tambling, Mattock knew that he only had until twelve-midday to charge Harry on anything other than possible drug trafficking, in which he was not caught in possession off. Without that proof, Harry Tambling would walk free.

A search warrant obtained the previous day while Mattock was down in Brighton had been obtained.

As the dawn opened next morning to daylight, police cars three in total descended on The Waddon. The banging on the doors to the pub, woke up not only those residing on the premises, but those neighbours who lived in close proximity of The Waddon with some of the public giving their voice to being disturbed so early in the morning. The reaction from within The Waddon brought about confusion. The sight of Terri standing in a nightdress confirmed that she was residing at The Waddon. Handing over the warrant, Mattock walked past the hapless Terri informing her that they were to search the premises. Terri looked on as the police waltzed in passed her, tempering the fury at the unearthly hour in which they arrived.

Someone provided her with a dressing gown to cover her modesty. This act only enraged her more.

Everything was turned over, every nook and cranny searched, every draw, cupboard and bookshelf in the home checked. The bar seating and tables checked beneath, the decorative memorable tack that sat on the window ledges behind the seating pushed or put to one side. Behind the bar, flower vases emptied. Flowerpots pot plants sifted and searched beneath for hidden substances in packets, the tills opened upon request and checked behind the till draws. Whatever substance they found that looked suspicious. They took to check out at the labs on suspicion of being illegal drugs. A list made of what they took and place in plastic bags.

An hour, two hours passed before Mattock decided his suspicions did not hold up and nowhere else to search. The police left the pub as they had arrived, the plants in flowerpots and vases left askew to inform the pubs clientele they are having been there. Terri on her mobile to her solicitor and legal advisor, as to her position if anything found, also seeking advice on what she could do to her dissatisfaction to the police raid and at the early hours of day taken place.

'Was worth the raid, just to see the ruffled feathers we produced in Terri Tambling's reactions,' Mattock said,

'Sir when questioned about the possibility of drugs on the premises. She did appear frustrated with our persistence in finding evidence to support her brother's involvement in drugs. Twice she tried to divert the charges towards Dan Prescott. First, she said that all these accusations of Harry running drugs, was a preconceived idea drummed up by the police seeking to frame her Harry. Second, that we only had Tom Brannon's version of events on what happened the night he overheard a conversation by assuming her brother had been in the booth behind, when he supposedly made the call on his mobile. Yes, her brother was there. But as no one has proof as nobody has yet to confirm from telephone records that he even made a call at that precise time.'

'True, her brother conveniently losing his mobile prior to our talking to him did not help our enquiries at the time. She cannot be stupid enough to assume we would not investigate that option, of ringing around the telephone companies for that proof,' Mattock said with a winning smile. 'That proof alone makes him more of a suspect than he is willing to admit. At this moment in time, do not reveal to Terri Chapman that we have a recording of the call, the time and place given the background noise,' Mattock said emphasising his wish for secrecy.

Helen looked towards Mattock, wishing to know how he could be so sure of his facts regarding his final comment. Held up in his hand was a mobile phone. 'Surprising what turns up in a search,'

'How do you know it is Harry Tambling's?' she asked

'Dan Prescott supplied me the mobile number a short while ago when we met up prior to Harry's arrest to the incident involving the car carrying drugs at the Five Ways crossroads on Purley Way' As he fumbled through his jacket pocket, Mattock produced a written mobile number on a piece of paper, and then rang the number with his own mobile. A shrill ringtone came from the mobile acquired in the search. Which he was now holding up to Helen, 'Check out the time of the relevant call which surprisingly has not been removed and listen to a recording he kept, not of his words. But of the recipients message that night, before Harry returned the call with his own message spoken and heard by Tom Brannon.'

Helen smiled. 'But with Tom Brannon now deceased we have only his written statement to the facts of the conversation he had heard, how do we get that repeated in a court of law and confirmed that we have not prefabricated this statement in advance of any trial?'

Mattock shrugged, 'That, Helen, is something for our experts to fathom, the fingerprints on the phone will confirm that it is Harry Tambling's mobile, the rest can be pieced together between Tom Brannon's statement and the recorded message pre-empting Harry's words or the threat spoken. We are making progress, the reason for secrecy at this moment in time is to provide the proof needed.'

As DC Alan Tatchell came up to the car and entered. Helen and Mattock both smiled at the possible outcome, before they set off back to the police station.

CHAPTER 18

Terri Chapman paced her room. Her thoughts on whether she could have done more to prevent the search, despite the advice received from her legal advisor.

Meanwhile, one mile away a figure was slowly coming around from an unforeseen impact of someone hit from behind. Waking up and tied to a chair in a room. Slowly he surveyed the room that held him. A blurred vision seen at first, disorientation and confusion, his head appeared to have been hit a heavy blow as the pain that ensued gave rise his vague memory of a trickle of blood seeping from a wound at the rear of his head. Dan's vision had improved to which he saw clearly his plight, for before him he found two men seated opposite across the room at a small table, both playing cards. Three glasses were set upon the table, which meant a third member was not far away. All the glasses filled to halfway. A thirst came over him at the sight. He wished to turn his head to track the whereabouts of the third person. The throbbing that came from his head wound conveyed opposition to this train of thought. Not wishing to convey his awakening from his ordeal, he quelled any pain felt that filled his head to any injuries. Biding his time to act. Dan closed his eyes until felt strong enough. Hoping that time would prevail in his favour, allowing his strength to return and his wish to voice opposition to the pain.

During the minutes that followed, twice words spoken as the three people present talked of the amount of time Dan had remained unconscious, one stating that Dan should be waking up anytime soon. Another deemed it enough to give the name of the perpetrator of his discomfort. 'Do you think, Ted, you may have hit him too hard on the back of the head.'

The reply from Ted showed no remorse as he said, 'Don't be stupid, was no more than a tap.' The voice heard, provided Dan with the precise location of where the third person was in the room, also his attacker's name Ted.

The third member of this trio called for the pair to stop talking openly, stepping forward towards Dan. Tapping Dan's chin and trying to arouse Dan, to promote any chance that Dan maybe awake already. Although the pain was intense, Dan managed to subdue any response and rise to the pain he was feeling. 'Nothing, not even a whimper, maybe you did smack the back of his head with too much vigour. He is still alive, enough to be quiet.'

That person returned to his seat. 'The boss will be here soon, we will wait and then wake him up, maybe the shock of cold water will revive him quicker,' he said as he sat back down, turning over his spread of cards onto the table. 'Shit, I'm sure you look at the cards while I check out the place. You win again,' said the man named Ted.

'You are saying I'm a cheat,' the person opposite called out as he raked in the winnings.

Ted retorted, 'It would not be the first time. Do not know why I play with you, the amount of luck you have playing cards.'

'Keep your mouth shut, before I rip your tongue out,' the response from the winner. Dan noted the fractured ego in his words.

Dan felt like retching, but kept down any possible urge to do so. While thinking about how he was to get out of this predicament. The three amigos had returned to playing cards. Dan kept up his pretence, but with his eyes slightly open to monitor the three as he tried to prise his hands out of the ropes binding the hands together. Due to a freak accident whilst in army, he was able to contort his thumb across his hand to allow the fingers to manoeuvre out of the grip the rope held. Wriggling his thumb under the rope and slowly loosening his fingers, he enabled to relieve the pressure on his wrists, as his left hand freed itself from its confines, enabling Dan to free both hands. His captors otherwise engaged. Opening his eyes fully Dan gaged how and where to discard the rope.

All three turned towards the main door as one, giving Dan the one chance to discard the rope to the rear of the room, luckily his aim found his target where a dark shadow fell over the rope. His legs not bound, Dan could move more freely. Ted reacted first as nobody was apparently entering, returned his gaze to the table of cards, then glanced over towards Dan unaware that Dan had discarded the rope from behind his back.

'Dave,' he called to another of the trio, letting slip as to the identity of the second captor. Dave responded to Ted's call to check Dan. As Dave approached, Dan flexed his fingers ready to lunge at Dave as he neared. The pain at the back of his head sufficiently subdued to give Dan no immediate concern. Tensed for action, the door opened. Everyone's attention, including Dan drawn towards the door as it opened.

Everyone turned to Dan as he uttered his shock response. The commotion that ensued as Mattock allowed a squad of police officers to file pass him into the room. Ted and Dave were the first to react. Forgetting their prisoner, they elected to go for the guns tucked inside the waistbands of their trousers. Racing to a side door in the room, Dave opened the door and ran with Ted in close pursuit, Ted turned as he passed through the door with the intention to shoot at the officers to dissuade them from following. The attempt failed, first, because Ted failure to see Dan Prescott following in close pursuit. The side doorway had already allowed Dave to pass through unheeded. Second, allowing Dan to take the extended arm holding the gun and rotate Ted using his momentum to prevent the gun firing by pushing Ted's body mass into the wall to the left of the door, forcibly ramming the arm into the open doorway, a manoeuvre learnt from his army days. Hearing a crack as the arm from the elbow down forced into the opening to release the pressure on the unfired gun.

'Thought you'd be tied like a hog to a chair, how come you're not?' Mattock queried, as he took control of the situation. Stopping Dan, from doing any lasting damage to Ted, now he had a busted arm.

Dan recovered from the two officers relieving him from his charge. 'I was and had just discarded the restraining ropes as you came knocking on the main door. How did you know where to find me?'

'I didn't. Helen's informed guess from a note picked up in a home visit earlier.' Not wishing to divulge the note found at the premises of The Waddon, stating a property acquired two days previously. 'Helen chancing on the fact it could be the place holding you. Luck was on your side and the rest as they say is history,' Mattock answered.

Luck may be on my side, but that is not always the case, thought Dan. 'How did you know I had been taken captive?' Dan asked

Mattock replied, 'A member of the public phoned into the station to say someone with your description had been hit over the head and bundle into a nearby car before speeding off.'

'Maybe I have a guardian angel; nobody can have that amount of luck.'

Mattock shrugged off the thought that luck played a part in all life's questions and answers of the unknown. 'Have only one question, that is do you know any of the three here in this room that held you captive.'

'Strangely enough before today I had not met up with any until the one who decided not to run out of the three revealed the name of two of my captors, the third omitted to name himself or aired his name as it never came up in conversation. Since you have taken him into custody, I am still none the wiser to his name yet. Of the two mentioned, I've seen him hanging around The Waddon on occasion, that is Ted, who apparently sought to cave the back of my head in,' answered Dan,

The room cleared of all evidence to the three men holding Dan, taken in one van to the hospital where Ted received medical attention to his broken arm. Ted left at the hospital with another two police officers while submitted to the A&E Dept. The other pair taken to the Croydon Police Station for questioning, held in a police cell until Ted was fit enough to join up later that day. Dan Prescott was escorted back home and left on the doorstep of his home. Mattock stated due to what had happened there were still questions unanswered, that he and DI Helen Smith would be back in touch later in the day. 'Your head may need seeing to. I know you are reluctant to go to hospital and have your head seen to, but you need it checked out for any more lasting damage that may have been done.'

About to drive away, Mattock stopped, 'Do you know a Gary Parsons?'

Dan faltered between strides walking to the door, turning he faced Mattock: 'Lives down south near the coast somewhere.'

'Do not know him personally?' enquired Mattock.

'Seen him in The Waddon once or twice, not in a while though… why do you ask?'

'How close is he to Harry Tambling? Does he help Harry in any of his criminal activities?' Mattock asked, ignoring Dan's question.

'Not that I know. No,' answered Dan, curiously.

DI Mattock drove off, leaving Dan looking on, as he drove left at the end of the road.

CHAPTER 19

Surprise fell across Dan's face as he saw his own car back on the driveway. Mattock had not mentioned the car's return.

Dan opened the passenger nearside door. To retrieve a mobile left there the last time he used the car. A spare Pay as You Go, since he had renewed the mobile earlier in the year. He used to carry a contract phone, but as he had habit of losing his phone on occasion, his contract withdrawn and insurance annulled and stopped.

He looked up at the downstairs window to his home, only a drawn curtain could be seen, likewise the upstairs windows. Not knowing the time, he noted the time on the dashboard at 7.30pm, the day now fading away and the night closing in. He could leave his problem until the following morning, but going indoors would produce more worry in another area. His appearance and the bruising to the back of the head, he knew would panic Samantha, Shirley on the other hand could help him by driving the car, as bruising could also be found around his wrists due to the exertion and strain caused by the pressure releasing his hands from the rope tied behind his back earlier.

Not wishing to cause any alarm, he decided to drive away as best he could to a side road, intending to sleep the night inside the car. His luck held out until he used his arm and hand to push the gearstick forward and back to reverse. Pain from around his wrist, due to soreness and bruising, the pain made him wince. He released the gearstick almost immediately. Dan knowing his intended plan had backfired. From the house doorway, he felt someone staring out at him. It was Shirley. Dan knew then, he would be going nowhere.

Resigning to staying put, he locked up the car before going indoors. Dan waved away the comments given out by the women to his condition and passed by both, stating. 'It is a late night and will talk in the morning. Goodnight to you both.'

Entering his bedroom, closed and locked the door behind him. The last thing he wanted was two women harping on and questioning where he had been and how he came by the injuries. Although the injuries looked bad, he felt all he needed was a good night's rest. They could give their jaws a rest and stop the nagging questions until morning. Sleep came over Dan before his head hit the pillow.

Dan woke up with a start. His head was pounding like it had been used as a punch bag in the past twenty-four hours. The room spun around several times before settling down until Dan was able to focus squarely at one point in the room. Raising his head, Dan rested on his right elbow. He allowed the pain that filled his head to settle down to a sore throb before attempting to leaving the bed. He grabbed and held onto the bedpost at the foot of his bed. To steady himself from the vertigo sensation. Declining to sit back down on the bed. He shuffled with a faltered hesitance each step taken towards the door. Gathering his thoughts, he then opened the bedroom door. Hearing nobody, he staggered slowly down the hallway to the bathroom. Only three steps taken down the hallway. He heard Shirley's voice boomed out. 'Not trying to sneak out are we.'

The suddenness of hearing Shirley speaking out, shocked Dan out from his fragile state. The result, Dan tripping up on the carpet falling headlong into the bathroom doorway as Samantha opened the door, to find out whom Shirley was speaking to. Recovering himself, he turned to face both women: 'Morning, girls.'

'You do not, "morning, girls" me, buster!' Shirley fumed. 'Thought you could get away with not talking last night and thought you could just sneak into the bathroom without bye-your-leave. What next, sneak out of the house?'

'Shirley,' Sam said, 'in his state I doubt he could go anywhere. Look at him, blood everywhere. The state of his hair like a bird's nest home gone wrong matted with blood. Could not even stay on his feet, he is going nowhere and all you can do his harangue him.'

'Harangue him. I haven't even started on him yet,' Shirley stated.

Sam looked at Shirley, challenging her to say something. Shirley relented, for now. She left the two, descending the stairs. Letting them both know exactly where she was, opening and banging cupboard doors, followed by a cup or mug landing on the kitchen work surface with a clunk.

Sam stared back down at Dan: 'Let it go, she is miffed about something. I do not know what. Therefore, you going to tell me what happened to you these past two days to be in a mess like this or are you going to shut me out like you always do when there is a problem.'

Dan staring back at Samantha as he made to move and winced. Samantha took hold of his hand then his arm as she struggled taking Dan's full weight in standing up. Once on his feet they headed into the bathroom. He sat on the corner edge of the bathtub as Sam sought the flannel, still damp from her use that morning. She rinsed the flannel out with fresh warm water. 'Let's have a look at that wound in your head, looks bad,' she said.

'Not as bad as it feels right now, only the heads thumping,' was all he could muster to say in response in his attempt to play down and make a joke about his appearance. 'At least I'm dressed.'

'Do not know whose modesty you are trying to save here, but I've seen it all before. I am a big girl now. I know the differences between a man and a woman.'

'Yeah, I guess you do. Look I'll fill you in as soon as I'm dressed and ready to face her ladyship downstairs.'

'For now, let's clean this wound as best as I can.' A few minutes went by, 'there, and you were right, not as bad as it looked on first appearances. I'll let you dress by yourself, you feel up to finding your bedroom on your own,' Sam proffered.

'Yeah, I'm fine. Thanks.' Dan rose and once he was up, retraced his steps back to his room.

Sam went and dressed herself, descending the stairs minutes later. No sign of Dan, she made coffee, walked into the front room and sat opposite Shirley, who sat staring off to one side tight-lipped saying nothing.

Nothing was said, until Dan walked in and then Shirley took in a deep inhale of breath and exhaled it down through her nose to mark her anger still. Drinking the coffee he brought in from the kitchen, he said nothing before getting up to leave. About to leave the room he stopped changing his mind and looked back on both Samantha and Shirley. Samantha stared back at Dan nodding her head side on in the direction of Shirley still looking away at the windows.

'Look, I could not face you both nagging me last night. All I wanted was to sleep I was not in any mood for another interrogation.' He turned his back to leave.

Shirley spoke, 'So, that makes it alright then does it.' Dan did not respond. She carried on. 'You asked me around to keep an eye on Sam, is that all I am to you, a carer for your cousin. You come in like death warmed up. The back of your head covered in blood and expect us to ignore the worry and questions we wanted to answer because you had a bad day at the office.'

Silence reigned over the situation Dan found himself, unable to answer. The sound of a knock at the front door saved Dan speaking out of turn and sounding callous in the way he kept problems and concerns to himself, avoiding the answers, he knew should be forthcoming to stop others worrying about him.

Samantha and Shirley both shook their heads as they also heard the knock on the door. Coincidence or fate taking a hand in Dan's favour again, 'Is someone going to answer the door,' Dan asked.

Shirley stifled a retort, but said, 'Well, you are nearest, why not answer yourself.'

Answering the door Dan opened to find Mattock and DI Helen Smith on the doorstep. Dan's face gave reason for Mattock to enquire. 'What, have we arrived at the wrong time?' Dan silenced at the question thrown at him, took a moment before recovering and opened the door fully to allow Mattock and DI Smith to come in. Both just walked straight on by and into the front room without Dan saying which room to enter. Finding Samantha and Shirley standing as he entered the room. 'Sorry, we have not come at an awkward time. We did inform Mr Prescott we would be calling last night when we dropped him off. You know DI Smith.' Turning to Dan, he said. 'I take it you have not told them of your escapades yesterday. How is the head by the way? Well do not let us interrupt. Might help us being here to fill in any gaps, the ladies might wish to hear, also help us on why you came to be in your predicament. I thought by allowing you to have the night to sleep, you would be receptive to talking this morning.'

'Thanks,' was all Dan could think to reply, trying to bring light humour to Mattock's appearance and encouragement to talk. 'Well. Now you have me cornered to speak up, how can I not.'

Mattock opened with a question and asked, 'What were you doing outside The Waddon when you received your friendly tap on the head.'

'I'd not call this a friendly tap,' Dan said trying to delay, but the facial expression on Mattock told him not to be obstructive. 'Just to speak to Terri Chapman who had come to look after Harry's pub while he was detained, held in your company, in the nick as she put it,' Dan answered.

With the bluntness of a question, he needed an answer too, he asked, 'Why?'

Dan knew then that Mattock had worked out the reason for the attack on him. Wondered whether he had himself, fathomed the answer to that self-same question. 'At first I was unable to meet Terri. The barman tried unsuccessfully to stop me from seeing her, saying she was not in. Unaware, he did not know I had seen her or someone upstairs. Looking up from outside and had seen someone draw the curtains two seconds before. When told, nobody was upstairs by the barman, not letting on I had seen someone. When he was not looking, I went behind the bar and went up the stairs. Found myself staring down at Terri in the upstairs room overlooking the part of the road, where I had been standing outside.

'I asked her why she felt the need for secrecy in staying upstairs and her living above the pub. She replied that she took it upon herself to keep an eye open following Harry's arrest. I think she blamed me for Harry's arrest.'

'Possibly the answer,' Mattock said in response.

'You think she was behind the assault on my head and abduction?' Dan said.

Mattock responded saying, 'Well, you said yourself. Terri considers you the reason for Harry being banged up in a cell. If she is devoted to Harry as she makes out to be, then it is conceivable she is capable of diverting the course of justice away from her brother. What's to say, you are not being set up to take a fall on his behalf?'

'That did cross my mind the last time I spoke to her,' Dan stated.

Mattock turned his attention to Samantha and Shirley with his next question. 'Have you two received any more of these telephone calls from our impersonator purporting to be Mr Dan Prescott?'

Both absorbed by the question and answers between Dan and the Inspector, expressed surprise at the new line of questioning aimed at them. Shirley spoke up first, 'No, no, we have not received any more calls, have we,' glancing over too Samantha to agree.

Samantha just gave a shake of her head. Mattock seemed satisfied with their answer, said nothing more than, 'Good. That's as I suspected.' Then with a certain curiosity enquired whether they had ever met a Gary Parsons or knew of him, heard his name mentioned. Both again shook their heads unison side to side, to say no.

While Mattock continued questioning Dan, Sam and Shirley. Helen watched their facial expressions on answering the questions. The answers coming across without too much suspicion of possibly lying. Looked casually around the room surveying for anything out of place. A photograph of Samantha and Harry Tambling in happier times caught her eye. This Helen found strange, as to why would Samantha still have a picture of herself with her ex-partner on show, when she was meant to be divorced from Harry Tambling and not part of his life? Did she still carry a torch for Harry? Did she have some pleasure in seeing the person who once knocked six bells out of her when angered? Noting, that the photograph was in Dan Prescott's home, could be she thought Samantha had brought it here with her while she stayed, doubtful. Mattock left to answer a call from the station. Helen asked Sam, 'find it strange that a picture of Samantha and Harry is still on show. I thought you were both divorced now. Am I missing something? No response came, just silence.

Shirley stood upright, a stance taken from someone assured, also the unwillingness to compromise if angered, as was the case, when Mattock walked back into the room. There was only a fleeting look, but Helen picked up, on the facial change. Samantha sat nodding her head up or down depending on the question. A woman who quiet, unassuming and few words to say about herself, is she in denial or had she known of the husband's past deeds, though were led to believe otherwise. The whole world against her, but with the help from friends like Shirley, not so much her family as apart from Dan, no other members of the family if any, all appear to be non-existent. On speaking with local drinkers in The Waddon, everybody knew Samantha well, but rarely saw her in the bar. Helen asked herself why she preferred to stay in the background when all the publicans' wives she knew worked alongside their partners. Samantha was excessively absolving herself from Harry's known criminal activity and any blame.

Mattock had left DC Alan Tatchell at the station to interview Harry Tambling, thinking him capable of asking the appropriate questions discussed prior to Mattock going to Dan Prescott's home.

A call came through on Mattock's mobile, a blue hazed screen highlighting Alan Tatchell in white glowing out from the screen. Mattock excused himself from the room, wishing for privacy while taking the call. Once outside Dan Prescott's home he picked up the call. Harry still pleading not guilty to the various charges held against him, his solicitor refraining him from saying anything more should it incriminate him. As they could not hold Tambling for more than twenty-four hours, had the choice either of charging him or letting him go. Thankfully, DC Tatchell decided to leave that decision to Mattock upon his return with DI Helen Smith. The only crime he was possibly guilty of was aiding and abetting drugs smuggling, the only proof being drugs found in a car he owned, and a picture of Harry with a known Asian drug dealer part of the Hou-Lin Hoi family under investigation himself.

That of Penny Connor's demise if the cause of her death attributed to Harry, organising it from a telephone conversation. This if true and phone records confirm that Penny Connor was the number on Harry's phone at the time of the alleged conversation. No other call made that night from Harry's mobile phone, establishes that he did not organise the death of Penny Connor. Not enough evidence to hold him, they had to let Harry go without charge. Mattock had Harry's house phone checked over a forty-hour period following the same conversation brought up six numbers telephoned, but the numbers rung made up of three BT land line numbers and three mobile numbers from various mobile companies, one to each. All registered call listed different users. Two were to known villains each had an alibi to their whereabouts on the night Penny Connor was stabbed. The third was register to a Steven Lauder, the name given was false as no record of such name recorded on the police records or on the NHS website with an NH Insurance number credited to him. The number when telephoned was dead, not recognised.

Mattock hung up and returned to the house. All three looked up, Samantha, Shirley and Dan Prescott. DI Smith saw the expression on Mattock's face and noted that he was in no mood to question the three further that morning.

'We are needed back at the station, DI Smith. Mr Prescott, we will be back, in the meantime watch your back and please have that wound looked at, even though your cousin has done a good job on cleaning the wound up. Just to be on the safe side. Morning, ladies, we will see ourselves out.' Mattock shut the main house door as they left. Only when back in the car did Mattock inform Helen the summation from the interview with Harry Tambling by DC Tatchell.

CHAPTER 20

Back at the station, news from the police enquires in Brighton had been made known as to the blood found at Highdown Road, Hove. A report received by fax was waiting in a file on Mattock's desk. Reading the report written up by the forensics established the blood results came up as 'AB' rhesus negative, a rare blood group, which narrows down the field if a body turns up suddenly. He handed the report over to Helen standing at his office door and who in turn passed it over to DC Tatchell standing just inside the doorway.

Mattock telephoned the police station in Brighton; they could not add anything further to what they sent over earlier. They had checked medical records and confirmed the blood type was not that of Gary Parsons, which meant they could now be dealing with another possible murder. Thanking them for the report and new information in respect to whomever the blood matched. Replaced the phone back on the receiver, informing Tatchell and Smith of the latest piece of added information. Brighton said they would be looking out for Gary Parsons treating the blood found as suspicious.

At that same moment, Chief Super Homer, barged into Mattock's room nearly knocking over DI Helen Smith standing inside the doorway. 'Well any news,' not even acknowledging the fact he had knocked DI Smith to one side.

'Pieces are now starting to come together, still need to confirm one or two areas,' Mattock said.

'Good, let's have a report on my desk first thing Monday morning sharp, and that is not a request,' Homer said as he stalked away from Mattock's office.

DI Smith quipped, 'Does not hold back in his demands.'

Mattock still thinking about the blood said, 'Alan, can we find out what the blood results showed up on our two dead bodies in the morgue. We can eliminate both our deceased bodies if there is no match. Small chance the blood could be Tom Brannon's, if so we have our murder suspect.'

'Do you think that's likely boss?' Alan asked as he headed for the door. 'Would appear odd for Tom Brannon to be in Hove himself.'

'The way this case is heading, oddities appear to be the norm. Gary Parsons a frequent visitor at The Waddon, which links him to Harry Tambling. Penny Connor found with a stab wound outside the Aerodrome Hotel.

'Parsons' car parked outside in the hotel car park is register as stolen. CCTV camera catches him driving away in the supposedly stolen vehicle. Only his name is not on the hotel's register. Are we to assume that a member of the hotels staff has played a part in her attack, giving information as to her whereabouts, which would confirm that Gary Parsons possibly did not stay at the hotel, but arrived under instructions to harm Penny Connor? Again, that link with Harry Tambling.

'Then we have Tom Brannon, who if his blood group matches that of that found in a house in Hove would indicate that he met with his death not at the lake, but in Hove. Then transported back up to Croydon and dumped in the lake behind The Waddon. Why, why go to so much trouble and to leave his blood lying about in an empty house, DNA check could pin-point him actually being in that house. At this moment in time, we are assuming without any hard evidence to contradict that theory. Carry on, Alan, we will access that prognosis on the outcome of the blood results or any other forensic evidence found,' Mattock responded, returning to the report from the Brighton Police Force. Helen, still standing in the doorway, stood waiting, but with no comment made by

Mattock, assumed she was to believe she was to take her leave, without Mattock having said a word to the contrary.

Helen had misconstrued his action and was waiting for DC Tatchell to leave. Mattock asked Helen to stay behind which reversed her assumption that Mattock was waiting for her to leave as well. Knowing Tatchell was now out of earshot, Mattock enquired, 'Helen, when you were hovering around Dan Prescott's home did you find anything of interest? I noticed you taking note of various items in the time you were able to search.'

Helen frowned at the misconception that other officers had of Mattock and found their assessment of him. That of ignorance on most counts. 'Sir, people in the office have a narrow opinion of you at the best of times; some prefer to think that you do not show interest in the cases we take on, but you have an awareness of what you see and what is happening around you is second to none.'

'I appreciate your candour and thank you for your vote of confidence, Helen. Whatever anyone else may think of me and how we work as a team together, we get the job done. I notice a few here are as dedicated to their work as me. Nevertheless, the odd one or two who seem content to sit around making out they are on the job and pick up the plaudits when others have done all the hard work, I have no time for. Myself, I do not give a shit what other's think of me, as long as I get results,' stated Mattock.

Helen allowed herself to smile at his frankness. 'Sir, you asked about what I found of interest. I found little oddities that seemed out of place, but then, could be a reason for these items to be still out on show. One was a photograph of Samantha and Harry Tambling. Rarely do you see a photo of a divorced couple in a house especially that of someone who has been using you as a punch bag for their troubles. Then I thought that with Dan Prescott friendship with Terri Chapman, could be the only photo on hand should Terri call in. I think that might be stretching that theory a bit. I cannot see Dan Prescott as that type of person who would rub salt into the wound towards his cousin or next of kin. Possible prognosis, he has no idea the photo is still on display.'

'Yes, I had noted that on previous visits, like you I thought it seems odd. Do a bit more digging on Samantha.'

'Talking off Samantha, you know some publicans and their wives. Have you ever met the like that did not work together in the licencing trade? He supposedly kept her away from working behind the bar, preferring to keep her away from the pub business, at home. The money in license trade is not as great now, as maybe in years gone by. So, the question is where did the money earned come from, to afford the lifestyle they had and a separate home away from the pub,' Helen said.

'Point taken, but I do know some publicans whose wives are not always seen serving behind the bar, they tend to help in the kitchen or play happy families with the kids and are on emergency bar duties if staff fail to turn up for work on any given night. Keep an open mind, but, keep digging,' Mattock answered.

Harry Tambling remained in his cell. Frustrated with the delay in his being released, his solicitor told to wait until Chief Inspector Mattock had returned to the station before a release time and date given. Despite the solicitor stating he had not been charged to date. Failing of his client not being charge, they only had twenty-four hours to keep him confined. Few visitors since being arrested. Only Terri and his solicitor had called in. Someone walking passed his cell. Took a quick look into the cell, then shut the vent opening to the cell door without a word and walked on down the passage. Harry called out, 'About time you let me go, you cannot keep me locked this long.' No response come, all he heard was the door at the end of the passage open and close behind, seconds later a key turned in a lock.

Harry kicked out at the cell door, more out of anger and frustration at the time kept in his cell. The desk sergeant on duty acknowledge the constable upon his return from the cells downstairs. 'Any problems or is everyone in the cells quiet for a change?' he asked

'Everybody but that Harry Tambling were sleeping like babies. I left Harry Tambling kicking off in his cell about wanting to be released and how he has rights,' the constable said.

Sergeant Price returned to the paperwork in front of him, screwing up a form he had just completed and threw it directly into the bin in close proximity. 'Just love it when you complete a form only when checking find, you have made some stupid errors. Need to complete another. Shit, I am going for a break, take over the desk Constable will you. Keep an eye on everything while I go have a fag.'

On his return found DI Helen Smith talking to the constable, 'Hello, DI Smith, how can we help.'

'Your health is not helped by your continued smoking,' she remarked

'Yes, ma'am. If your life was taken up with the constant need to complete paperwork instead of assisting your people out in the field, you may be back on the occasional cigarette to calm your nerves against the monotony of office work,' he stated.

'I'm not down here to argue the point. Mattock will inform you of whether to let Harry Tambling go or not in the next hour, we have kept him longer than are allowed. May need to let the community police on the beat be aware to keep a look out if and when he is, give out a photo to provide a likeness, should they see him and watch what he does.'

'Heard, he could be responsible for that Tom Brannon's death.'

'At the moment that is all it is, just rumour. Harry Tambling was locked up downstairs when Tom Brannon met his maker, Sergeant,' Helen said to waylay the rumours from escalating further.

Mattock came down the stairs meeting Helen as she started to ascend them. He was with the Chief Super

Intendant, narrowly avoided walking into him, coming up short on facing Mattock, as she moved to one side to allow the Super to continue his progress down. 'Helen,' Mattock said, 'we are to let Harry Tambling go. On the evidence, we have, it is too much conjecture, with no substance to prosecute. Keep him under close surveillance and watch every move he makes when he leaves these premises.'

Helen reacted as if she expected this outcome. Mattock call out as he left the building along with the Chief Super, 'Helen, let me know if anything transpires on his release, also have Tatchell check up on Tom Brannon's ex-wife follow up on his assumption mentioned earlier,' the door to the station closing behind him.

Watching the door close behind ended her chance to ask where he will be found if needed. Her fascination to find out the destination of where the Chief Super and her boss were going quelled before her curiosity could surmount a spoken word.

Harry Tambling released without charge, with him stating after his release that his solicitors would be getting back to them about the unreasonable length of time held. Helen smiled to herself saying, *Just try Harry, just try*.

Already in place, the undercover police followed Harry from the building as he proceeded to hail and enter a taxi headed for home, The Waddon. Community police already advised and plain clothed police kept watch when Harry appeared in their locality. Two plain clothed police officers from the investigation team sat in The Waddon keeping track of the comings and goings, alternating with two others at intervals at differing times. Trawling as much information as they could muster from The Waddon regular clientele, Terri catering behind the bar was unaware, but had her suspicions.

Harry arrived thirty minutes earlier, not stopping he avoided the attention surrounding his appearance by going straight upstairs. The bar was busy, with a man down from behind the bar. Meant Terri had to forestall her wish to talk with Harry. Another hour passed before she could retire and vacate herself from the bar. For a lunchtime trade, today was busier than the norm. Enquiring with her regulars established that a big convention at the Festival Hall in Croydon. The convention held in one of the bigger halls. Nobody supplied the answer as to what. Terri knew the information would be forthcoming later. The pints kept flowing and the extra income for the pub from the food passing over the counter. A welcome from the recent problems, good business for the pub.

Terri excused herself, leaving Toby to cater by himself, Sally having pulled a sickie that morning, left them slightly exposed to a sudden rush of drinkers. Told Toby to call up if needed, knowing Toby more than capable to manage.

Upstairs Terri found her brother snoring away in one of the upstairs bedrooms. Typical she thought. Deciding to leave him there, she turned to leave. Mid-turn, discarded that notion. Nudging Harry awake, Terri called out, 'Come on wake up, Harry, you can sleep later. We need to talk, you got some explaining to do and you are not going to do that in la-la land, while I am downstairs slaving away in the bar.'

Awakening from his sleep, disorientated for a few seconds, unsure of his whereabouts, flaying his arms fending off a shadow that was not there, Harry's eyes focused upon Terri standing beside the couch. Holding a glass of cold water; preparing to throw it over him. 'Hold on, woman, you do know I've been banged up in a police cell.'

'Yeah and let's remind ourselves, how the hell did you get there?'

Harry refused to back down to her response. Sitting up, he gave her a hard stare. 'Why don't you tell me? I've not had a good night's sleep, since the old bill invited me into their hotel accommodation,' he said, his left arm pointing, as if pointing to the hotel in question, but referring to the police station.

Not lying down, she gave back as good as she got, Terri continued, 'Sleep, that's all you have done, since you took up their offer. Bet you even had your three meals a day while lounging about at my expense.'

'What do you mean at your expense?'

'My taxes go to pay the police and provide you a place to eat and sleep at his majesties pleasure. Plus, I have to take time out from my pub to ensure your pub does not go under.'

'Not my fault I got banged up.'

'Then whose is it stupid. What were you up to? What have you gone and got yourself involved in that was so important. You did know the cops were onto you and your Chinese friends. From the expression on the face it appears no, well I am surprised.'

Harry threw his hands up, 'I can't be doing with all this. I'm going out, anywhere but listen to you picking holes.' Not waiting for a comeback from Terri, he was out of the door, ran downstairs and left the building in seconds. Terri stood watching angered at the flippant manner in Harry not willing to stay and talk. She heard the main pub door, and then watched from the upstairs window Harry strike out along Epsom Road, heading towards West Croydon. She stood there for a few minutes watching, looking, also noticed two others leave shortly after and head in the same direction as her brother Harry. For a few minutes, did not give any thought to the two men, realisation dawned on her that they were cops sent in after ten further minutes of Harry leaving.

By mid-afternoon, the clouds were amassing across the skies, dark and menacing, with the threat of a storm. Dan had quietly sat drinking his coffee at one of the tables outside his favourite coffee bars, when he went inside to purchase another. Thirty minutes was all the time heartbeat, teemed down, hailstones followed. As he made to return to his seat, he looked out on the torrential rain, now descending from the sky. In a corner seat at the window unnoticed by Dan before, he noticed Harry Tambling looking down into his cup. His initial thoughts were to ignore him and find another seat, the café had little room provided to hide from Harry's sight. Too late, he found Harry looking up at him before he could move. Decided to pull up a chair opposite Harry and sat down. 'You're back out then?' he said.

Harry sat for a while saying nothing, just stared back at Dan. Dan sensed that Harry was clearly unprepared for this meeting. Dan looked around the coffee shop, only two others sat at a table near the coffee bar. Both on occasion periodically lifted their eyes in his direction. Guessed they were police officers by their observing eyes. 'Seeing as you're not in the mood to talk, I will take my leave.' Not a word spoken Dan made his getaway, leaving through the main door back out on the street. The torrential rain had eased to a few specks of raindrops. Turning left once outside, saw a rainbow had formed high up in the air, its archway formed across the sky, slightly fading, but still eminent in its appearance.

Dan walked into the High Street, continued through down a side alley leading into the Whitgift Centre. His coffee in a takeaway cup still in his hand, bought a newspaper and sat down at a table outside another café, only told to move on unless he wanted to order something. Declining the offer, Dan sought another place to drink his coffee. No seating available he took up a position beside the upper floor safety balustrade while leaning his elbows on the rail itself as he watched the shoppers and office workers go about their business. A child in a pushchair was making merry hell for his mother trying to navigate her way around the shopping centre. An old man took umbrage at a young boy, racing passed on his skateboard, had just clipped him, as the boy tried to weave in and out of the gap the old man had not intentionally provided. Not quite making the gap when the opening closed too early, the young lad caught the old man's elbow. Leaving behind, the old man waving his walking stick in the air in

176

anger, remonstrating. A passing woman, thought to see if he was okay only to be sent away packing with a flea in her ear, with the old man turning his venom on to her. She left berated.

'That will teach you to interfere in a minor accident. Some people just do not wish to be given a helping hand,' Dan thought to himself as he watched on.

Placating his position on the balustrade rail, Dan discarded the coffee cup into a nearby refuge bin conveniently placed alongside an occupied bench. A television in the nearest electrical store had a face Dan recognised on the screen, being outside the store was unable to hear what was said from where he stood on the opposing side of the centre. Walking around the walkway, by the time he stood in the doorway, the News item just finished and concentrated on the next story. A man and woman standing just outside the store went to leave themselves. Dan apologised for stopping them and asked whether they had heard the news item on the TV just seconds ago. Both seemed mystified, so Dan explained that he was talking about the man, a Detective Inspector moments ago, speaking on screen. Both shook their heads, claiming they had not been listening. Allowing them to leave, he thanked them. Disappointed at not knowing, Dan stopped himself from showing his disappointment at the not knowing.

His mobile phone rang in his trouser pocket, answering the call, he said, 'Okay, I am not far away. I will be with you as soon as I can.'

Walking from the Whitgift Centre, Dan made his exit at the rear, continued on up towards Festival Hall. A commotion had built up outside a building, Dan remembered the building accommodating The Blue Orchid night club, memories of them days flashed past him, but reality struck knowing the club had long since closed down. He found Shirley standing over Samantha lying on the ground. 'What happened?'

Shirley could not contain herself on seeing Dan, 'A youngster on a skateboard, a boy, went flying passed them as we were walking into Croydon. He came up fast on his skateboard, snatched Samantha's handbag as he passed, knocking her to the ground in the process. Left her with a twisted ankle and me not knowing whether to give chase or hold back and care for Samantha. Next thing, I look around from checking on Sam and the boy has gone, disappeared into thin air.'

'I came as quick as I could, you okay, Sam?' Dan enquired.

'Yes, just twisted my ankle hopefully, apart from that feeling stupid and angry for being so helpless in letting it happen,' responded Samantha, looking gloomy and in agony.

'Shirley, I take it you have phoned for an ambulance. Cannot risk moving her should it cause more problems to her ankle. What did the boy look like?' Dan asked.

'Just like your normal lad on a skateboard, young looking, longish dark hair may have been in his early twenties at most,' explained Shirley.

Dan convinced that this was the same boy he had seen earlier in the Whitgift Centre, causing mayhem. Shirley's description more or less confirmed that. A passing police car stopped Seeing the crowd of people gathered around Sam laying down on the pavement. Dan, left Shirley to explain what had happened. One of the officers on the phone communicating with the station. Whilst leaving the other to disperse the crowd forming and moved them on.

Only when the ambulance came and went did the officer succeed in that department. Dan enquired as to which hospital they were driving to. When told St George's, he asked why not Maydays. Not given an answer, he saw Shirley jump up into the ambulance as requested by Sam. No room for himself said he would make his own way to the hospital.

Watching the ambulance follow the one-way system, around the crossroad intersection and back up the other side of the central underpass going under the intersection. Continuing onto the second of two roundabouts and then right, going on along the flyover towards Waddon. Dan was unsure that the ambulance was taking the quickest route to St George's Hospital.

His eyes saw an outline to a skateboard to the right side of Festival Hall on the opposite side of the road to where he stood. Without giving a thought to passing traffic, Dan raced across the intervening road sections narrowly avoiding two cars that braked, pulled up hard. Jumping over the barrier surrounding the roundabouts, due to minor roadworks. The commotion caused by Dan in crossing, brought a response from the skateboard as it crashed to the ground as its owner took a glance around the corner of his hiding place, at where the commotion was coming from. Dan recognised the youth as the one he had seen earlier. The handbag he held confirmed him as the one who had attacked Samantha. Moments later saw Dan running hell bent towards him, unsure for a second he hesitated before throwing the handbag to one side. Started to race away from Dan, Dan had fifty metres to gain on the boy. He found the boy was a lot fitter as he started to pull away.

Dan maintained his speed, knowing that the boy would tire eventually. The army training coming to the fore, he claimed back the advantage the boy had gained before, continued to claw back the ground between them, when the boy made the mistake of looking over his shoulder to see where Dan was, he tripped up clipping the kerb on passing the entrance to the underneath car park to Festival Hall. As the boy slowly got up, Dan took grip of the boy's hair in passing and propelled the boy into a lamppost conveniently stationed alongside the road. His head hit hard and bounced back off onto the floor. The contact with the lamppost with his head, the boy was out cold before he hit the ground. Now laying their sprawled out, legs akimbo, hardly the menace he was earlier. Dan phoned Mattock, told him he had just apprehended a petty crook seen snatching a handbag from his cousin near Croydon centre. Mattock asked him where the boy was now.

Dan looked down at the floor, 'I am standing over him. Not far down the road to the Magistrates Court, or Fairfield Car Park back entrance. The boy, crashed out on the pavement, where he can't cause trouble.'

'What have you done to him?' Mattock enquired, then said, 'I'm on my way now, don't go anywhere.'

Dan remained silent a few seconds, Mattock thought the line had gone dead, but then Dan spoke up. 'Do not rush; I'm going nowhere and neither is he.'

'What do you mean?'

'Just that he is out cold; I told you he had a run in with a lamppost, possibly wake up with a sore head.'

Mattock arrived within minutes, accompanied by DI Smith. When they arrived, the boy had just stirred, waking up bleeding from the wound to his forehead. 'I'll help take him back to the hospital,' Dan said.

Mattock stared up at Dan, using his mobile Mattock called for an ambulance whilst Dan just watched on unconcerned. 'We'll let the medics do their job; you've done enough damage already.'

Ten minutes later Dan had filled Mattock in on what happened in the events that led up to the boy laying out cold on the pavement. Mattock then asked, 'Did you have to hit him?'

'Did not touch him, the lamppost did, ran straight into it. Should have seen it, the boy never looked where he was going then smack, collapsed like a house of cards,' Dan said.

Mattock stared at Dan Prescott. Shook his head, 'With a little help from yours truly.'

Dan showed his disbelief at the assumption Mattock was making: 'I told you I never touched him.'

CHAPTER 21

Standing around outside a hospital ward was not one of Dan's strongest areas to comply with; he could only remain calm when in motion. Dan had walked up and down the corridor six times already. Waiting outside the ward, due to two others crowding around Sam in the ward. Matron on duty was sticking to her rules, only allowing two relatives per bed at any one time. The Matron not a person to trifled with stood overseeing the visitors at the bedsides of their next of kin or friends.

Dan had brought her handbag along wishing to tell her that her life was his main priority. Cousin she may only be, but he would always protect family. Samantha lay up on a bed ankle strapped up by the nurse. Mattock had transported Dan to St George's hospital. He sat down calmly watching Dan pacing up and down the passage. 'You are going to sit down at some point.'

'How's the case coming along?' Dan said, changing the subject.

'As if I would go and tell you,' said Mattock. 'I give you what I know and you tell our target. Yeah, nice one.' No argument or debate to the contrary made by Dan, the silence that ensued for several minutes. Mattock took the opportunity to make his absence, saying that he needed to get back for the boy, join up with his other officers watching over the sustained injuries to the boy's head.

Dan asked whether the boy had been named. 'No ID was found on him. Until the boy wakes up, then and only then will the name be forthcoming, and he is due to go up for a brain scan.' Answered Mattock, continuing, 'this is standard practise because of the injury to the head, which he would not need if you had not helped happen.'

Dan listened to Mattock's assumption repeated over again. Dan responded with what he had said earlier. 'I told you, Mattock, I never touched the boy. He tripped and made contact with the lamppost. Not my fault he could not look where he was going. I was too far away to prevent the accident.'

Halfway down the corridor and not looking back Mattock just waved with the back of his hand as he continued his exit saying, 'If you say so.' He disappeared through a door to the left. The only sound that enforced the fact that Mattock had left Dan to his own thoughts. The soft thud of the door closing too behind him.

A police constable sat outside the cubicle in A&E containing the boy. The X-ray completed and now back inside a side ward. The boy had come to and was sitting upright in his bed, when Mattock sauntered into the room. His first reaction on seeing the boy sitting up was to ask the constable why nobody had come to fetch him when the boy had come around from his ordeal.

'Nobody knew where you were, Sir.'

'The Medical staff knew.'

'Sorry, Sir. Did not think to ask.'

Mattock gave the constable a look of dismay, refraining himself from conveying his thoughts he asked: 'DI Smith, has she been in at all?'

'No, Sir,' the constable confirmed.

'How long has the boy been awake?'

'About twenty minutes, Sir, shortly after he returned from the scan.'

A doctor overseeing his patient looked from the boy on seeing Mattock appear in the room. Leaving the boy, he motioned for Mattock to go out into the corridor, the doctor followed behind him. When outside the room, the doctor told Mattock that the boy would need some rest before answering questions. Mattock asked whether the boy had provided them with a name.

'Ricky,' the doctor replied. 'Ricky Thompson.'

'Thanks,' Mattock replied in response.

'If you can leave any questioning for a couple of hours, then I can access whether he is fit enough to answer any questions then,' the doctor said in response to the silent question formulating in Mattock's head. Before he could utter a spoken word the doctor added, 'Ricky Thompson will be taken up to the wards in the meantime, possibly to a side ward once a room can be found for him to transfer to.'

'It's that serious then?' asked Mattock, noticing the name Dr Masood on the badge pinned to his white coat.

'DI Mattock, I do not think you realise how much of an impact to the head Ricky Thompson took. He appears to be okay, but until the X-rays come back from the scan. We need to be aware that the scan could come up with a long-term injury. The results will be with us within half an hour. Until then we need to keep the patient calm and provide rest from any stress or damage emanating from any injury to the brain.'

'I will need to have someone at the door to his room, if that is not inconvenient. As he will be required to answer a few questions, appertaining to a crime committed earlier today. Just so we know he is not left unattended,' said Mattock.

Dr Masood stated, 'Whether a crime has or has not been committed, my patient's health comes first whilst on the premises of St George's Hospital.' He saw no given reason, not to allow a police constable to sit outside the patient's room providing they did not interfere in the medical staff working at the hospital during the time Ricky Thompson was there.

Frustrated as Mattock was to the encumbrance in completing this crime saga. He relaxed his motives for conclusion. His mobile rang inside his left side jacket pocket. To his delight, the caller was DS Tatchell. 'Good, Alan. What have you come up with? Good news I hope.'

'Yes, Sir, at least I think I have found the possible cause to Tom Brannon's death,' came the reply.

The silence was deafening, only seconds passed, it could have been half an hour, but the impatience told when Mattock spoke again. 'Come on then, the suspense of not knowing is killing me.'

DC Alan Tatchell prolonged the suspense when heard to fumbling with the notes, shuffling in the background.

'Be with you in a moment, Sir.' Mattock groaned inwardly.

Tatchell continued, 'The blood results showed that Tom Brannon's blood did not match that of the blood found in Highdown Road, Hove. An autopsy revealed that Tom Brannon's body had been in the water for several hours. Stabbed in the left side of his body before dumped into the pond, the weapon described as a long skewer, or similar instrument, which penetrated through into his heart. The murder weapon has yet to come to light. I have taken the liberty of having the area around Waddon Pond searched for the weapon. Nothing found yet, but still awaiting the pond being dredged and searched.'

Mattock never usually praise his own officers in their endeavours to show initiatives of when the need to be working by themselves. But on this occasion, he could not restrain himself from smiling at Tatchell's own initiative. 'Good thinking Tatchell, I'm leaving the hospital now and should be with you as soon as traffic permits. Keep me posted if your men come across the weapon.'

He drove along Croydon Road, turning right into Beddington Lane, Mattock pulled into the service station to fill up on petrol. His thoughts elsewhere as he did not notice a car pull up behind and without staying reversed and pulled up short of Mattock on the opposite side of the petrol pumps. Only taking the hose from his car and replacing the hose back it in the petrol stand save himself from the gunshots fired through the car window lowered, coming between the petrol pumps missed him by whiskers. As he dived down, he saw the last glimpses of the offending car driven at speed out of the service stations exit without stopping for any traffic passing by.

By the time Mattock had recovered to take action, knew as he run across the forecourt to the road. The car had disappeared around the corner up Beddington Lane and up the hill into Hilliers Lane. Mattock placed a call from the radio in his car, reporting the incident and providing the first five digits of the number plate. Not able to catch the last two letters as the car had taken the hill at speed narrowly avoiding a truck, coming down from the opposite direction. The shots fired and the suddenness of the attempted murder of Mattock. Unsurprisingly no one claimed to witness the event. Claiming what happened was over too quick and the witnesses panicked on hearing shots fired.

Mattock when contacting base was notified to Helen driving over to Waddon Ponds via The Ridgeway entrance. On advice from DC Tatchell, Helen knew that Mattock was expected and would be over there. On arrival, Helen and DC Tatchell informed each simultaneously of Mattock not being present. News filtered through that concerned DI Mattock, having gunshots fired at him from a passing car. The car stopped for several seconds at a service station allowing time for someone to take a shot at Mattock from a firearm, then drove off. This happened when Mattock by chance stopped at the service station in Beddington Lane. The news spread around the ponds. Helen panicked, pleading a need to see DI Mattock. She left Waddon Ponds, explaining why she thought it necessary, to leave Tatchell at Waddon Ponds. To head off and see whether she could help Mattock and mainly to check he was okay.

Touched by her concern Mattock smiled and ensured he was okay, that he was unharmed. The Crime Scene Investigators were making a surveillance of the service station checking the scene for the shots fired. The bullets imbedded in a fence post and Mattock's car, only two fired. The investigative team had concluded that Mattock must have a Guardian Angel looking down him, to have been so close to the shooter and that the shooter missed their intended target. On reflection, he felt he knew who the shooter was on this occasion. A face loomed up in his mind, apart from not seeing a scar on the left cheek hidden behind a headscarf, the face reminded him of someone he locked up several years earlier, who had made the point that when released he would enact revenge.

His chosen route coming down Beddington Lane, would not have been known. So how could someone know his intension, in driving this direction if the destination were unknown to anybody other than at the HQ he had called into earlier. The only person who would know that he was headed over to Waddon Ponds would be DC Tatchell, but then Helen informed by Alan Tatchell of Mattock's intent on driving to the Ponds. His thoughts still could not come around that someone knew he would come via Croydon Road, Beddington Lane. Only reasonable explanation was his assailant by chance must have seen him at the hospital and followed him.

Leaving the service station, he told the officers remaining, to deal with the fallout from this crime scene. That he was leaving for another at Waddon Pond, his intended destination prior to the opportunity that ended in a failed attempt on his life. Informing DI Smith, he was leaving to meet up with DC Tatchell, she said she would follow him as she then opened her car door. Both drove down The Ridgeway, opposite what Mattock remembered as being Poppets, the chocolate sweet factory, now Brydon Tiles. Once driving down into The Ridgeway found the entrance to Waddon Pond within minutes. A number of unmarked police cars parked up near the entrance to the area gave notice to the local inhabitants that their lives actively intruded upon once again. Ignoring the barbed comments, Mattock walked on passed the local gathering of residents.

Going under the cordoned blue tape that surrounded the recent murder scene, Mattock and Helen approached

Tatchell as he talked to two of the divers who had been dredging the pond. Looking around the whole pond area surrounded by posts supporting chicken wire affixed to them, fencing the pond off completely. A deterrent should people and children attempt to encroach into the pond itself. Tatchell acknowledged Mattock's presence as he came up from the blue tape along with DI Smith. 'Sir, we have found another weapon whilst searching for the object that possibly and could ultimately have killed Tom Brannon. The diver has come up with a knife, found it hidden between the undergrowth and the overlying willow tree protruding several feet out over the pond. The branches stretching from the trunk looked skeletal and worst for ware with its naked leafless appearance. Posts around the pond in uniformed manner and also across one side of the pond. Seagulls in the vicinity felt obliged to use the posts to rest upon, all but a few. Pigeons littered the park towards the annex to the pond area, along with Seagulls. Took flight and flew off in panic, when frogmen resurfaced and came too close.

DC Tatchell's voice brought Mattock's attention back to the task in hand. 'Maybe the weapon used on Penny Connor. We have sealed and prepared the knife for forensics to look at.' Mattock nodded and told Tatchell to carry on with that assignment. Two Crime Scene Investigators drove off with the knife.

Happy with finding the possible weapon used on Penny Connor, now the focus was on finding Tom Brannon's murder weapon. Mattock felt they would not find that weapon in this location and killer. Gary Parsons was not guilty on this occasion in respect of Tom Brannon's death. In Penny Connor case, Mattock held the view that the jury was still out on that one for now. With luck, DNA will solve that with the possible knife found. Mattock knew the ring was closing in and almost within touching distance.

A crowd of onlookers watched on. Mostly from The Ridgeway homes residence that lived close by and looked onto the Green, other home owners and nearby businesses on the trading estate occupied the opposite side of the pond. A walkway separating the two sides of the pond. For those that did not wish to walk all around the ponds. Police constables asked onlookers to return to their homes or too move on. Allowing the police to carry on with their work investigating.

A couple of youths, seen playing around, kicking about something in the grass opposite to where Helen and Mattock stood. Alan Tatchell had just joined them both. Mattock prompted Helen and Alan both walked around to the spot. Not requesting the boys to stay put. The three boys left leaving behind whatever the item of interest was seen kicked about by the youths.

They found nothing to warrant them continuing with their search. DI Smith and DC Tatchell returned to Mattock who remained where they had stood, both reported nothing out of the unusual hidden in the grass, only the odd discarded soft drink can, flattened.

Mattock stepped onto the parapet staging built on the Ridgeway side of the pond. Stared into unclear water, but able visually to see clearly the bottom of the pond in parts. accepted that the ponds to be unclear in most parts. Sensed the knife used in the stabbing. Was not, discarded in the pond on the night of the stabbing. Only a recent acquisition of the pond, strategically place near the willow tree. Not thinking the police would return to dredge the pond.

The search completed with nothing else found, the Crime Scene Investigation team left. All that remained was the ducks, Mallards and Coots on the pond. Geese scattered on the pond and the nearside recreational parts. Mattock considered how the body had been dumped and not seen dumped in the process. Be difficult to position the body close to the willow tree. Without incurring some damage to the surrounding chicken-wired fenced boundary. Pathways on both sides of the ponds likewise the old small bridge that spanned the pond with small arched tunnels underneath, separating a smaller pond. No mudded footprints or shoe print markings, given the lack of rain.

He supped at a pint of lager. Observed only a few patrons sat at tables around the premises. A staircase, central to the main bar area. To lead the way... upstairs to another bar, closed for now. Assumed it was open during the evening and on into the night, relying on club scene of the nights, mainly weekend. A narrow section extended to the rear, twelve feet wide and thirty feet in depth. The décor had seen better days, a dark interior. Never seen the light in many a year. Lighting held a sombre glow; just enough to see what one ate off the plates. Dan turned to see those seated behind him, a lone figure sat to the rear. A black person wearing darkened sunglasses. Dan reflected as to whether people could see through the dark lenses when in enclosed places away from sunlight. The darkened Oakwood Veneer colouring to the surrounding wood panelled throughout the bar, a corner seating as you walked in to the right, the uninviting subdued lighting kept the person unseen, submerging him into the dark interior, but for the few people who came with the purpose of buying from this person. Always money and drugs dealt with under the tables.

Looking into the mirrors behind the bar. Dan could see clearly each time anyone came into the pub and made a beeline to this person. One individual seemed to act mysteriously, approaching the bar signalled for two drinks, not revealing where the drinks were headed as he walked away from the bar without paying, circled the bar before setting himself beside the black person. Heard the name Leroy mentioned in talking to the black person. Dan assumed this the name of the black person. Talk turned to friendly banter, to a hostile reaction in what, was not said shortly after. This happened within minutes. Dan thought of this mysterious person living on the edge. Reacting to whatever said to the extreme. Then the person stood up. Leroy stood also, thanked Jerome for coming along.

Telling Jerome not to worry, that the deal was a done deal and in the bag. Hands shook and Jerome left the pub. At the main doors, Jerome hesitated, looking back once then disappeared to the left.

Dan stayed, his eyes returning to Leroy. Leroy had sat back down rifling, counting the paper money notes accumulated in his pockets, in the time Leroy had spent doing business within the pub.

The girl behind the bar approached Leroy with another drink, Leroy hidden from view by the girl. Dan glimpsed a finger pointing in his direction, vaguely heard her telling him, alerting him that Dan has been closely watching at the bar. Leroy acknowledged the girl's piece of news. Dan not wishing for trouble drank up, thanked the girl and sauntered out of the pub not looking back he allowed the front door to close, headed to the left as if following the other guy Jerome. Not Dan's intension, Dan sought out an opening to stand within a shop entrance opposite the pub and watched. He moved slowly further back into the store feeling conspicuous where he stood previously. Not too far inside, enough to be able to still watch for Leroy to come away from the pub himself. Nobody from the store questioned him about being there. That wait, came sooner than later to a close as Leroy alighted from Yates's and headed towards Croydon Centre. Leroy not stopping continued, with Dan following from a short distance behind led the way to West Croydon Station, Dan checked himself that nobody else followed, kept his distance.

Leroy disappeared into the station, closely followed by a short distance by Dan. Only a police car pulled up several metres away. Mattock and DI Helen Smith came from the car as soon as the car stopped. Mattock walked up to Dan, persuading him to stop and saw his quarry taking the stairs two at a time as he raced out of site down the stairs. Trying hard not to allow his annoyance to being stopped in his track. Dan momentarily looked to the sky and exhaled. 'Not a problem,' he countered. He followed Mattock back outside into the street.

Mattock asked Dan if he was in a rush to be somewhere. Dan said, 'Why should I be in a hurry to go somewhere,' when he, Mattock and his partner DI Smith happen to prevent him from following someone he saw now slipping away.

'Was it something important you stopped me for or is there another reason you just happen to pull up in front of the station for?' Dan asked,

'No, just saw you in passing. Thought I would ask or see what you were up to,' Mattock said in response.

'My lucky day then, you wishing to pass the time of day chatting,' continued Dan.

'From your comment, I feel we have come at a bad time,' Mattock looking at Dan, 'perhaps you wish to convey with us what you were really up to when we happened to arrive here.'

Dan resigned himself to reveal he was following a suspected drug dealer selling in Croydon bar and following him to ascertain the dealer's source.

'So why do you feel the need to do our job for us, when all you needed to do is contact the nearest police station for us to proceed on your, the public's behalf,' Mattock said in askance.

'Thought, I would be helping in some small way.'

'Do not, I repeat do not interfere. We have a police force to do your bidding if only you would allow us to do the job. We have a police work force and resources to work a lot faster given the information. Look where it got you the last time you tried to help.'

Dan listened knowing that Mattock and his police force were nearly always, caught up in paperwork and red tape to act quickly. That he could and would try using his training in effect to good use irrespective of Mattock's concerns. 'Working outside of the box can help and work when used side by side of the police also,' Dan said in response to Mattock's words.

'Just give us the name of this dealer you claim to have seen in a bar. Which bar did you say?' asked Mattock.

'I didn't,' answered Dan. 'Yates's for your information. The person was a black person named Leroy. Did not get his surname, was never mentioned.'

'Leroy Williams if it's the same person. Has been trafficking drugs on and off for a number of years. Helen, check the name out, thought he was still inside. Seems he never learns, spends more time in prison than out. Has a sister Sharon, who watches over him, not clear as to whether she knows how to? Was there a black girl working behind the bar?' Mattock asked.

'No, a white girl and appeared to be his lookout when working. I think she let known I was watching him from the mirror behind the bar. I left to avoid unwanted trouble. Kept watch unseen from across the road. Then, intended to follow him, only I came as far as here when you pulled over.'

'We will question her. Have someone go over to Yates's, Helen. She may well be working her shift still. If not, get hold of her address. Dan, anybody else working with him, maybe not alongside, but within close proximity to Leroy or sitting near the bar, other than the girl?'

'No not that I could tell,' Dan said. Then recalled what transpired while he was in Yates's pub. 'Leroy arrived alone around 11am and knew where he would be sitting to carry out his business. The girl knew his poison, what he drank. Pulled his pint of lager without any acknowledgement and took it over to him. He was there for four, five hours. Punters coming in and out off the street for the arranged buy and sell under the table. There was one black person came in around 2.30pm, appeared agitated to extreme. Leroy knew him as Jerome, again no surname mentioned. Leroy kept trying to placate him by saying the deal was a done deal. Could have been an arranged meet. Jerome did not seem convinced. Maybe he felt Leroy was playing him. Only he left some forty minutes later. He never bought anything of Leroy, no drugs, nothing. Had one drink, unlike Leroy bought his at the bar, then sat with Leroy discussing the arrangement they had going, not in anger, no harsh words spoken by either. Just noted Jerome was acting very nervous and Leroy keep telling him everything was okay. As I said he left about forty minutes later.'

No interruption came from Mattock as he listened. The name Jerome he had heard before, but could not recall where the name had cropped up before. Not taking notes down, just recording and locking away the information until he was back at HQ base to write up.

CHAPTER 22

Helen had little trouble finding the information on Leroy's living accommodation. He lived in a one bedroomed flat in Honor Oak Park. Midway down a side road around the corner to the station. Once known the local police sent a car over to pick him up.

Leroy from previous experience, sensed that police were outside his pad. Panic had the better of him as he walked away from the scene before Helen could challenge Leroy at his front door. Now observed by one officer, backtracking in the direction he had come, making his escape. On Helen's word, nobody gave chase as Helen had a car stationed nearby at the other end of the street, from whence Leroy came. Not wishing to harangue him near the train station at Honor Oak Park, soon after his departure from West Croydon Train Station and making him jumpy. Leroy heading for his home, appeared luck played a part in Helen's guesswork. Already notified that their suspect was running back in their direction. Police officers were told to follow and not apprehend him yet, just see where he led them.

DC Tatchell made enquires in Yates's to where he could find the white girl working behind the bar earlier. Told her name was Mandy Warner, had been working there for six months, hardworking, liked by the punters who came in, always happy, no previous convictions given from background checks. Lives local in flats on Duppas Hill, a car arranged to pick up the girl for questioning. Mattock listened intently to all Tatchell had to say, whilst thinking of the name Dan had provided earlier, he had checked with records of all known friends of Leroy Williams. None came back with Jerome being the Christian name to one of these friends. Somehow, the name Jerome struck a chord in Mattock's mind. Mattock brought his mind back to the present as he focused back on what Tatchell had just said concerning Mandy Warner.

Mattock thoughts wandered again – within walking distance to The Waddon, could be her own local. Local Recreational Park with its own sports playing fields provided. Playground for drug distribution or dealers selling drugs to the young and vulnerable, drugs knowingly sold on the premises of Yates's by staff. Harry Tambling association with drugs and drugs haul going down somewhere tonight. Harry Tambling's associates, the Hou-Lin Hoi family the suppliers of Leroy Williams drugs dealing – Mattock mind turning over recent events around in his head, processing the probability of his thoughts being correct. Knife crime appeared on the up, as another two young members of society lost their lives in Thornton Heath in the past three weeks. A black youth caught for the crimes. No apparent reason given other than mistaken identity, unharmed and that in their case, they showed no respect to the attacker. Mattock summed up his use of the word. (Respect, a flippant word used in today society, a throw away word for those who have no respect for life, but wish to be respected themselves for who they were. Ask anyone, when did the respect for those innocently killed by the knife go?). Used by the disturbed psycho's, carrying knives in the name of protection, but, judge innocent bystanders on not being respectful.

'Sir, Mandy Warner has just been brought in. We have put her in the interview room,' the Sergeant on desk duty said.

His thoughts broken into, Mattock asked, 'Can you ask for DI Helen Smith to come down and meet me outside the interview room, Sergeant.'

'Sir, DI Smith left earlier. Said she was heading over to Honor Oak Park to apprehend a Leroy Williams. Can have someone track her down on the switchboard and have her come in.'

'Yes, do that. Let me know when she is likely to be back. In the meantime, have someone stationed inside the interview room. Keep an eye on Mandy Warner while I'm waiting for DI Smith.' Mattock was taking no chances with Mandy Warner, could have caused harm to herself while in custody. Hedging his bets Mattock asked the sergeant whether there had been any word, concerning a drugs haul coming in anywhere. Sergeant Price knew nothing, which Mattock thought would be the answer. Not sure as to why he thought to ask the question in the first place.

DC Tatchell, seen coming down the staircase into the foyer presumably from the Detective's main room, on eye contact with Mattock knew he had initiated his services needed. Not given the chance to say anything, Mattock conveyed to the sergeant that DC Tatchell would be helping him talk with the girl Mandy Warner in the interview room.

Leroy's failure to see the unmarked police car, led to Leroy's downward turn in fortune. Followed by a plain clothed police officer. He unwittingly was to direct them to the warehouse where a drugs operation was in progress. Outside activity to the warehouse gave nothing away, no cars in the street showing signs of the activity going on inside. Any deal on-going inside between the drug rings. With guns on show and at the ready, should trouble ensue. Too much at risk in police showing unexpected. Helen on catching up with Leroy as he entered the warehouse?

As Leroy entered the warehouse everyone inside turned around with guns at the ready to fire on the intruder. Unaware that a deal had been in progress his actions on seeing all guns on him. Was too slow to see the gun coming down on his head from behind as one of the watching guards came from behind a tower of boxes near the doorway he had entered. Slumping to the ground, Leroy was out before he had hit the ground.

'What the hell is going on? Who is this person? Anyone know him?'

'Seen him around,' said Chang. 'Works with a syndicate in and around south of the River Thames. Deals more locally in Croydon.'

'Check outside and clear this mess up and get rid of him,' looking down at Leroy, blood trickling from the ear. 'If anyone saw him arrive there may be trouble following up behind. Only thing in our favour is the goods already have left,' George Parsons said.

Chang quickly disposed of Leroy's limp body into the boot of the Merc. One of two cars parked, just inside the warehouse on the right-hand side away from the main area involving the drugs deal earlier. 'He's still alive, has a pulse,' Chang instructed one of his men to take the car and dispose of him somewhere a long way from there.

A heavy-set man moved forward to pick up the limp body of Leroy and stuffed him into the boot. Leroy's, head made contact with the boot lid, sounding with a thud. 'Chung, have a heart, I said get rid, not give him more to grouse about when he wakes up. Don't make the injury any worse.' The sight of the blood intensified as a fresh wound run blood freely behind the other ear. The heavy-set man checked Leroy over and found he had punctured his neck, caught behind the ear. Leroy left with a small incision along with the injury to the other ear earlier. Not saying a word the boot lid came down and shut.

Abdul standing at the closed entrance pulled on the handle to open the large metal sliding doors fully. Abdul saw two police officers hovering about at one end, checked the other end without revealing himself, nobody at this end. Drawing the attention of the two police officers to Chang, that the police were at one end of the lane. Chang himself came over to the entrance strolled out into the lane, taking one look himself to confirm, also turned around checking as Abdul did the other end. An unmarked car stood on the corner close to the kerb on the warehouse side, two people sitting inside, both in conversation while one looked down the lane towards his direction. Retreating back into the warehouse, Chang confirmed that police were outside watching. Then motivated everyone in the warehouse to move it. 'Get away from here, fast.' He shouted out. Chang reasoned that they followed the person now tucked up in the boot of the Merc. Everyone inside swung into action as one. Pandemonium had broken out as calmness shattered and the fear of capture took over. The Merc sped out from the warehouse turning right once outside and headed down the lane towards the unmarked police car.

Aware, but not expecting a car to suddenly appear and race out of the warehouse and head in their direction. With the unexpected sight of a car speeding out from nowhere onto the lane, the pair of officers sitting in the car, unprepared, were galvanised into action. They were both drinking coffee. The suddenness of action shook them as they were reacting fast, the coffee flew up everywhere inside the car including over themselves, panic set the scene. The hot coffee in close contact with flesh, down the front of their clothes and trousers and drenched through to the skin. The car sped by them at speed. Other officers behind them on the corner of the lane stood up and tried to force the car off the road into another warehouses that lined the lane. Not stopping the officers, themselves, were forced to jump out of the car's way as the car driver drove true, straight at them without deviating. Uniforms branched out in all directions to avoid being run down.

Most of those inside escaped out the back of the warehouse and up over the adjoining roofs. Those that chose to follow the car out through the main entrance found themselves confronted by police. Chang and Chung took their chances as they escaped inside the Merc. Helen supervising the small operation as it unfolded, not expecting the quickness of movement. She felt let down by the uncertain way other officers reacted to stopping several escaping including what she thought the main people involved. Rounding up those that failed in their attempt to flee, Helen arranged for back up to bring the prisoners into the station. One or two stragglers picked up from coming down off the roofs straight into police covering some back-fire escapes and windows. The speed of the Merc that escaped from their clutches around the corner, unable to catch the number plate numbers as those used were temporary plates used by most motor garages.

The warehouse checked out for any other persons on the premises, Helen reasoned that Leroy must have been in the escaping car, but nobody saw him in the car itself as the car sped passed them.

HQ informed to expect prisoners following a capture of people found on the premises of a motor repair outfit. As they were all running out and no fire, assumed that they were up to no good. Arrested for possible drugs, or stolen goods.

Mattock, when informed, made his presence known as he watched the prisoners handcuffed come through the main doors. Logged in and taken down to the cells. Helen brought up the rear along with the officers driving back with her. Mattock beckoned Helen to join him once all prisoners were booked in. 'What have we got here, Helen? You seem to have had a productive day.'

Helen grimaced at Mattock with a wry smile. 'Not as productive as I'd like it to be, several escaped including one Leroy Williams. Followed him from his home, must have got wind of us being outside his home as he backtracked before reaching it. Told our people not to confront him, as he turned back the way he came. Followed him to a warehouse where he was seen gaining entrance. We positioned ourselves outside, while I made contact here to have more of our people sent out to us to help should there be trouble. Ten minutes we stood outside when all hell broke loose. They must have spotted us there as two came out one after the other, must have seen us. As panic and pandemonium, broke out from the warehouse. It could be something was going down there, possibly drugs.'

'Where is our friend Leroy?' Mattock enquired.

'Not sure. He was seen going into the warehouse by myself, but, not seen leaving. Had officers check out the warehouse and its connected buildings, nothing found. Suspect he was inside the Merc that escaped our clutches. Only he was not inside occupying the car back or front passenger seats, suspect he could have been, enclosed inside the boot. If he was and we have not seen him since. Leroy could have inadvertently walked in on a deal going down. We cannot determine if that is good news or bad. Leroy was not found inside the warehouse.' Helen said. 'The car was driven away by one of the Hou-Lin Hoi family.'

Mattock saying nothing as Helen summed up her recollection of events. Waiting until she finished up with the prisoners safely housed in the cells until questioned. She joined Mattock back in his office. She sat opposite Mattock who had begun to sit back waiting for her to say something. Nothing came. He raised his eyebrows venturing her to say something, but still nothing came out, remaining silent.

DC Tatchell came to the door and stood hovering in the doorway. Not knowing whether to come in and join them or his gut feeling that this conversation was private. Mattock looked at DC Tatchell standing there, still no word uttered from Helen. 'You have something to contribute to the silence, DC Tatchell, come on come in, please someone speak to me.'

DC Tatchell said there had been a call reportedly seeing a car that fit the description of the Merc, seen driving away from the warehouse. The car's been found abandoned on the outskirts of Bromley on a disused building site.'

'Well if we are finished here, we had best go have a look. Go fetch the car, Alan. We will be behind you shortly. By the time, you fetch the car around the front we'll be downstairs waiting,' Mattock said.

As Alan Tatchell left the office, Mattock turned to Helen. 'So, was there something you wished to talk to me about, before we head off?'

'No, it can wait,' Helen countered. 'Let's go.'

As if on cue, the car driven by DC Alan Tatchell came out of the compound and pulled up outside the station as DI Tony Mattock and DI Helen Smith pushed the door to HQ and walked out on to the pavement. Both entered the car simultaneously, driven off as soon as the car doors closed, Tatchell driving set the car in motion. As they pulled around the corner, both Mattock and Smith already buckled up. 'I take it you know where to go?' Mattock asked.

'Roughly, the satnav will guide us as we near Bromley, Sir,' Tatchell responded.

Helen sat quietly as they drove through Croydon to Beckenham and Addiscombe. Mattock not used to the quite broke the silence by asking again, about what happened at the warehouse that morning. Helen's reply was, 'Nothing.'

'So why the silence, is there a problem?' Mattock probed.

Helen opened up, 'Not really just that if it was a drugs deal going down or a shipment of illegal gear. Why did we not find any incriminate evidence in the warehouse? Then why did they see fit to disperse and make a run for it, if no crime was committed, the place was spotless,' Helen said, responding to a question with a question.

'So, that's your problem, the reason for the silence?' said Mattock, looking over to Helen.

'I told you, there is no problem, was thinking about Leroy Williams and the warehouse,' she insisted.

'Possibly be, the handover had already taken place. You happened to appear as they cleared up. Only Leroy entered the warehouse at the wrong time and set the cat amongst the pigeons. Someone panicked on seeing the police outside.'

Helen nodded in agreement to the scenario panned out by Mattock. If Leroy was not meant to be there. Turning up unexpectant.

Tatchell appeared to be in cruise control mode as he navigated the roads they travelled. At times, they used the siren to get around local travel hold ups, due to road works or the red traffic lights. They arrived on the building site thirty minutes after receiving the call informing them of the car's whereabouts. The Special Investigation Crime Squad was on the scene already going over the car. Dusting for prints and pulling it apart suspecting powder remains from transporting drugs. Mattock noticed the boot still closed. Not sure why nobody had seen fit to open the boot. Pointed it out to one of the Crime Scene Investigators. Mattock spoke to the senior officer in charge. Not given a chance to speak, the investigator put his hand up to stop Mattock from saying a word. He was speaking to another on his mobile. Another ten minutes transpired before he closed down the mobile. 'Sorry, I am DI John Hanlon, and you must be Detective Inspector Mattock,' introducing himself before explaining the call he had been having. 'Family, never know when not to telephone, even when something more important than their point of crisis.'

John Hanlon shook Mattock's hand and for whatever reason Hanlon began to clean his hands on his jeans, directly after shaking Mattock's hands. Wearing casual clothing of T-shirt and jeans, John Hanlon guided Mattock back over to the Merc. 'I know what you are about to say. Why is the boot, still unopened?' then continued after allowing Mattock time to refocus on the car. 'We found the car boot locked with the car key still stuck in the lock. We are waiting for someone from the local Fire Brigade to turn up and force it open. Probably with a crowbar, we do not have one to hand.' Pointing over to the unmarked police van near the exit to the building site.

Taken aback by the fact John Hanlon had not seen fit to have this in his equipment needed for this kind of drawback in his field of crime detection. 'A mix-up in communication signals,' Hanlon said, seeing the expression on Mattock's face, as his explanation.

Helen had stayed quiet until after these exchanges of words were spoken, was when John Hanlon moved away to check on his colleagues, that Helen smirked at his back. Smiled at Mattock, as they looked at one another, she said, 'I thought these people, were the crème de la crème of our police force investigators.' Walking away as a fire service truck came through the gates and then directed by hand signal over to the Merc, by waiting investigators. News media teams had by this time, got wind, or notified of something going on at the building site. One or two of the news reporters determined that they would be first with the impending news that they would convey or report on.

The drill and part to pop the lock out from the car boot lid, that John Hanlon had long been awaiting came from the fire service truck. Brought over and within seconds, pop the lock with minimal effort. The expectation of what they would find enclosed when opened took Mattock, Helen and DC Tatchell by surprise. Expecting to find the body of Leroy Williams enclosed. As the boot was lifted by Hanlon, the reality stared up at them from inside. Nothing was inside, no body inside, completely empty.

Mattock stood back from the car, resigned to find the trip over did not have the expected result he had envisaged. To find Leroy Williams not inside proved a wild goose chase had been the result. He headed back to the police car, on route he called out to John Hanlon, telling him to relay anything found on the car to him, any fingerprints found, which should reveal who was driving or connected to passengers carried. Anything that could relate to drugs or drugs transported within the boot or any part of the vehicle. Getting into the car, he then sat waiting for his partners to arrive, thinking on what or where to go next. Mattock almost convinced that they would find the body of Leroy Williams. No sooner than Helen and Alan

Tatchell returned to the car, they were on the road back to HQ.

Helen took the heat out of the relief and disappointment by asking how the interview with Mary Warner went earlier. Mattock remained silent as he left the talking to DC Tatchell, all the way back to HQ. 'Mary Warner had said she was not involved in any drug dealing, claiming she only knew Leroy by him regularly coming into the pub. She never saw or noticed him dealing drugs, inside Yates's or outside the premises. Seen him around all the time she worked there, always friendly, kept himself to himself generally, but known by all the punters. Denied seeing anyone or Dan Prescott watching anybody, just did her job at the bar. Nothing found in her flat involving dope of any substance, with nothing to keep her, they let her go. It was her word against Prescott's,' he said, his voice tailing of as they entered the police yard.

'There must have been others in the pub that could bear witness to what had or has been going on in Yates's?' Helen enquired as they all three alighted from the car.

'We have not yet followed up that line of enquiries,' Tatchell responded.

Mattock picking up on that answer, 'Okay, DC Tatchell, you can make that your next task. I'd advise you to go now, while that thought is in your head. Helen and I will be in my office when you return going over and piecing together the information we have so far, plus what we are to do next ourselves. Why you are at Yates's see what you can find out about this Jerome character. Someone must know him there.'

While Tatchell left for Yates's, Mattock commented that that question was not put to Mandy Warner earlier. 'Helen, I have looked myself, but check records again and see if you can find any information regarding a Jerome, see if I missed anything. I had not found a thing. Pity we do not have a surname. That would narrow the search more profoundly. All we have is a brief description of him from Dan Prescott.'

CHAPTER 23

Clouds high above in the sky appeared to be forming and closing ranks in an attempt to hide the sun. A storm could follow, as some were dark and grey, the first hint that the day did not bode well.

Shirley came up from behind Dan as he stared up skywards. Dan remarked that the day ahead promised to involve rain, maybe even a storm. Shirley wrapped her arms around Dan, a rumble from the heavens confirmed Dan's storm warning. The rain descended, the patio rain free one minute and the next spots of rain appeared to join together until the spattering of raindrops turned to a downfall, totally transforming the garden from a place to sit out in and enjoy the sunshine, to a place to take a cold shower, should anyone go from the sublime to the ridiculous.

With the patio windows already closed, the inside of Dan's home was more appealing to the elements outside. Dan turned around on Shirley and said, 'Amazing how the weather can change one's mind from their first thoughts and set of options including sitting outside in the early morning sun, to another more obvious in a split second, resigning yourself to staying behind closed doors.'

'Samantha is back, came back earlier. Appears she is only suffering a sprained ankle, should be okay in a couple of days. Told to rest up but try to walk around let her ankle get used to her weight,' said Shirley.

Dan responded saying, 'Meaning we have company upstairs. Are you trying to put the mockers on my wishful thinking?'

Shirley letting go of Dan said, 'Not entirely just saying, we could always take advantage and return ourselves to the bedroom, take a hint from the rains open invitation to stay indoors. Possibly need to keep the noise down a tad.' Her smile so inviting to concur with her wishes, Dan followed her back up the stairs.

Passing Samantha's bedroom door and it wide open. Sam looked up as they both passed by, Shirley with Dan in tow, hand in hand. On seeing them, Sam voiced her thoughts, 'Ooh please! I do not wish to hear you cavorting around the bedroom. If you must, try to keep the noise down. Better still, I'm going downstairs where hopefully I will not have to listen.'

Although sore Samantha came back down the stairs unaided. Not wishing to be a party pooper and interfere.

Downstairs Samantha thought of making tea, but changed her mind. 'With a cup of tea for company and them two upstairs grunting and groaning, no thanks, I am going out.' Her mind made up she put her coat on and called up the staircase from the banisters post, that she intended to go out. Outside she pulled and fastened her coat around her. Looking up to the heavens, Samantha cursed the rains. Finding the car keys to her own car inside her coat pocket, took no time to decide she was driving.

Dan had brought the car over to his home, parking it in the driveway, off the road until she was well enough to drive again. She sat in behind the steering wheel and closed the car door. Panic set in as she put the key into the ignition, steeling herself she turned the ignition on. Surprised the car fired at the first attempt. The ankle bared up despite the discomfort and slight ache around her ankle. *Here goes*, she thought and released the handbrake and placed the car into first gear, slowly the car moved forward. As the car rolled out from the drive onto the main road. She turned left and straightening up. Samantha, despite the long interlude waiting, she pushed the gearstick up through the gears as she increased speed along the road.

A car driving towards her head-on and at speed and she had nowhere to pull in. Sam panicked. Suddenly, the oncoming car pulled into a space Sam had not noticed between two cars on the left. Averting Sam's fear and panic from escalating to a sheer state of horror.

Sam looked for a second to the sky thinking if she had a guardian angel, felt they were watching over her at that moment. The opening probably seen by the oncoming driver and distance between them allowed the time to avoid a head-on collision.

No clue to where she was heading and no thought driving all day. The crisis and panic dissolved, she was able to calm down and her heart rate reduced to a normal beat. The only pain from her ordeal was her ankle that still ached from the pressure applied, to the gas and brake pedals. Not wishing to ease up kept driving for another ten minutes, the driving became second nature. She had been driving twenty minutes before realising where she was driving to. Seeing a signpost leading to Croydon, coming up from Purley High Street. Continuing she drove on to the Croydon High Street following the road and manoeuvring into and parking up inside the Whitgift Centre car park. Followed the other car park users leaving their cars behind and enter the Whitgift Shopping Centre.

Dan woke up, leaving Shirley in bed. Clothed, dressed he headed downstairs only to find him and Shirley left in the house. Calling out for Samantha, knew she had gone out by the unanswered response. Shirley not wishing to be alone descended the stairs. 'Sam's gone, not in the house,' he said.

'Yeah, she said earlier, something about going out,' Shirley answered. 'She can't have gone too far with her ankle sprained.'

Five minutes elapsed before Dan decided to walk outside the front door. Looking up and down the road, he ran over to the junction turning and still found no sign of Sam. Only returning indoors did he notice Sam's car missing as he reached the doorstep and looked onto the driveway.

He came in reporting Samantha's car had gone, not in the driveway. Shirley said it was only a matter of time before Sam drove the car again. Picked up the coffee Shirley had made, and placed it back down almost as soon as he had picked it up. Found his coat and keys, while informing Shirley he was going out to look for her.

Dan's concern over his sister was in Shirley's mind was well intended, but felt if Sam was able to drive, then the sprain in her ankle was not as bad. Shirley's mind interrupted by Dan speaking up.

'Then why take the car?' asked Dan. Then the both looked towards the front door, hearing the lock turn.

Sam opened the front door, her appearance alleviated Dan's concerns. 'Popped into Croydon, did some window shopping and allowed myself some thinking time. I'm going back home to my own place.'

'Why?' asked Dan. 'There is no rush to go back.'

'I'm well enough to return to normality, besides you don't need me around. Cramping your own lives,' Sam answered. 'No, I've made my mind up, I'm going.'

Sergeant Price rang Mattocks Office, Helen picked up, 'Yes, Sergeant.'

'Just had a call that another body has been found in refuge bins on the Roundshaw Estate, could be Leroy Williams, who you've been looking for.'

'We are on our way down, fill us in when we get there.' Helen replaced the phone down. 'Come on, seems Leroy Williams has resurfaced over on Roundshaw Estate.'

Mattock was out of the office before Helen had put the receiver down. Downstairs they were filled in to where Leroy had been found, Wilson Sports fields, Mollison Drive.

The Special Crime Scene Team were already on the scene as Mattock and DI Smith turned up. George Balding who oversaw the Special Crime Scene Team was found talking to the person who found the body. 'What have we got George?' asked Mattock.

'Hi, Tony, been a long time. Arrived as soon as we had word of a body found. Immediately changing tact when making an offbeat enquiry about Mattock's home life. How is the wife these days, still with her?' George enquired.

'Yes, she's okay, doing fine,' Mattock answered slightly confused. Ignored the enquiry and turning George's attention back to the here and now. 'What's up George, what have we got here?

George was into investigative mode as the formalities were over. Reported 'What we have here is a black person, male of about thirty years of age, identified as Jerome Williams.' Then followed with a question, 'This person is not the one you've been reported looking for?'

'No, George, it was not, but the name Jerome is someone I've definitely heard of recently. Helen, I never knew that Leroy had a brother, which I'm assuming they are.'

'Would appear he has, must admit I never saw that one coming,' Helen said, as confused as Mattock as to why and where he had been staying. Leroy was always in trouble with the police, no time has a brother been mentioned or seen at their home or any occasion when Leroy brought in for questioning.

George not listening or spoken in reference to the body before him between Mattock and his colleague DI Helen Smith. Catching only a reference between two brothers. Leroy and Jerome, the person in the refuge bin. 'So, this one has a brother and the brother is the one you were expecting to see here?' George asked, stating the obvious.

George spent a further ten minutes checking out the deceased Jerome Williams, he murmured to himself throughout the time taken to examine the body. 'So, what do you have for us, George? What can you tell us about the deceased?' Mattock said, probing George for a conclusive answer.

'Obviously, he is dead. I will know more when I have taken a closer look at the body back at the morgue, on how and anything else that contributed to his death. On first impressions, I would say Jerome here died from two knife wounds. One wound to the right of his abdomen, and another up into his chest. He would have died, almost instantly, probably seven hours ago,' George said, as he supervised the body's transfer to the morgue.

Mattock stood watching and listening to George, in his immediate assessment. He himself had seen many of these deaths, by more knives than he wished to remember. 'He has lost a lot of blood, that's before we get a closer look.' Until the Crime Scene Investigation Team were content with the decision to move him, a more thorough examination would take place later. Helen kept a discrete distance away from the scene. Although not squeamish found the amount of blood sickening to look at.

'This, Sir, Tony has all the hallmarks of Tom Brannon's death. Only the knife we have back at the station was not the murder weapon used on this occasion.'

'Helen this case is becoming a bloodbath, murder on a scale that we are just allowing to escalate out of control,' he stated,

Mattock stood staring around at the current crime scene, thinking this is more than random killing. This was someone who has set out to make a point. This was someone local, just by the nature that all the deaths so far had been within a two, three-mile radius of Waddon.

'George, did you handle the autopsy on Tom Brannon?'

'Yes, Mattock, I did. You are thinking do these two cases have similar markings in the way they both died. I would say as I have already stated, on what I have seen, on that analysis that I concur with your prognosis. See you back at the morgue later when I can confirm that theory.' George left the crime scene, leaving behind Mattock and DI Helen Smith.

'If I was a betting man, Helen, I would back Harry Tambling as being our man. Knowing he never actively commits the actual crime of putting the knife in. After Tom Brannon's death, you could not, and with his having the perfect alibi, places him at the bottom of the pile of suspects.'

Mattock let Helen take the car back to HQ, electing to walk back towards Wallington Police Station. His hands entrenched into his coat pockets, ignoring the raindrops that fell as a pre-warning cursor of the heavens opening up anytime soon. On reaching the crossroads off Mollison Drive, Stafford Road, Mattock turned left and crossed the road. His attention now focused on the rain falling from the heavens. Two options presented themselves to him, either take cover in the small café in Mellows Park or retrace his steps back to the sports facilities. A mental note made him aware that the social club was open in the sports facilities. Where the chances that the small park café would be open when rain made, its presence known was unlikely. The social club could reveal answers to some probing with club members. Mattock retraced his steps.

Opening the door to the social club brought some unwanted stares from within. Not put off he entered, ordered a pint from the bar, sitting on one of the provided stalls set along the bar. His coat dripped from the sudden deluge of rain. Taking it off Mattock directed to a coatrack by the bar manager. Placing his coat on the rack's peg, he returned to the stall. Mattock, having been seen investigating the crime scene earlier. Felt eyes on his back as he supped the beer in his glass. Slowly some sort of normality transcended back into the club. Finishing the first, Mattock asked the bar Manager for another of the same. Several other punters entered the bar, all the talk centred around, the news of a body found in a refuge bin on the sports ground. Mattock just sat, knowing that someone would open up and ask him a question on the case. From the whispers, he heard clearly, known to frequent the club often. This prompted Mattock to speak up, rather than wait. 'Can anyone tell me if they knew the person found inside a refuge bin earlier, name of Jerome Williams?'

The bar Manager spoke, stating that Jerome was last in the club the previous night, sat in the corner feeling sorry for himself, spent the night with a pint of lager in front of him. Left, without hardly drinking a drop.

Mattock asked if Jerome lived around Roundshaw, or on the estate. The bar manager said he lived alone up near Douglas Close in a flat. Asked if Jerome had a brother, the manger declined to say. 'Jerome never came into the club with anyone, always alone. Never had much to say, generally known to use drugs on and off. Not around here though, I'll have you know'

Intrigued by the manager openly saying Jerome was into drugs. 'Are drugs commonly in use at this sports club?' Mattock enquired.

'No never, we have a zero tolerance to drugs use here. Anyone caught is told to leave and banned from the club indefinitely,' the manager said, affronted that he and the club asked. Undeterred by his provoking questions, that would cause harm to the club's reputation. He asked: 'Was he a dealer of sorts in drugs?' He saw the manager blanch in question to his continued line of enquiry.

'You are thinking why this copper insists on asking questions when told of what the club expects from those that use these facilities. I will tell you shall I. When someone informs me that Jerome was a known drug user on and off, then stipulates the intolerance level that the club operates, I have to ask whether the club has a selective hearing process that allows people like Jerome to continue using these facilities. Your policy appears hypocritical in respect of Jerome Williams.'

One or two members of the club sensed the trouble Ted the manager was in, digging a hole ever deeper for himself. Allowing Ted, to steam up, with the words thrown back in his face incensed Colin Turpin. Scraping back the chair that he sat in, Colin rose from the seat. Let Mattock know that the fact he was a copper made no difference, Colin approached the bar. 'Now why don't you leave just leave Ted be, he has told you nicely what we do with drug takers.'

Mattock took one look at Colin Turpin, from what he saw, took the man to be into bodybuilding by his physical presence. He had never thought that anybody would have the nerve to question the law. This day he knew, he was to prove wrong, 'Whom might you be, Mr? I don't believe you heard me present myself, I'm Detective Inspector Mattock. Now if you wish for me to stop with the questions, maybe you would like to enlighten me with first your name, then you would care to fill in the blanks which Ted failed to answer.'

Colin went to move closer; his movement was to provoke Mattock to hesitate. However, the only response that came from Mattock was a warning. 'Now, Colin, I'm sure that is your name. I remember now. Bit of a hard case. Well before you do something you will regret; I will warn you only once, son. Don't think, just leave it alone and walk away if you have nothing to contribute in answers, then leave quietly.'

Neither Mattock nor Colin saw the social club door open, or the person who walked in unannounced. Apart from Ted the manager, who remained silent, the man had walked up behind Colin. The first Colin knew of the man's existence came with the words. 'You heard the man, Colin, now do yourself a favour and leave.' Colin turned to find who had spoken. His reaction to act met with the words. 'Colin, do not make your second mistake. If you are looking for trouble, then I am your man. Now do what the Inspector suggested and use what little brain you have and clear off.'

Colin went to react, then a second thought changed his stance into leaving the club through the main door.

Mattock took one look at who the person was, 'Dan Prescott, your timing is exemplary. Thought it was going to turn nasty there for a minute. You frequent this club a lot, do you?'

'Maybe,' answered Dan.

213

'Then I take it you have never seen a Jerome Williams in this club?' Mattock asked.

'Should I,' answered Dan, not committing himself.

'Nobody has filled you in on why I could be here then as you drove into the sports facilities?' Mattock not receiving any communication from Dan agreeing or disagreeing continued, 'There was an incident on these premises earlier, a body found in one of the refuge bins outside, turns out to be a Jerome Williams. According to Ted here, Jerome came in on occasion, lives not too far from here. The rain outside prompted me to come in and make enquires as to what anyone knew about him. We spoke before, when you were stopped earlier. You claimed you saw and heard the name Jerome mentioned at Yates's, was wondering whether he could be one and the same person.'

Mattock ordered a pint for Dan Prescott and one for himself. Motioning to a table towards the back of the club, Dan led the way with Mattock following. Not before telling Ted the manager, he would need to ask further questions later and not to leave the country in the near future.

He sat alongside Dan facing the inside of the clubhouse. Taking in the clubhouse surroundings inside, noticed the bar for the first time from the back. A long bar was split by a pillar in a central position. Which probably helped to support the ceiling, the club itself inside had a dance floor, the lighting together with usual crystal mosaic ball in the centre of the dance floor held up high above the dance floor, indicating social functions where held there. Tables and chairs took up most of the furniture; the wood panelled flooring and carpeted around the dance floor added the overall feel. The sports facilities next door the main reason people would come and the adjacent playing fields, to the social club bar. As a club, itself, like most social clubs Mattock had seen helped bring the communities together. Brought money to the venue to help fund activities. Needs a good lick of paint outside too compensate for the drab interior. 'How come you are here, Mr Prescott?'

'I came here sometimes to use the social facilities, get away from the house. Different and more social aspect, with the club members who come here from whatever sports actively involved in. Whereas the pub scene although more social towards the drink and for the general public use. I used to play here many moons ago.'

A mobile rang, both looked at one another, a shrug from Mattock said it was his. Several minutes passed by while Mattock spoke into the mobile, every now and then Dan could hear the other person speaking. Closing his mobile, Mattock got up, 'Have to go, another lead came in to who killed our friend Jerome. Seems the same weapon was also involved in Tom Brannon's death. That weapon a knife, has been found in the undergrowth, a short while ago in Waddon pond, same place we found a similar weapon in the last two days.'

'Can I help?' asked Dan. 'With anything.'

'Maybe better if you stayed out of it for now. I may need your help later in tracing a Gary Parsons with the people you know. He does not register on police records. He could like yourself, be ex-army. We are not always privy to them.'

Passing Ted behind the bar, he said. 'Oh, Ted, tell your friend Colin, the next time he pulls a stunt like that again, I will arrest him for threatening a police office and I will make it stick, got it.' Seconds later, Mattock was standing outside the club. Remembered he had no car, he returned inside and called Dan Prescott over. 'You came in a car. I need a lift to Police HQ in Croydon. Can you oblige?'

Retrieving his jacket, Dan drove Mattock back into Croydon. The traffic taking its toll on the journey Dan pulled up outside Croydon Police Station fifteen minutes from the outset. 'Thanks for the lift,' Mattock said as he alighted from the car. 'I will be in touch no doubt, oh and let me know what information you can find on who we spoke about earlier.'

'Sure thing, have not seen or heard from Sam's ex. Sam has moved back into her own place,' Dan mentioned.

'Have the women received any more mysterious calls of late?' Mattock enquired.

'No. Not a word,' replied Dan.

'Probably a crank caller, I'll have someone check in on Samantha now and then.'

'Thanks, Sam may not be happy about you checking up, but will make my life easier.'

Mattock walked into the station, while Dan pulled away merging into the traffic as he drove off. One other motorist offended by the sudden appearance of Dan pulling out in front of him sounded his horn. Dan smiled as he left the motorist behind driving at speed into the outer lane and down the underpass. Not wishing to return to Wilson's Sports Fields, he turned left at five ways into Purley Way. Avoiding the chance of stopping at The Waddon, better to check on Sam and inform her that she gets will have a visit on occasions from the police.

CHAPTER 24

Fingers tapping on the bar, along with a tune played out over the airwaves. Coming from the speakers, sound outlets around the bar. Bar not open yet for business, but a meeting arranged for staff members and management alike. Hastily arranged in light of the interest the pub was generating due to the number of crime related issues in and around Croydon of late. Yates's bar involved in possible drug dealing. A new reported death of somebody found on a nearby sports facility. A missing person, known to have used Yates's bar. That of Leroy Williams, well known to the punters that used Yates's as their watering hole as some punters deemed to think of Yates's.

'The disappearance of a regular to Yates's, news had surfaced that Leroy was using Yates's premises, dealing drugs to punters off the street also possibly with clientele of the pub. To some of the bar staff unknown and gone unseen as Leroy kept his secret dealing, but in that he was never as discrete when passing to complete strangers, his secret was known by one staff member.

'The recent police interview with a member of staff in connection with Leroy. Management have called this meeting to discuss what needs to be done to stop this problem with drugs and possible dealers using Yates's happening again.'

Mandy piped up by saying, 'This has not been proven, that Leroy had been dealing in drugs. I never saw him dealing myself and I've told them this.'

Her boss Peter who had called the meeting and listened to all the comments said during the hour set aside. Everyone told to come in two hours before work started. Nobody could say that he or she not allowed to air viewpoints without discrimination. To say openly what was on his or her mind.

After the talking went on for the best part of an hour, Peter raised his hand to instil silence before he spoke, 'I have heard all your viewpoints; fail to see what this has to do with safeguarding the reputation of this pub. This pub has a reputation for no drugs allowed on the premises for dealers and takers alike. The fact a dealer was allowed, openly on these premises dealing openly and with respect, Mandy, I find it offensive that you had not owned up or not report we had this problem in Yates's bar. I had the police into my office informing me that you denied knowing about this Leroy, and he was up to no good. But Mandy, they have a witness to the fact, that you not only knew what was going on, but encouraged the person by providing drink for him as soon as he walked in through the bar doors each day regular as clockwork.' He stopped to pause. 'To confirm what this Leroy Williams was up too, I am informed that he has disappeared, presumed missing, an act of which is suspicious to say the least,' Peter stated,

Peter looked at Mandy, 'I allowed all to speak up, but as I see the situation. The position of one employee has left us with one option only. From this day forward, Mandy, you do not work here, your services are no longer required. Let that be a lesson to the rest of you. We at Yates's have a zero tolerance on drugs use here. Meet me in the office after this meeting, to collect your cards and pay.'

The silence from everyone to Mandy's termination of employment, sent out a message to the rest of the staff.

DC Tatchell sat waiting for someone to serve him. Told the previous night that Mandy's shift began early the next morning, but a meeting was due before opening time. He had waited half an hour and still Mandy had failed to show for her shift. Asked the barmaid on duty that morning what time she expected Mandy to appear for work, Teresa said she was her replacement; brought in at short notice due to Mandy's dismissal that morning by the pub landlord Peter. Teresa could not say why Mandy had left. He would have to take it up with the manager. DC Tatchell asked Teresa if he could speak to manager, producing his ID card stopped Teresa from asking any further questions. 'Can you tell him I'd like to see him please?' The barman who sat outside banged on the door. A voice came from behind the door shouted out, 'What is it?'

'You're wanted out here,' was his answer in response to his irritation, by a flippant remark of insignificance?

Peter came out, his next question answered by seeing DC Tatchell standing outside his office. 'Yes, how can I help?'

Producing his ID again Tatchell said, 'Would it be more private to talk in your office?'

Peter stared at the ID shown to him. He started to allow Tatchell into his office. Then had a change of heart, telling Tatchell he had nothing to hide. 'We had a talk before we opened the bar for business this morning. I take it you are here concerning your talk with Mandy Warner. As a consequence, we the management, decided to terminate her contract with us, she no longer works here.'

Alan raised an eyebrow at this and said nothing. Remained silent about the news of Mandy Warner's sudden departure, that had been imparted to him. Changing the subject asked did Peter know Leroy Williams. Peter refrained from committing, stating he had not met Leroy Williams or knew of him.

Tatchell then enquired whether Peter worked behind the bar himself or did he take a back seat. Letting his staff have free reign over the bar, while he sat in his office.

'No, I work behind the bar when busy and when extra staff is needed,' Peter replied.

'So, when you have worked, when required, you had never set eyes on him. I find that strange. That you as manager and from what information we have received, you're telling me that you do not know this person, who has been a constant fixture in the bar for the past year,' Tatchell said.

'Yes,' Peter replied.

Tatchell reaction of mystified shock, then asked, 'Why was Mandy Warner sacked by you?'

'Apparently, she knew the person missing to be a drug dealer; we have no wish to be associated with drugs,' Peter stated.

'Well perhaps you should come down to the station with me and answer some questions in respect of Mandy Warner, fill in the blanks to information and help with our enquiries,' Tatchell said as he got up to go, expecting Peter to follow. Peter declined DC Tatchell and his request.

'No, I have nothing more to say. I have a business to run.'

'No, well now I'm not asking you. I'm telling you that I will expect you back at the police station in one hour or I'll have you arrested for concealing information that could possibly end in closure of your premises.'

The rage that had shown on Peter's face, dissolved as the implication of not conforming to the police officer request. 'I'll get my coat.' As Peter turned, Tatchell smiled.

Mattock met up with Helen as they ventured into the morgue, knowing that an answer to several questions would be the result of this visit. Helen could see something played on Mattock's mind as they entered the morgue itself. The intense look on Mattock's face. Realised also she would only have answers when and only when he decided to open up.

As the door opened into the morgue, the attendants transferred the body off the trolley on to the table. Laid out Jerome Williams looked a lot less worried than when Mattock first laid eyes on him, a calmness and peace replaced the fear and shocked look on his face.

George Balding head down stared at the body of Jerome before instructing his attendants to go fetch out the body of Tom Brannon, and transfer him on the table behind him against the wall. Looking up at Mattock and Helen, he noticed Helen take a step back as he examined the body, while Mattock moved forward and watched on. George, pointed out the similarity between the wounds on Jerome and then Tom Brannon. The size of the knife wound and again the similarities to which the knife wounds bore the exact tears to the extraction of the knife, leaving a telling imprint. Confirming the same used on Jerome was the same knife in both incidences. Whoever the assailant was they had medical background.

Helen looked up at Mattock from the news imparted, as they both knew the implication now was that the knife found in Waddon Ponds was not the murder weapon used prior to Tom Brannon's death. Mattock chanced a question when throwing it towards George Balding. 'We have a knife in the lockup which we thought the weapon used on Tom Brannon, as you have proved this unlikely, can you look at Penny Connor's X-ray and tell us whether the same knife was used in that murder case.'

'I would need to see the body of Penny Connor and reports by the hospital coroner,' replied George.

'I will arrange for that with the hospital, will produce some drama in that her funeral has been set for this Friday morning.'

'You could have words with them in my going to the hospital and use their facilities with their own coroner present to witness. Might make life easier,' George answered.

'Yes okay. Thanks, have the results sent to my office, George. Thanks again, will be in touch.' The police station morgue door closed behind Mattock as he left. Helen followed up behind him.

Tatchell was sitting in the main office at the detective investigation desk, beside him sat Peter Sims, manager to Yates's bar of Croydon. Peter a typical Publican, not someone who would stand out in a crowd, a T-shirt and jeans during the morning hours of work, generally spruced up for the night-time trade. Today was the attire of a casual worker, more lax and open, confined to his office. The doors to the main office pushed open as Mattock, backed up by DI Helen Smith, who came in closely behind. On seeing Tatchell with someone standing by the sergeant's desk, Mattock veered course to stand over Tatchell. 'DC Tatchell, you have company I see.'

'Yes, Sir, this is Peter Sims Manager of Yates's bar, have brought him in to help us with our enquiries. He dismissed Mandy Warner earlier today in light of us bringing in and talking to Mandy Warner.'

'Direct Peter to my office and yourself also. Perhaps arrange coffee to bring in. Then we can all sit down and hear the explanation to why he Peter Sims would dismiss someone so talented over a police investigation,' Mattock said as he and DI Helen Smith sat down to listen to Peter Sims' explanation in his compact office. Nowhere else to sit, DC Tatchell hovered by the office door.

Peter Sims allowed into the office had little room to manoeuvre in. His first words at relocating to Mattock's office, was that he did not need to give out information as to his reasons for dismissing a barmaid. He was acting in the best interest of Yates's bar.

'Mr Sims, Mandy Warner as far as we have established, did nothing wrong in her duties as a barmaid. Leroy Williams, disappearance also had nothing to do with Mandy Warner. Why you thought this so, I cannot imagine. We know he was a dealer in drugs on more than one occasion. Yates's bar was not the only bar in Croydon where he carried out his operation. What Mandy Warner's dismissal tells me is that you are covering up for someone. You state you know nothing of any drug dealing within your bar, we know this to be a lie. As you know yourself, Leroy had been going into your bar for the best part of a year. That is what my sources tell me.

'Mandy Warner employed by you for the past six months, before that she was a student. My take on your

222

sacking her is she is the fall guy for your bar's own incapacity to control who and what goes on under your roof in respect of drug abuse, goes beyond Mandy Warner's employment with you. My sources also tell me that, and we have confirmation from your own employer, that you have also been in charge for little over a year, which appears to coincide with the appearance of Leroy Williams at Yates's. I would think that would mean you had more knowledge of Leroy's activities than any other working at Yates's bar.'

Peter Sims remained silent. With all eyes on him, the response of silence to their unanswered gaze on a man digging his own grave deeper. His actions earlier placed him in a position of a guilty man with something to hide. Prompted by this silence, Peter said, 'I may have been employed for the last twelve months and as you claim Leroy had been seen by various members of staff including Mandy. Informed by one of your officer's that Mandy had revealed that she had known of Leroy activities in our bar. True drugs can be a problem for Publicans like me who try to maintain zero tolerance in this area as we have a duty to eradicate drug dealers. I still maintain that I was unaware of the extent of Leroy Williams's involvement. As for my staff, I would have thought that if someone were dealing with drugs in one of my establishments, I would be told and informed of this so that I could act on the information I received. If not then our relationship with the police, in clearing the streets of this dangerous pursuit is in jeopardy.'

Mattock was not aware anybody had informed Yates's of police information given about the interview with Mandy Warner. He looked at DC Tatchell with a frowned look, to enlighten him into how the information of an interview made available to her employer. More to the point was how the information provided was false, as Mandy had not admitted she knew of Leroy Williams dealing in drugs. Tatchell gave him a shrug of his shoulders in response.

'Mr Sims, can you tell me which officer gave this information you said you received, was a name provided?' he asked,

'Detective Inspector Mattock, I have not come here to talk about who informed me of information regarding Mandy Warner. I am here to help in enquiries connected to Mandy Warner's recent dismissal on the grounds that I may be able to assist. I'm not the one in trouble,' Peter stated.

'Your actions, Mr Sims, were premature, as we had not released any news in connection with Leroy Williams. Mandy Warner never claimed to know Leroy Williams other than as a paying customer. I do not think any information came from one of my officers, the only person who could possibly, would be Mandy herself. Knowing her job would be on the line, I would say that would be foolhardy on her part. Especially as Mandy, was not charged or guilty for any wrongdoing to date. So, I question where your information would come from, could you please elaborate for us?'

Helen sitting nearest the door to Mattock Office, received a note from one of the other inspectors who asked for the note to be passed on to Mattock by the desk sergeant. The note revealed that a Leroy Williams found bound and gagged in an office to a disused Office Block, recently vacated when the last tenants left a year earlier, found by a building inspector on behalf of a company wishing to purchase.

The note stated Leroy was at St Georges Hospital, Tooting, London, recovering from concussion from a head wound received. Police, only notified because of the possibility the wound came from a vicious attack that was of a result from a crime committed.

Peter Sims face showed signs of desperation, written all over it. His defence and character broken apart by Mattock's line of reasoning to his actions. Knowing, once he admitted knowing Leroy, would question the rest of his statement as being false, a total fabrication to protect himself from involvement to a the drugs operation.

Mattock read the note, then he refocused and spoke to Peter, 'I am not finished with you yet, Mr Sims, but you can go for now, back to your bar. Something has come up that needs our attention. Should you do anything stupid, it will only confirm our own suspicions. You are free to go. But refrain from leaving the country.'

Mattock waited until Peter Sims had left the building, before he spoke. 'Helen, you can come with me to the hospital. Leroy Williams could be well enough to answer a few questions now, if not now then as soon as he recovers sufficiently. Alan, I want you to find out whether anyone from inside the station has been to Yates's bar and spoken to Mr Sims, double check his alibi of receiving information from a source within.'

CHAPTER 25

The A&E Dept. at St Georges was abuzz, the afternoon busier than normal. The drink related cases seen more often on the night shift than expected on any given afternoon shift. A wedding celebration held at midday had hit trouble when the ex-partner turned up unexpected and unannounced at the reception. All hell broke loose as the former husband and bridegroom decided to air their differences on the dance floor. Within ten minutes, the hall was awash with blood where some hapless relation used a broken glass-bottle to enforce his own justice upon the brother-in-law.

Mattock and Helen walked into the hectic scene in A&E, threading their way through the crowd. Helen pushed a male patient down on to his seat to avoid walking into her from the side. About to start more trouble, on producing her badge and ID, thought better of it. Reduced to mumbling profanities under his breath.

The receptionist on the front foyer desk pointed the way to the lifts, stating that the patient they had come to see Leroy Williams was in a side ward off the corridor, on the second floor. Two minutes later found them waiting for the ward sister to determine whether Leroy was up to questioning. Mattock bided his time while hoping that Leroy could provide answers. Mattock's face had become recognisable by the number of times he had been in St Georges Hospital the last few days, in the number of staff that took time to speak to him. Helen picked up on Mattock's popularity around the Hospital. 'Okay, Sir,' she smiled, 'play your cards right you could be on a winner tonight, plenty to choose from and I'm sure there is possibly a raffle going on for the lucky winner to be wined and dined by you. Your popularity is high from the number of smiles and favourable comments from some of these nurses.'

'One problem I foresee, Helen, her indoors might take offence at the celebrity status I am acquiring if known,' Mattock said, staving off the witty comments from Helen.

'Only, if someone informs her,' she answered.

Lift doors opened onto the second floor and the ward sister on duty walked from the lift to speak to Mattock before entering the sideward, telling him she would only allow Mattock in if she felt Leroy was well enough. The sister came from Leroy's room within minutes, beckoning both Mattock and DI Smith into the room. 'He appears to have recovered significantly enough to be discharged,' entering the ward found Leroy sitting up in the bed. Looking in better shape health wise than Mattock expected.

Leroy knew Mattock through arrests for past crimes. Helen, he met for the first time. 'Detective Inspector Mattock, I must say your taste in partners has improved over the years to a new high,' he stated, while taking in Helen and her smile towards his comment. 'Maybe we could meet up and talk sometime soon. I could fill you in on his bad points,' he said, smiling back at Helen.

'Leroy, I am not here to talk about my love life. You know why I am here?'

Leroy peered back at Mattock, then spoke to Helen. 'There you have one of his bad points, right there. Always makes a negative from a positive, does not likes a complement to his taste in women. Maybe he is not up to the job.'

'Leroy do not try to change the subject. My love relationships, is not what we have come here about. We are here to talk about where you have been in the last two days and why you were seen going into a warehouse near Norwood,' Mattock said, trying to turn his discomfort away from Helen's amusement to the reality of Leroy's situation. Coupled to that, Leroy may not know that his brother was now no longer alive. 'You need to talk to us, about why and who you were to see or meet up with in the warehouse. So why were you there in the first place?'

Leroy shook his head, 'Wish I could tell you, but I have no memory of what you are talking about. What warehouse, Norwood, where in Norwood. Sorry, man, no can tell, my mind is a blank.'

'You were seen in Yates's earlier that day. What were you doing there?'

'Again, brother, I've no idea where you are coming from. This bang on the head clearly took my memory away,' Leroy said showing no interest in helping himself.

Mattock only had one card he could play to get Leroy to talk. 'Then maybe your memory will filter through and reveal insight into who could possibly want your brother Jerome dead.'

This had the desired effect Mattock wanted. Leroy at first stopped talking when his brother's name when first mentioned. The surprised look on hearing his brother Jerome was dead. Questioning 'What are you saying, my brother is dead, he cannot be, not my brother, Jerome he would not hurt a thing. Dead, you messing with my mind man.'

Mattock stared down at Leroy laying down. 'Leroy, someone found your brother's body up at Wilson's Sports Facilities. No easy way of telling you, but you are the only one who can bring justice in locking up the person who pulled the trigger.'

'Mattock, if I say anything, my life is of no importance, like Jerome I will be a dead man walking, you hear me.'

'If your life is of no consequence, then do something to make your mark for when you are gone, if not for you, then for Jerome. Do not lessen his death for some lowlife who does not give a fig. Leroy, you owe nobody by keeping quiet. If your brother Jerome was in trouble, more likely your life is at risk also. Saying nothing, only serves to help those who wish you harmed. You will not gain any favours from these people. You walked into some deal going down, which you were not to be a part of, a bang on the head for your reward. Are these people so important that your own life is worthless, along with your brother's life, you do not owe these people anything, help us to help you, your choice, Leroy?'

Leroy just stared into a void staying silent, resolute in his remaining quiet. Mattock looked up to Helen knowing they were going nowhere fast.

Tatchell put his head inside the doorway, mentioned to the constable on the door something and passed a message onto Helen standing in front of the constable. She looked up from the note and caught Mattock's attention. Beckoned Mattock to step outside the room for a moment.

'Appears news travels fast, our friend Leroy in there has been mentioned into day's evening press. The fact he has been arrested on suspicion of killing his own brother.' Having read the note, Helen passed the note over to Mattock.

Mattock did not even look down at the note, just screwed it up and threw it towards a corner. Just stared down at the evening paper report 'I would like to know who and how the papers have been informed of this garbage. The only thing they have right is his being a drugs dealer for some gangland mob and all I want is the information to which one. Helen, once the hospital has given Leroy clearance to go take him to the nick for questioning.'

Ten minutes later saw Leroy escorted out of the hospital, gently pushed into the squad car onto the back-passenger seat. Then sped away to Croydon Police Station. Helen placed the newspaper under Leroy's nose. 'Still think being silent is going to help now?

'Go down that list of names we have seen at the warehouse, check whether Harry Tambling has any connections with any of them. Then get me Dan Prescott, he may shed some light on Harry's background history that he has not told us before, Helen. I will be up in my office.'

Walking passed the interview room Helen called out to Mattock, 'What do we do with Leroy in there?'

Mattock stood still, staring at the door of the room. Then he said, 'We let him go, if he will not help himself, then maybe if we throw him to the lions out there. He will hopefully stay alive long enough for us to find out who is his paymaster in all this. Have someone follow, keeping a distance. He may lead us to them, Helen,' he said, continuing on his way to his office.

Helen remained standing as she saw Mattock walk off. Tatchell came up beside her and they both helped to release Leroy back onto the street. Tatchell saying, 'I don't think this is a good idea.' Then said he would follow Leroy. While Helen followed up on the list of names involved in the warehouse meeting, at the same time arranged for Prescott to be collected and transport back to the station.

Mattock was on the phone when Helen came into to his office. In the conversation, she overheard the name Gary Parsons spoken about. Mattock pointed at the spare seat in his office, motioning for her to sit. Ten minutes later Mattock hung up. 'How did you get on with the list of gang members seen at the warehouse heist?'

'Two names come up as frequent drinkers in The Waddon. The rest, Harry Tambling has spoken to all on odd occasions, including the Hoi Sin family. Terri Tambling claims that Harry had only been in her establishment on rare occasions since his release at Wallington nick, but maybe if we talk with other drinkers we may get to prove whether he has been there more often than she states.'

'Which two have you establish to be constant drinkers in The Waddon, apart from Dan Prescott?' asked Mattock.

Helen pulled out two pictures taken from CCTV cameras in the locality. 'One was Mandy Warner, pictures show that she has met up with Harry Tambling on more than one occasion. Nothing of proof to say any romantic goings on between them. Just good friends.'

Looking through the notes on the wall, Mattock unpinned one. A picture of Gary Parsons, which he passed over to Helen. 'Gary Parsons, I have just been having an in-depth conversation with CID in Brighton. They tell me that Gary there is part of the Tambling family. He is a distant cousin to George, Harry and Terri. Turns out their mother had a sister who lived over in South Wales. Turned up unannounced three years ago, moving into Hove and contacted the boys shortly after moving into Highdown Road. Making the trip up from Hove on the Monday, returning back there on the Friday, stayed with friends in Croydon. I suspect that the tattooist may have a spare room that he rents out.'

Mattock waited for a comment from Helen, nothing said he continued: 'A closer analysis on the blood found at Highdown Road, carried out by Brighton Constabulary has highlighted some discrepancy on the initial test carried out. Whoever, the blood belonged to. They appear to have been dying from Septicaemia, a kind of blood poisoning. The cause from a systemic infection attributed to an infected part of the body circulating in the bloodstream.'

Helen frowned, silently weighing up the odds that the same condition and blood could have come from Penny Connor's wounds. Nothing ever mentioned by the St Georges Hospital in relation to septicaemia being in her bloodstream.

Speaking up she said, 'Tony, could the blood found have come from Penny Connor's wounds. Penny, stabbed from behind, prior to her being dumped that night, could have occurred in Highdown Road and not as we have been, led to believe. She claimed that she was attacked from behind by her assailant and leaving her for dead at the Aerodrome. It is in the realms of possibility that Penny got her stab wounds in Hove. Would then confirm her statement of transported up here unconscious. Gary

Parsons knowing that the possibility of her loosing too much blood when travelling up here, could have resulted in her been dumped at the Aerodrome Hotel on route. The hotel had nothing registered to record of her staying there. The sight of Gary Parsons seen driving away from there in the early hours would indicate that he is guilty. If we can prove the blood from Penny is the same as that in Highdown Road, Gary Parsons would not have a leg to stand on. In a court of law, he could not prove otherwise.'

Nodding his head in agreement, Mattock held up one finger. 'There is one problem at this moment in time. Nobody has seen neither hide nor hair of Gary Parsons. The Brighton Constabulary said nobody has been near the property since we first went in and found the blood on the floor, which tells us he has either left the country, living in other accommodation elsewhere in London, or the blood is his own, but we have no body to account for the latter.'

Helen standing in the doorway said, 'Mattock, I think you'll find that what you said previously, the blood group did not match that of Gary Parsons, this was confirmed by Brighton Police upon our return from Hove. Are they likely to get that wrong, I cannot buy that, if they have had that wrong from the start. Then we would have to dispense with their other results and double check on all the blood and DNA tests again ourselves.'

Shifting the papers around on the wall chart Mattock found the note in respect of the blood results. Then went over the results given by St Georges Hospital, 'Helen, where are the results on Penny Connor's death?' he asked.

'Never gave any information in regard to her blood type, or to what actually she died from. We just accepted that she was given a lethal injection of poisoning through the intravenous needle.' Pausing for several seconds, as Mattock digested what Helen had just said, 'The hospital denied responsibility in causing her death. They maintain that they had done everything possible in keeping Penny Connor alive. The poison broke down her resistance quicker than they had expected,' Helen said.

Coming around his desk, Mattock looked out of his office and surveyed the main detective's room. Staring back at Helen he said, 'Can you find out what information you can on Penny Connor's medical records from the hospital, what her blood group and what poisoning had caused Penny Connor to die. Also, have Tatchell and someone to go with him drive down to Brighton Police Station and get us the hard copy on the blood stains found and double check Gary Parsons' blood group and whether he was suffering from septicaemia.'

'I will get what information I can in medical records from the GP's office. On all three deaths, Penny Connor, Tom Brannon and Jerome Williams, we may as well have the results kept by the local centre as backup. I will also have records go over the last phone calls made by all three from their respective telephone companies. See if any or all have been in contact with someone connecting the three. Could be Gary Parsons or someone closer to home?' Trying to stay positive, Mattock thought that with luck they might be progressing in the case to a conclusion.

The phone rang on his desk the name Super Chief Inspector Homer verified as the caller on the phone. 'Yes, Sir.'

Several minutes passed by with the occasional yes and no spoken. Mattock listening to Homer remonstrate. Doing most of the talking, seemed Mattock had been given an ultimatum. Mattock switched the phone on loudspeaker in error, too late to turn the sound off. Mattock left it on, '*find the results on the case within the next twenty-four hours. Then it would be passed over to the Serious Crime Squad at Special Branch.*' Homer said.

Mattock replaced the phone back onto the receiver. 'Well you hear Homer. Appears someone upstairs above him in the force is wanting immediate results; As you heard, we have a time limit to get the results on his desk or the case goes elsewhere, Special Branch.'

Dan Prescott stood downstairs in the police station foyer waiting patiently for Mattock to show his face. Dan reasoned that Mattock had still not sorted the problem of Harry Tambling yet. The call came from DI Helen Smith that they needed some help from him. DC Tatchell noticed Dan standing as he came into the station, looking worse for wear. 'The boss called you in a while back... has he seen you yet?'

Dan smiled up at Tatchell, 'Does it look like it? Apparently, he has been told. Been here nearly half an hour and I am still waiting.'

Tatchell said, 'Have had a lot on, I am sure Mattock will inform you when he does come down. I will remind him when I get back to the office in a moment.'

'What's the story on the commotion around Roundshaw this morning?' Dan asked.

'Mattock will be the one to ask,' was the non-committal response from Tatchell, then he disappeared up the stairs.

Within two minutes, Dan sat before Mattock and in the small confines of Mattocks office, DI Smith and DC Tatchell were seated either side of Dan Prescott. Photos of both Leroy and Jerome were place in front of him by Mattock. Dan looked down on both. DI Smith placed a photo of Mandy Warner on the table, side by side all three photos stared back up at Dan.

'Do you recognise any of these three people in the pictures, Mr Prescott?' asked Mattock.

Dan pointed to Leroy and Mandy, 'These two, this one pointing to Leroy was the person you stopped me from following the other day. The girl, name of Mandy. Believe she works in a bar in Croydon, same place as where I saw Leroy, same day you stopped me as I recall. Mattock, I informed you of this woman a few days ago.'

'Yes, been a few developments since then. Are you telling me you saw Leroy Williams for the first time that day in Yates?'

234

Dan could not help retain a piece of sarcasm, 'No, I have known him to be a dealer for many years. Yeah, that is why I told you I was following him that day, to find out where he lived. That boy would have known me on sight. Mattock do you think for one moment that if I had known Leroy that I would need to follow the man back to his home. The woman Mandy, as far as I knew she was just a barmaid at Yates.'

'Never met her anywhere else in this locality?'

'Not that I recall... am I meant to?' Dan responded.

'Not very observant, appears to drink in The Waddon when not working. Do you still maintain you have not met Mandy before?' Mattock impressed.

'Never seen or recall seeing her at The Waddon,' said Dan.

'I find that strange, Prescott. The Waddon not being a big pub, would find it hard for you not to notice one of their frequent social drinkers.'

'So, what has happened to Mandy, she been bumped off? You think I am responsible in that I have colluded with these other two in having her bumped off. Is that about the size of it, Mattock?'

'That is not why you are here, Prescott. I am trying to establish whether you can help in our enquires, you have knowledge into the world of Harry Tambling, every time a body turns up at present, has Harry Tambling's lurking in the background. Three murders have come into question in recent weeks and all point to Harry Tambling and his associates. Only one provides the ideal alibi, that murder is Tom Brannon. His alibis we cannot refute as he was in one of own police cells. His family who seemingly appear to sit in the background guarding and covering his back. To his sister, Terri providing his alibi and cover his actual involvement in each murder directly. Everything is circumstantial evidence.'

DC Tatchell seated to the right of Dan broached the subject of Mandy Warner. 'I went along to Yates the following morning to speak with Mandy Warner only to be told that she had been given the push out of the door at Yates's, sacked. Her duties already terminated that morning. Through her interview with us the day before, the finds her employment terminated. Mandy denied ever knowing Leroy Williams or the other fella you said you had seen in the bar, but clearly known to Leroy. That was his brother Jerome. Mandy claimed that she only knew them through drinking as punters in the bar. You said Jerome looked nervous about something when you were there. Transpires he had a cause to be worried. He was last seen dead in a refuge bin outside a sports clubhouse facility on the Roundshaw Estate.'

'That would be Wilson's, where the body of Jerome Williams was found. That explains the commotion over there,' Dan answered.

'Then again Mandy reveals that she drinks at The Waddon when she did not work,' said DI Smith. 'You can see a regular occurrence appearing in the fact that Mandy has connections with The Waddon currently used by yourself and owned by Harry Tambling. Mandy who states that she never knew Leroy and that he was a drug dealer. From sources, close to Wilson's his brother Jerome dealt in drugs, strongly denied by Wilson's bar manager. Evidently, gets himself killed and unbeknown to us here he is related to Leroy, a known criminal. We were unaware he had a brother until confirmed by Leroy. Who now, is living in denial to the danger imposed on his life suggested by his brother's death, claiming if he points the finger at anyone involved, then his life will be in jeopardy.'

Seeing the look between DI Smith, DC Tatchell and Mattock as their eyes met. Dan's intuition, told him they want his help and they were trying to manoeuvre him into working alongside them. 'So where do I come in and why can't you just arrest those you suspect and do what you are known for. Playing good cop bad cop setting one up against the other to get results.'

Then acting as if the penny had just dropped, 'This is where I come in. You throw me into the lions at the expense of letting the other side think that the police have backed off. Leaving me to infiltrate and to stir up a storm, also taking the dissension should all goes awry,' Dan said.

'Eloquently put,' said Mattock, 'could not have put it better myself. I think something is going down. Maybe drugs deal or heist. Someone out there is organising something. We need to find out what. Your knowledge of Harry Tambling, what he is now capable, and the other various factions out there, we need someone prepared to go in for us. We need to catch them all red-handed.'

'You give a good reason to help. What information do you have that gives you credence that something is going down?' Dan enquired.

Mattock knew he could pull Dan Prescott into bringing in Harry Tambling and all other associate criminals to boot. 'The day we stopped you from following Leroy Williams, we, I mean DI Helen Smith followed up on Leroy from your information. I personally have a list of crimes we have arrested Leroy and put away in prison for over the years. He has been in and out of prison more times than I can remember. Helen followed up in your pursuit. Went over to Leroy's home and stood outside waiting for him to arrive from that train ride home that day. Before he started to walk up his road, then backtracked to the station before he reached home. Must have been aware, that something was up, spooked.

'We traced his way to West Norwood, getting there, we found him entering a warehouse. Waiting and watching for a while. We assumed he left in a car, exiting within twenty minutes of his arrival. When we rounded up those left on the premises, we found no sign of Leroy Williams which backed up our theory that he left inside one of two cars, we thought the boot. Coming out of the warehouse doors no one saw him in the car itself,' Helen stated.

Accessing the information received, Dan weighed up the roll he was to play in Harry Tambling's downfall.

What part did Leroy played in Harry's life? Does not answer the question, as to why Leroy refused to talk or plea bargain talk his way out of his mess. If he feels his life is in danger. His brother's death, would surely give a clue as to his life expectancy and sway him to protect himself. Mandy Warner, was never in The Waddon whenever he drank there. Possibly in the other bar. Since Harry's marriage to his cousin had ended and when Harry moved out, he himself had not been a frequent visitor to The Waddon.

Commenting on a reason for his absence, Dan said, 'Could be if Leroy was in one of the boots of the cars, he may have been incapacitated at the time of his confinement. If his life was in question, he could have plenty of reasons for keeping his silence. One reason for his not talking, could be he has another roll to play, maybe to do with this deal you feel is about to go down. Now knowing his brother has died, as a result off your suspicion, there is a connection, to the drug dealing. Could be that Harry Tambling is the least of his problems.'

Mattock sniggered to himself, 'What, do you mean that the Hou-Lin Hoi family were involved in his temporary disappearance? You could be right, following the drug theme. So, I take it that means you will help us?'

'That is if I have freedom in what methods I use to obtain the information.'

'I would rather you go through me when it is time to the use of force,' Mattock emphasised.

'Then that could be a problem, because while you and your people are deciding to go into action. The chance to apprehend anyone will be over.'

'You have no faith in the police have you, Mr Prescott?'

'Not in my experience. No.'

Helen and Tatchell remained silent, but smiled at the cheap shot. Mattock looked at both and then at Dan.

Dan asked, 'What information are you working on that gives you the notion that a drugs deal is on the menu? I have heard nought to confirm any drop going down. Need to show my face in The Waddon, if only to meet up with this Mandy Warner here in the picture. You could be right and need to start somewhere.'

The photos taken from the desk, replaced by a map of Croydon and surrounding area of South London. 'The warehouse used in the last gathering of local hoods is over here in West Norwood,' Mattock said pointing to the road. 'The warehouse emptied out when we rounded up the local criminals. If Leroy is used on the job, I can only assume that his role will be as a driver.'

Perusing and scanning the map. His fingers cast their net over the map stopping at various locations. Dan's thoughts kept to himself to what he was focusing on, his demeanour changed towards the work ahead. 'Mattock, if you are expecting Harry Tambling to start getting his hands dirty and be hands on, then you will be disappointed. Harry prefers to let others take the initiative and stay in the background organising. The Hoi Sin family if organising the drop, then that is where our main problem will come from.'

'Special Branch have been tracking the Hou-Lin Hoi family for a while now, they may have influence in whether you achieve whatever you have in mind. We are talking hypothetically of course, as until we know something for sure is going down. Nothing can be done,' Mattock said.

'Do you always look on the bright side of a situation, then go and pour cold water over it,' responded Dan.

'Just trying to point out the obvious, if you start stirring up trouble in any plans they have scheduled. They could hamper any scheme you have planned or instigating to infiltrate on the inside. If they thought you were not helping, Special Branch could and would fit you up, incorporating you in any crime they see fit and then hang you out to dry,' Mattock reinforced.

'While you are sitting their contemplating, Mattock, you better give notice to Special Branch before I set foot inside the inner circle of Harry Tambling and his world,' Dan said in response.

Helen still sat watching and listening to the talking going on said, 'Consider it done.' Stated on impulse and before Mattock could utter a response himself. Tatchell just nodded in agreement with Helen. His movement reflected in a glassed fronted photo of Mattock's family on the desk.

Rising from his chair Dan said, 'I am going down to The Waddon, with a little luck Terri will still be there. Dust over any problems Harry might have, in my presence being questioned by Harry or amongst any others.'

Leaving the door wide open when leaving, Mattock, Helen and Tatchell remained in the office. Mattock made the call to Special Branch, consulted with someone questioning them on their involvement. Plans made, soon turned over in light of Special Branch instructions not to interfere.

CHAPTER 26

The Waddon, as usual that evening had a close vibrant atmosphere from the clientele within the pub, all local to the pub, either through residing and working nearby, the few that venture by the reputation of past visitors. The landlord instigating the friendly atmosphere by providing free cooked bar snacks, finger food. To keep the flow of money coming across the bar for alcoholic beverage in recompense, men replenish their glasses with beer and lager, the small occasional shot. Women tend to prefer the wine, cocktails, vodka, rum, incorporating bottled mixers of tonic, coke, fruit juices. The occasional pint of lager drank by those few women that drank beer and lager.

Any noise would cease on the pub door opening. As recognition unfolded, the noise resumed unabated. Dan Prescott entered this night unannounced, his welcome no different to anyone else coming into the pub through those doors. His face well known to most. At the end of the bar in his usual place sat a cheerless Harry Tambling. Unlike his other clientele, Harry on this occasion did not look up. Dan noticed that Terri was still in town overseeing the bar staff behind the bar. Busy refilling the shelves with clean glasses from those returned to the bar, washed and ready to use again.

The Asians, Dan assumed them from the Hou-Lin Hoi family as he recognised two from his last visit. Approaching the bar Dan asked for a pint of his usual. Terri got up from filling shelves on hearing Dan voice. 'So, what do we owe the privilege of seeing your face in here?' Terri asked.

'No reason. Just thought, maybe it was time to reacquaint myself with the place. Is Harry busy?' he asked,

Terri looked down the bar at her brother, 'No more than usual, not sure he will want to see you though. You here to cause trouble, none of your friendly coppers waiting outside to come in?'

'Not tonight, they are just keeping tabs on Sam's welfare,' Dan proffered as an answer for the police attention in his recent life.

Terri asked, 'How is Sam these days?'

'A lot better. As long as Harry stays away.'

A look on Terri's face said she was not happy with his responsive remark. She turned her head towards her brother. Noted that he was staring up towards the sight of Terri speaking to Dan. Her head gave a slight nod, the movement towards Dan.

Leaving his Asian friends behind at the bar. He motioned to Dan to join him to the seats situated to the rear of himself. A truce made with a handshake. Harry pointed at the seats for Dan to sit, by a motion indicated with his hand. To Terri he asked for a round of drinks and two more for Dan and himself and sat down.

A moment of silence fell between both, both gaging the other as to why Dan was there. Harry spoke first as the drinks arrived and Terri began to sit down alongside Harry. 'Not now, Sis, need to talk with Dan alone for now.'

Terri looked towards Dan then rose to go, 'If you're sure, Harry.'

'I'm sure, no problem with Terri's absence from these talks, Dan.' Dan said nothing. 'Good,' Harry said.

'Heard a friend of yours left for the heavens above?' Harry commenced.

'Yeah, not sure as to why he was head hunted,' Dan replied.

'Guess his time was up, when you have to go, your name is on the ticket for that ride to the stars,' Harry said.

'Never heard that quote before, something similar, not bad for you, Harry, shows you are all heart.'

Another lull began, before Dan enquired, 'So, what are you up to now, are you joining the rank and file going over to smuggling drugs these days.'

'What gives you that idea?' Harry commented.

'Possibly the company you keep these days, seems they have influenced in that direction. Never thought you would be a hypocrite and turn on to drugs and dealing. Another bow to add in your world of crime.'

'Drugs was never my game, you know that better than anyone, Dan.'

Having seen the evidence on film, Dan knew different. The striking resemblance between the man in the CCTV film and the person sat before him. You never could be mistaken to the identity. The person in the film showed a photo-match to the man before him. Intuition told Dan, Harry had lied.

The way this meeting was going Dan knew the chances of him ingratiating himself back into Harry's world, would not happen soon. The meeting continued in small talk, until Harry went up to the bar. Dan had learnt nothing to go on. The Asians went to leave, when Harry approached them. Standing up the Asians spoke to Harry. Dan could not believe his luck. The hint in their last spoken words before the Asians left. The Asian called Chang asked if everything was okay. Harry replied yes.

'Good, then all is okay for this weekend. The Thamesteel Warehouse, Sheerness, time one o'clock after midnight, early morning alongside the dock.' Chang shook hands with Harry and departed.

Dan heard as clear as day. Time and place. The words not softly spoken, not hushed down enough for Dan's ears not to pick-up. Dan remained silent to this information. Time slipped away as Harry, Dan and Terri who joined them once the Asians had left. Dan and Harry carried on with small talk, recalling how their paths had met in their youth. Remembering the games and the trouble, they got into while young, until Dan joined the Army. Then their paths took a different turn. Dan joined the Army, Harry and shortly after Terri went into the Publican trade. George the other brother, Dan had not heard or seen him since they were young. Dan refused a drink observing the closing time at The Waddon. Pleading his time needed, to get up early next morning for a job at home, not elaborating on what the job was, he left in a cab ordered.

As Dan walked in through the front door, all was quiet. Arriving home to find the girls not there. They had retired or in Sam's last spoken words left. Recalled Sam stating she would possibly move back home that day. Shirley could be upstairs. One last drink before retiring he thought pouring out a long cool drink, dark rum and coke.

Waking up to the sound of his bedside alarm clock upstairs, Dan woke up still in the armchair. He knew the alarm would continue if not turned off. Made his way into the hallway, the alarm stopped as he set foot on the staircase. Relieved the alarm had stopped, also meant Shirley had stayed on behind, sleeping over in his bed. Ascending the staircase, he entered his bedroom and looked down on Shirley spread face-down on his bed. Hearing movement, she stirred and looked around to see Dan staring down. Shirley smiled as she opened the bed covers to allow him to get in. Dan stripped and got in beside Shirley and pulled the sheets back over them. Moving over she put her arms around him, across his chest. Then proceeded to slowly kiss him on his chest, lifting her chin Dan pushed Shirley over onto her back. Aroused, he slowly caressed her left breast before pulling her in closer and proceeded to make love, slowly at first until Shirley was aroused through foreplay.

The sun was out and Shirley sat across from Dan in the garden chairs, two cups of coffee on the table. They had been up for an hour. Both sat soaking up the rays from the heat given out from the sun. 'What have you planned for today?' asked Shirley.

Dan sat quietly for a minute before answering. 'Will call in on Samantha, make sure she's okay. Then have business with DI Mattock to attend. I will be out all day.'

'What business?' Shirley enquired.

'Cannot tell you at this time.'

'Cannot or will not?'

'Be best if you did not know. I am just doing this for a friend I hardly knew.'

'You mean Terri Chapman I assume.'

'No, Tom Brannon. His death was needless, he got in over his head and I need to make amends,' Dan said leaving the garden for the house. Dan made the call to DI Mattock and relayed what transpired the previous night, arranged a time to meet up. DI Mattock stated his need to speak to others.

Three minutes later Dan was on the road, driving first to Samantha. He arrived in time to meet her at the doorstep, the postman delivering the post that day allowed Dan to go up the path as he came out. Samantha seemed glad to see Dan, leaving the door for Dan to close on his way in. The kitchen was a mess, 'Thought I would clear out the cupboards and clean the kitchen, freshen up the place.'

'Okay by me, thought I would drop in to make sure all was okay.'

'Yeah I'm okay. No need to check up on me all the time, you and Shirley have your own lives to live,' Sam said. 'You know the calls that were made to your house, was thinking about that. Who would have known about me staying at your home other than you, Shirley and myself? The police obviously would.'

Dan intervened, 'Stop thinking about that, you're home now and need to forget them. That is all in the past. No calls have been made since then. Get your own life back.'

Samantha smiled. 'Thanks for your help, thank Shirley for me also. Want a drink, kitchen is a mess but I think I know where the tea bags are?'

'No, there is no need besides I'm meant to be elsewhere. Just thought,' Dan could not reveal where he was heading. 'Just thought, I would call in beforehand.'

Dan gave no more thought of Samantha as his mobile reverberated in his pocket. He was driving and halfway to his meeting with Mattock. Pulled over and answered. 'Yes, I'm on my way. Be with you shortly.'

Ten minutes later pulled into the roadside café, a Little Chef south of Croydon. Dan entered the Little Chef and after a quick surveillance found Mattock at a table close to the window, to the rear, overlooking the car park. Dan sat opposite Mattock who was sitting relaxed and calm. DI Smith sat down beside Mattock staring out through the window onto the car park. The waitress had taken the orders and gone. Dan went over again what he had learnt from his evening visit to The Waddon. 'I can't see me and the Tambling's working together in the near future, both Harry and Terri appear to bear a few grudges towards myself. The Hou-Lin Hoi family have become a permanent fixture in the place. Their feet well and truly under the table, very cosy.'

At that point, the food ordered arrived. No talk engaged while the food was set before them. The drinks ordered followed shortly after. Only then did Mattock speak up: 'Mr Prescott, Dan, following our talk last night, I spoke to Special Branch, to someone I thought connected to the surveillance going on with the Hou-Lin Hoi family shortly after you had left. Special Branch instructed us to leave well alone and not to get involved. Following what you told us earlier, appears things have moved on a pace. Spoke again with our friends at Special Branch. They reiterated what they had already stated in that we are to do nothing that may hinder their own plans, they are already aware of this drug drop going down.'

'So, what you are saying is that despite Special Branch surveillance on Hoi Sin and his family this past few years, nothing will be done. If they have watched over the family

246

for the past two, three years and done nothing to stop what has occurred prior to this drop. How can you be so sure that action and justice will happen this time?' Dan questioned.

Helen listening said, 'If we act gung-ho and ignore what we have been told to do. Then the likelihood is we could undo what Special Branch had planned. The Kent police will be involved, I am sure.'

Dan shook his head, 'Now you know why I get frustrated with the police, so much red tape and lack of purpose in their actions. What is to say someone is not on the take, getting a piece of the deal?'

Mattock and Helen looked at Dan, both at the same time, before Mattock spoke, 'Why are you taking that view, as if a conspiracy is going on?'

'When we spoke, after the Penny Connor woman died, you told me then not to interfere in police work. Now Tom Brannon has died. I have come close to death myself, when beaten unconscious. Then you have a third killing left on your doorstep with Jerome Williams. How many deaths do you want before you stop crawling to them Neanderthals in Special Branch to ask permission to act. Special Branch seem only interested when someone is bringing in drugs into the country or international gang related incident. Are they going to do something about the Hou-Lin Hoi drug empire or are they just seen as sitting on their arses as the last three years of inactivity suggests? Watch this space, only that appears to be all they are doing.' Dan stopped his rant, knowing frustration and being inert, the cause to his own actions.

Pushing his meal to one side almost untouched, Dan considered the options, he did not feel happy not involving himself in some degree. Thought how he would have dealt with Harry Tambling and the Hou-Lin Hoi family if he had gone along alone to Sheerness on the Isle of Sheppey.

Prescott looked from the window and at DI Smith. 'This warehouse, where you followed Leroy. Did you say there had been a meeting in progress, what if that had not been a drug deal or shipment going down. What if the meeting was amongst dealers, negotiating the split of an impending shipment. Could the warehouse be the place one would split the drugs with the various gangs in receipt?'

Helen answered, 'Could be. You're saying that the meeting was just to negotiate between the rival drug gangs. Would be the reason nothing was found on the premises.'

Listening to the talking, whilst, he finished the meal on his plate, Mattock set his plate underneath Dan Prescott's plate and untouched meal. 'Instigating a stakeout around that warehouse, what if they decided not to use that particular warehouse, plenty of others to choose from in and around South London and not necessarily Croydon. What is to say that a supply of drugs had not already been shipped in? Spliced up between the dealers that day, could have taken to the road before you turned up following Leroy. So, why choose that warehouse. Your, presuming that Special Branch will choose not to be on the Isle of Sheppey, if and when a shipment comes in tonight?'

Paid for the meal, they stood around the police car outside. 'Look, the way I see it,' Mattock stated, 'I have no reason to suspect Special Branch in pulling the wool over our eyes on this. Unless there is Government interference, in which I doubt. I will check with friends in the Kent force when I get back to the office. If anything, comes to light. I will ring you. In the meantime, keep your head down.' Both Mattock and Helen got into the car and drove away with Helen driving, leaving Dan standing in the middle of the car park, his own car at the far end, furthest from the Little Chef Cafe.

Driving back Dan put on some music, an Eric Clapton CD – Clapton Chronicles, one of several CDs from varied artists stored in his glove compartment. Playing was the track – Pretending - one of Eric's older tracks. Deciding to drive into Croydon Centre, he parked up in the Whitgift Car Park and walked out into the main High Street, found

The Fox opposite West Croydon mainline station. In the corner, he found Tiny and Mitch Sanders, buying a pint he walked over and sat next to Tiny, facing into the bar. 'How's tricks Tiny. Harry, still keeping you busy.' Dan acknowledged Mitch looking at him and with a nod of is head, saying, 'Mitch.' Raising his glass to both he added, 'Cheers.'

Mitch stared back at Dan, his pint of lager raised in mid-air, midstream to his mouth. Now open, in surprise at who sat across from him. Tiny just sat undeterred by Dan's appearance. Dan spoke to Mitch Sanders, 'Mitch, either drink your pint or shut your mouth and put the drink down before you pour it over yourself.' Mitch did the latter.

'So how come you are not with Harry?' Dan asked Tiny.

'Not needed, Boss is not around. Told us to go have fun and here we are,' all Tiny would say.

Dan laughed, 'I can see you are having a ball in this place, must get more excitement in a graveyard.'

Tiny responded, 'Is that why you're here then, to add to it?'

'A funny comment coming from you, Tiny, not normally known for your wit, wasn't bad at all,' Dan said as he drank from the glass of his raised pint of beer.

A relaxed atmosphere once the alcohol was free flowing came across the three and the two barmaids immersed themselves into the friendly laughter. Dan despite misgivings in allowing his defences to come down sobered up when confronted with his mobile phone ringing in the background. His demeanour changed almost at once. He could hear Mattock saying something down the line, the noise hindered his hearing what Mattock was trying to convey. He found sanctuary when taking the phone outside. 'Sorry, could not hear a word you said, had to come outside. What was it you were saying?'

'For someone seeking justice for a lost friend, you have a strange way of showing your commitment. Last thing I expect is his champion getting drunk. You have two hours to present yourself at the warehouse mentioned earlier in West Norwood. When you have sobered up and it had better be soon. Expecting to see you completely sober at the warehouse. Have spoken to our Super Chief Inspector and he has given me some men, too man outside in an unmarked car in the street nearby observing the comings or goings. Have also asked a friend in Kent to keep me posted as to whatever transpires at the Sheerness end,' Mattock said, internally questioning whether Dan was on board with their attempts to bring about a conviction.

'Great news, have been immersing myself with two of Harry's men, establishing links with those within Harry's circle of friends. Harry himself is in Kent taking a hands-on approach. Appears the Hou-Lin Hoi family are using Harry and his contacts to further their distribution of drugs up and down the country,' Dan said.

'Thought Harry preferred staying in the background?' enquired Mattock.

'Seems he has been given no choice, maybe the Hoi Sin family connections have something on Harry. Could be the reason to why he took his temper out on Sam. No one is saying what that hold is, could be more to do with his actual involvement. He looked comfortable with his lot when chatting yesterday, that could be a front he has put up, a shield to cover some deep underlying problem,' Dan declared.

'Whatever. I want you here outside these warehouses tonight completely sober. No weapons,' Mattock reiterated.

Dan took one look at Tiny and Mitch. He caught hold of Tiny's elbow and said he was leaving, while his mind was still intact. Leaving the Fox, he sought a late coffer bar near East Croydon Station in the foyer. He asked for two cups knowing one would not be enough to help him sober-up. Buying a ticket to West Norwood, he sat on a bench outside East Croydon Station watching the late trams running that night come and go. The timetable said the next train due in half an hour, delayed due to a disturbance at a station further up the line into London. The coffee drank he felt no better and ready to retch up on the pavement. Seeking a place to empty his stomach, he sought out an alley to slip down. Choosing a side road across the road from the station between two buildings. Close to the Polytechnic College.

When out of sight, he placed two fingers down the back of his throat to induce the sickness to the surface. Retching into the gutter, he then returned to the station and down onto the platform. Ten minutes later, Dan was on the train for West Norwood.

CHAPTER 27

Sheerness was a small seaside town on the Isle of Sheppey, adjoined to the mainland by a bridge, on the northern Kent coastline. Sheerness the main town on the coastal isle was quiet. Night air cool, not exceptionally cold for a coastal resort at 12.30am. The residence of the town blissfully unaware that their small port was about to liven up shortly after midnight. A small fleet of vehicles, made up of three cars and two 1500 weight Luton vans transcended onto the port side area. Men alighted from the vans. Whilst others stayed within the cars, all waiting for the shipment due to arrive. Wait was shorter than expected, as a small cargo ship berthed alongside the harbour side, within an hour of their arrival. The activity went from miniscule to frenetic within ten minutes as the gangplanks, gave access from boat to shore. Those actively involved in this drug harbour operation, blissfully unaware of the police presence who seemed to be nowhere in sight, as the shipment came of the boat to the waiting vans unhindered, without a hitch.

Kent police under instructions from Special Branch were to wait on instructions from them to intervene in the operation as it unfolded. Watching the proceedings from rooftops of the warehouses and overlooking the small harbour, an unmarked police van stood stationary at the far end of the docks. DI Ken Harman from the Kent constabulary watched through the van front windscreen along with two other members of the Kent police force observing. Special Branch saw fit to play the part of those unconcerned, which alienated themselves, signified by their absence from the dock area. The cargo of drugs along with other goods smuggled in the cargo. DI Ken Harman saw movement from the entrance to the dock, assumed that Special Branch, the newcomers making their play. His enthusiasm quelled, as they were early morning workers coming in to start work. Pandemonium spilled out over the dock area as port workers and the men under the Hou-Lin Hoi family saw each other. The port workers not meant to start for another hour. Hou-Lin Hoi family completing with the final shipment, stowed into waiting vans. Harry Tambling drove a waiting car up alongside Chang, one of the Asians and his co-partner, his brother got in and then made their way to the rear of the docks to alight at the furthest point of the docks back out onto the main road and onto the mainland road routes to London.

DI Ken Harman at that moment received his cue to act from Special Branch. Acting too late, as the two vans last seen driving out of the dock into the night, only leaving the remaining two cars prevented leaving the docks. As DI Harman and his van pulled out in front, his men closed in and surrounded the two cars coming out from within the warehouses.

His anger at the late call spilled out and reacted with venom at the Special Officer on the line. DI Harman punched in the number for Mattock's mobile. His anger still shown in his voice, he relayed the events of the night to Mattock not without airing his views on the operation and to him told not to interfere.

Mattock hung up, turned to Helen, 'Appears Kent police were stopped from interfering until too late to arrest anyone, the response we received when enquiring into the drugs problem with the Hou-Lin Hoi family.'

Helen said, 'Are we to assume someone in Government is behind the Special Branch stance in this?'

'It appears that way, which would agree with Dan Prescott's reasoning. Could be someone knows more than we have been informed to date. Still does not explain the inactivity from Special Branch. Would someone in Government be on the take and involved in Special Branch, but who?' Mattock said in askance.

Both stared ahead from their place of concealment. The shadow of someone walking down the Lane sprung up on the wall of a warehouse. Alerted to the intrusion of a man walking along the lane, saw Dan Prescott emerge from the moonlight casting a shadow ahead of him. Mattock pulled down the window to the passenger side door to their car, 'Get in the car, no need to advertising your presence.'

Dan proceeded to get into the car seat behind Mattock. Helen acknowledged his arrival with a nod of her head. Dan nodded his in return.

'So, what is happening, are we just sitting here. Do you see them coming to this warehouse knowing that you caught them here before?'

'This is the only place we have a lead on. When we raided this place before, all the known villains had gone. Those left behind were their men cleaning up the place. The cars seen driving out from this warehouse, included Hou-Lin Hoi family connections. We assumed that by Leroy Williams leading us here, we only missed the top men in these gangs by a whisker. Our contacts in Kent Constabulary tell us they, like us, told to observe and not to engage. Only when told to engage with the opposition, it was too late to act on the main targets as they had already departed from the premises. When told, we assume that this is their destination. The boat has been commandeered and prevented from leaving the dock, the crew held and the remaining criminals in one car that failed in its attempt to leave along with the other vehicles, three I believe, are on their way to police headquarters for questioning.'

Two cars appeared and turned into the lane, heading in their direction. Drove passed and parked alongside the warehouse. The occupants alighted, four from each car. One looked up at the warehouse. One continually looked up and down the road. Another two walked away from their cars across the road from the warehouse and disappeared into an alley. None of the people was familiar to Mattock or Helen who witnessed the arrival from their vantage point. Dan Prescott watched sitting in the back of the unmarked car. Not a word spoken as the play panned out before them. Dan could not contain his silence, saying. 'They appear to be over dressed for this caper.' They all wore suits that did not fit the descriptions of a criminal. More of business persons turning up for an auction. Late at night and dressed up, Mattock remaining silent agreeing with Prescott. One of a trio of people, the one central, turned around and observing the vehicles in the lane up and down, then pointed in their direction. The two either side started to walk in their direction, guns pulled out at the ready, they had been spotted in the car. As the two men approached with their guns at the ready, one shouted for them to get out from their car slowly. The change in their manner showed these men to be professional in their stance and movement. Mattock stepped out first followed by Helen then Dan. Both men guarded as their guns rose further, as they came out of the car. The man on the left told all three, Mattock, Helen and Dan to turn around and place their hands on the car. This instruction alone told Mattock they were facing police officers. Three other men came up behind these two facing them. Again, guns came into view.

Knowing he was faced with officers from Special Branch. Going for his inside pocket. Mattock spoke up, 'We are police officers, at least two of us are.' His comment floundered into the night air, ignored out of hand, as all three forced to put their arms behind their backs, their hands handcuffed and forced to get down and lay face down on the ground. The poor street lighting gave out an unclear vision to this area of West Norwood. Mattock found himself frisked as the officers fumbled finding his ID badge giving credence to his being a police officer in his left inside coat pocket, giving his name and rank. Passed to the person behind, who in turn gave it to the officer leading of this force. 'What are you doing here Mattock?' come the question.

'We were following up on a tip off we had received into an ongoing investigation,' Mattock replied.

'Good, Mattock, what part of the words stay away, do not get involved did you not understand?' The officer passed back Mattock's ID badge.

'And you are part of Special Branch I take it.'

'Pity your observation skills could not be extended to following orders when given. You are correct in your assumption that we are Special Branch. Now we have sorted that out, you can run along. We can take it from here. No need for you to be here, we have it all under control. Someone un-cuff them, make sure they get back into their cars and direct them away from here.'

Not wishing to leave, without knowing to whom he was speaking to him. Mattock stayed where he was standing, compelled to say something he asked, 'Can I have your name?'

No name escaped the man's lips, but Mattock sensed that something was wrong with this set up when not revealing his name and rank. 'We are Special Branch as you have guessed my name is irrelevant he said.'

'You are nothing special, you may be Special Branch, that saying you should have no objections to revealing a name and rank. I will assume you are up to no good and arrest you if you insist in not complying with my question,' Mattock intimated.

'Mattock, take a look around you. I do not think you are in a position to make demands. Now leave before I have you arrested for obstructing our police work tonight.'

'So, you say the name is irrelevant. If I wish to converse with my boss I will need to know who has given me my marching orders from a criminal act unfolding, due to information I and my colleagues were made privy to,' Mattock said, smelling something not quite right.

'All you need to know, DI Mattock, is that Special Branch is on the case overriding any activities to any drugs case you are currently involved in. If your superiors have any doubts, then let them take it up with my bosses in

Special Branch.' With the officer walking, away from Mattock, his actions dismissed Mattock who remained standing beside DI Helen Smith and Dan Prescott.

Mattock turned to Helen, 'Use the mobile, Helen, and phone head office to see whether we can find out whether operatives in Special Branch are currently working on a case in the West Norwood area. I do not like what I am hearing. Something fishy about them being here; why were they not at Sheerness dock earlier. Why not apprehend these people at Sheerness, why allow them to sail right in, unhindered?'

Listening to Mattock, Dan could see the reasoning and understood where Mattock was coming from. If you knew a drug shipment was coming into this country, you caught them at its point of entry the shipment came into the country, unless Special Branch had reason to allow them to enter and trace the franchise to its depot of distribution, that way, not only do you get the drugs. You also close down every operation that will emanate from that first deal, before it has a chance to be sold onto the highest bidder and filter into the public domain, through the dealers and shakers on to the street.

Speaking up Dan said, 'If you think about it, Mattock, the deal could be that by letting the drugs come to the warehouse known to be used by your enemy. You catch the Hoi-Sin family in the act of the biggest heist, concluding with all the dealers known to the Hoi-Sin family.' Dan stated and continued, 'That could probably be why no action was taken at Sheerness until after the shipment had been moved away from the docks. The fact the ship and crew were impounded and taken away to Kent HQ, Chang Hoi-Sin would be unaware of what became of the boat and crew following their departure from Sheerness Docks.'

'Mr Prescott, you are too trusting where the police are concerned, I can smell a bent cop when I see one. Don't start making any excuses for those I suspect of being one,' responded Mattock, who continued in watching the

Special Branch officer sloping away, without looking over his shoulder and talked over the possible acts of deception by Special Branch.

When both Dan and Mattock sat back in the car, Helen drove the car away and as instructed by Mattock. She parked in the road opposite. Pointing out as she drove away that Special Branch had also removed their vehicles from outside the warehouse entrance and out of sight.

Sitting in the car once parked and the engine switched off, Helen pointed out the two cars in which Special Branch had come in, parked adjacent across the road. Sizing up options before them, Mattock hankered to hang around and watch the scene play out. He never liked to be sat on the outside just looking in, Mattock much preferred to be in the bigger picture, involved. Thoughts of leaving and obeying Special Branch instructions to leave, in his mind was not an option. The more his mind questioned his role and the murder cases, the more he swayed to stay and see what part Harry Tambling played in this escapade.

Dan slowly walked back the way they had driven and parked up in the road two hundred yards on the left-hand side. Approaching the crossroad intersection watchful from a distance of the Special Branch and their officer's movement in and around the warehouse. Took in where he felt they had staked out the place. Noticed two on the roof opposite as well as occupying several other buildings across through open windows. Mattock and DI Smith crept up alongside him. Dan noted the time as half past two in the morning by his watch. 'What time did your people in Kent Constabulary call you?'

'About quarter to two give or take a minute,' Mattock answered.

'Say they have been on the road half an hour, still leaves possibly another hour at the outside for the convoy of what, two vans and one car to arrive. Special Branch appear to as they say, have everything tied up in this being the place they are heading to. What happens if somehow

Chang Hou-Lin Hoi and his family are headed elsewhere and not here?'

Mattock smirked and said, 'That would be very unfortunate.' Thinking over the question Dan had posed, he continued, 'Why do you think we have been watching the wrong place for the drugs haul to be distributed?'

Dan did not immediately answer Mattock's question posed. Helen not wishing to wait for Dan to reply prompted Dan to answer Mattock. 'Well, why not here?'

'Sorry I was lost in thought. If you were intending for this warehouse to use, seeing as we have not seen anybody coming or going even close to open up and prepare for a delivery prior to the arrival of the merchandise. With only half an hour for the expected delivery it seems very quiet around here.'

'Maybe they have someone on board one of the vehicles who has the key to open up the warehouse on arrival,' Mattock said giving a plausible response.

Dan not satisfied with this answer to his query, continued, 'Where are the clientele, the dealers and expected gang members that they are working for? I would expect to see one or two vehicles parked up with these people waiting inside.'

The way Special Branch had staked out and watching over the warehouse, Mattock could not envisage a member of the underworld going into where trouble was with police presence. The Hou-Lin Hoi family's own lookouts would have taken note of police activity in the area. A young couple decided to take a sexual relationship a step further on the corner, moved on by verbal contact from a member of Special Branch.

Shaking his head, Mattock likened Dan Prescott to someone who would look into a problem and create a solution that defied logic and come away with a bigger problem to work with.

At that precise moment a call came through on Mattocks mobile, breaking into his thoughts. It was DS Tatchell.

Taking the call, 'Hello,' he said then let Tatchell speak. Helen and Dan remained silent waiting to hear what Tatchell had to say. After several minutes with Mattock muttering something down the phone interrupting every time he needed clarification. Mattock motioned to Helen to get the car and take them to the police station to pick up Tatchell.

'Appears Gary Parsons has resurfaced, been found and seen in the tattoo parlour. Tatchell was going to head there with another car and officer. Told him to wait and we will pick him up on route. A constable is watching the Tattoo parlour until we arrive.'

Helen spoke, 'What about the warehouse? Do you want me to stay around here?'

'No, Helen, we will let Special Branch do their job despite my misgivings. Let us get out of here. If they mess this up, they cannot lay the blame at our feet. As they said, they have it all under control even though I like Dan have doubts as to this warehouse being the base for the handover. I think that we may have deterred them, when you Helen dropped in on them several days ago.'

CHAPTER 28

Driving off and no words said between them. They drove to the Croydon police station. Tatchell was surprised to see Dan Prescott in the back when he got into the car and sat behind Helen. Said nothing, but relayed what had transpired between the constable watching the tattooist shop and himself should Gary Parsons move on elsewhere. So far, Parsons had not moved on.

'Have you notified Brighton Police of the new developments?' asked Mattock.

'Yes, informed them as soon as I was off the phone to you. They have told us to keep them informed while they were sending someone up here,' Tatchell answered.

The constable watching over the tattooist's entrance had remained posted there since calling into the station. Told to wait the arrival of DI Mattock and DI Helen Smith arrived minutes later. No screech of car wheels to show the urgency of their arriving and the quickness of the time elapsed between first contact and them arriving. Noticed two others with Mattock.

DI Mattock asked slightly peeved. 'Mr Prescott, why are you here, this is a police officer matter now. DC Tatchell, you had no right to tag him along.'

DC Tatchell started to respond, when Dan butted in, 'Do not blame your Detective Constable here, I left him no choice in the matter.'

'There is always a choice, but only one he should choose. You do not fetch along a member of the public on police work,' Mattock enthused. 'So, kindly leave and allow us to do our job.'

'Has anything happened since you contacted DS Tatchell constable?' asked Mattock as they took up space in the doorway.

'No, Sir. Gary Parsons has remained in the same position since I saw him through the shop's front window. Nobody else has entered the shop. Their talking appears heated between them at times. Both have raised their fists, more so Gary Parsons, Sir, but no blows have come out from any argument they may have with one another. Almost, like they are talking in agreement about another issue,' responded the Constable in answer.

'Can imagine whom and what they may be talking about, Helen. It is late for someone to have a tattoo done at this hour of the night. Well done, Constable, and well spotted. Detective Constable Tatchell, you come with me, about time we had words with our friend Parsons. Helen, we may need backup should trouble erupt, wait here with the constable. Mr Prescott, you stay here also, no need for you to be involved at this time. Ready, Tatchell,' said Mattock.

Walking out from their cover, Mattock and closely followed by DC Tatchell behind. Halfway across the road and they still stayed remained unnoticed by Gary Parsons or Fred Carver the owner in their approach. Once across was interrupted by the arrival of two of Harry Tambling's men, Tiny and Mitch Sanders.

Dan Prescott on seeing the pair almost went forward, Helen taking note also. Placed her hand and held Dan's elbow to ward him off from continuing stated: 'Not yet, see how and what happens. No need to advertise ourselves yet.'

Mitch and Tiny stopped as soon as they witnessed DI Mattock and Tatchell approaching the tattooist shop. They hesitated, but too late, seen by Mattock as they were also walking in the direction of the tattooist shop. Inside the tattooist Fred Carver had not looked out the shop window. Mattock made no break in his stride in continuing crossing. Lifting his left hand, he beckoned Tiny and

Mitch to join them inside the shop. Making no move to run Mitch and Tiny came closer and entered ahead of Mattock and Tatchell. Hoping Helen had taken her cue, they would be coming up the rear. As they neared the shop, Gary Parsons had risen from the seat he occupied with Fred Carver mouth gaping and about to remonstrate until he eyed Mattock he recognised from a previous visit.

Helen in the meantime had radioed ahead to police headquarters, for back up should there be trouble. They remained outside the shop door looking on in through the window. Two minutes had elapsed before another two police cars appeared. Helen watched them drive up and as they alighted from the police cars, she cautioned them from entering the premises, put a finger to her lips indicating her wish for silence and wait. From her position, adjacent to the shop entrance. Helen had a clear view. 'No noise, I may have jumped the gun in requesting your assistance as all is quiet in the shop at this moment.'

Sergeant Price standing beside Helen was one of the two police officers in the two cars that had arrived. 'Mattock and Tatchell are inside, not much happening yet,' Helen informed him.

'I think you may wish to change your views on it being quiet in there. Appears Gary Parsons, is reacting in their presence,' the sergeant said when looking through the shop window.

Helen had seen Gary Parsons remonstrating at the sight of the police entering with Tiny and Mitch Sanders. Not about to wait for any cue from Mattock, Helen was prepared to go in there and then refrained a second later. DC Tatchell had covered the front door should Gary Parsons decided he would make a break for freedom. Parsons silenced his anger reseating himself. 'So, what happened there?' Helen asked aloud.

She received no reply in response. Fred Carver seated, both Tiny and Mitch stood towards the back of the small shop. Mattock, seen slowly walking back and forth inside the front window, doing the talking. The view Helen had, she could not make out what Mattock was saying.

'What are they doing here?' cried out Gary Parsons as Tiny, Mitch followed by DI Mattock and DC Tatchell, to Mattock he said, 'You can't just go and barge in here any time you please.'

Fred Carver standing up at the time they all trouped in could not believe the outburst from Gary. He stayed quiet in case Gary turned on him, unaware that the police presence unsettled Gary. 'Gary Parsons, we finally meet,' said Mattock, not ruffled by Parsons volatile manner of words. 'Seems you were about to have happy reunion with friends coming to visit. Although with our appearance, you are unhappy at our joining the party. But before you go and burst a blood vessel, why don't you just calm yourself down and we just have a friendly chat.'

Gary still angry at the intrusion, 'Fred, you tell them to bugger off, you know your rights. They need a search warrant to go over these premises.' Making known his wishes. While trying to influence Fred in his will to turn the situation around in his favour and the police told to go.

'You have something to hide Mr Parsons. That the reason you wish us gone. Otherwise why so vocal in wanting us to go? Mattock enthused in his question.

Parsons quietened down, holding back his wish to reply. Stared at Mattock, as he sat back down. Fred not following Parsons wish to oust the police from his shop. Given what they had been speaking about prior to the police interruption. The police presence put any trouble he envisaged on a back burner. But, saw the decision quelled any further trouble from Gary.

'Good,' Mattock continued when Parsons sat down, assuming that he had put off the ensuing trouble that could happen.

Not letting the cobwebs form in his calming effect on Gary Parsons, he said: 'We had knowledge of your presence here, in this shop by one of our constables on the beat seeing you here. We merely need to have a talk with you, about your whereabouts this past week. You have a few questions to answer. Now you can come quietly with us or we can arrest you for obstructing the police in their work. Either way you are required to come with us down to the police station, to answer as I say a few questions,' said Mattock.

The question and the expected answer took time for Parsons to register before he looked up from where he sat. Tiny and Mitch started to close ranks behind where Parsons sat. DC Tatchell saw the pair close, but Mattock also saw the pair move closer. One look from Mattock, made both stop in their tracks. A wry smile on his face, as he said, 'Boys, you two should know better than try anything. Well appears I may need backup to take all four of you to the station.'

'DC Tatchell, good timing,' Mattock said, as Tatchell entered. 'DC Tatchell, make the call to the station to have backup sent.'

'No need, Sir. DI Smith is one step ahead of us, take a look outside,' Tatchell said in response.

All four of them including Mattock turned following Tatchell's gaze outside, any thoughts Gary Parsons had off talking his way out of going to the police station ended there. Opening the shop door wide, Tatchell moved aside for Helen and several other officers as backup if needed to stop any problems arising. Lastly, Dan Prescott walked in through the door. Gary seeing Dan Prescott brought no immediate recognition to mind. Mattock told Dan to wait outside until he told him otherwise. Returning his gaze onto Gary Parsons, he asked the sergeant to take him back to the station, along with DC Tatchell. Mattock deciding that Fred Carver would accompany him in his car along with another police officer to be his driver. Helen then asked to take both Tiny and Mitch back with her and another constable. Warning them both should trouble be on their minds.

Mattock requested Fred Carver to lock up. Keeping a presence of two constables outside the premises. Whilst the owner was down at the police headquarters. Tatchell drove Tiny and Mitch, back to the station for questioning. Instructing Helen to check the shop over before they left. Look for anything that could link Fred Carver to Tambling, including Gary Parsons.

Inside twenty minutes, Mattock had all parties on arrival in separate interview rooms. Ready to talk to all, Mattock instructed DC Tatchell in the meantime to ascertain if any developments had occurred, emanated from a recent raid by Special Branch on a warehouse in West Norwood earlier that night. He did not provide Tatchell with all details, wishing only to establish whether Special Branch had operatives working within in stopping the drugs haul smuggled in, or whether they were diverted to another warehouse since there departure from Sheerness. The destination for the drugs to be split; around other leading known villain's in London and leading villains further up north and corrupted ministers within Government circles.

Mattock before he spoke to Gary Parsons and Fred Carver. Told Helen to carry on with the interviews, while he had a chore in his office awaiting his attention first. Going the photos and news clippings pinned on the wall-chart. Mattock was appraising himself on the crimes as they unfolded before he went down to interview the suspects involved. The only person not down in the interview rooms was Harry Tambling.

Dan still sat around the foyer of the police station waiting for Mattock's return. He too was waiting for answers in respect of Harry Tambling and Tom Brannon. He wished to go up with Mattock to his office. Told to remain in the reception area, until called. He talked to Samantha on the mobile phone whilst walking out of the station. She confirmed that Shirley had returned to her own home. Dan said he may be out for the rest of the day and that he was down at the police station helping them with criminal developments and he would explain later. Dan asked Samantha, whether Harry before there split had confided in her to any association with a drugs ring in South London.

Silence was his response, 'Well, you have gone quiet all of a sudden,' Dan said.

'I was not quiet, I was thinking. In answer to your question, Harry never did drugs or even talked about the subject. Nevertheless, I remember on one occasion he was speaking or shouting down the phone at someone from whom he had a received a call. The word drugs never come up throughout the phone call, but he was getting more agitated the more he spoke. Could not tell what the theme of the call was over, but never knew he was a criminal himself until Shirley enlightened me to why his attitude and character changed for the worst. All I can remember was the name Hou-Lin Hoi came up,' Sam recalled.

'You sure that Hou-Lin Hoi was the name that came up?' asked Dan, adding importance to the question by speaking in a raised voice.

Sam noted the change in his voice, 'Yeah, I am sure. What has this to do with Harry now?'

'I cannot say too much now, will fill in the gaps later. Harry has himself caught up with that family somehow. I think justice will be done soon,' Dan stated. 'Will call you later,' Then Dan turned off his mobile before he re-entered the police station.

Mattock sitting across the table from Gary Parsons, alongside him sat his brief. Beside Mattock sat DI Helen Smith who had returned from the tattoo shop with Tiny and Mitch, who were booked into another interview room. Finding no evidence of drugs being on the premises. A constable stood stationed outside each room.

A knock at the door interrupted them before they began, as the constable opened the door a piece of paper, a note passed through the opening directed towards Mattock. On receipt, Mattock opened the scrap of paper revealing a message. Upon reading the note, Mattock was up and out of the room excusing himself. 'Sorry, this can't wait. Something has cropped up that needs my attention. This interview will have to be done later, unless…' looking at the officers from Brighton, 'you two wish to step in, I am sure you have questions that need an answer.'

At the reception desk, he pulled the sergeant to one side away from the front desk. 'Who handed this note in?'

'Nobody, D I Mattock, we had a call come through expressly stating we had to get a message to you. We had a call, Sir, stating that we needed to get your attention with this message to you urgently.'

'Did the caller reveal a name?' asked Matlock.

'No, Sir, it was an anonymous caller.'

Helen came up beside Mattock, having left the interview room to find out what was so urgent for Mattock to walk out. 'Sir, what's going on?'

Mattock did not say a word, just passed the note over to Helen to read. At this point, Dan appeared, looking over her shoulder, glimpsing part of the message conveyed on the note. Mattock was on the phone when they both looked up. His quarry answered on the first ring. 'What went wrong at the warehouse? I thought you said you had it covered. What part of covered did you mean?' Mattock said as he recognised the person's voice on the other end.

'DI Mattock, I am not answerable to you. The assignment just did not turn up as expected. We had no other leads as to where else they could have transported the cache to. All the leads we had of places other than the warehouse have drawn a blank also.'

'Basically, you're saying, Special Branch have fucked up,' Mattock said raising his voice.

'Mattock, all I am doing is retaining your knowledge of where else they could possibly go from your own contacts.'

'Why should I help? You let your main chance at Sheerness pass you by with not even a glimmer of an active participation, my services were of no consequence or of use earlier, your words. Now you have pissed on your own grave, my knowledge is required. I will get back to you when I have asked around. Maybe I can clear up your mess without your own interference.' Mattock hung up.

Helen with Dan and the rest the officers in the foyer stared at Mattock as he got off the phone. Not realising he had been shouting into the phone. 'Well, what is so special about Special Branch?' Calming down from his little rant, he continued, 'Helen as you can read from the note, we are back to square one. The drugs never showed up at the warehouse, as we suspected they would not. So, Mr Prescott, where do you think they have likely been taken if not the warehouse, any clue?'

'The people they arrested at Sheerness, could they likely know as to where?' he asked, Mattock replied, 'Good, call Mr Prescott. I'll get on to DI Harman. Helen, you look through the information from the warehouse notes you collated and contact your people and ask around following your visit there earlier, a few days back.'

CHAPTER 29

Mattock telephoned DI Harman of Kent Police. 'How did you go in the smuggling operation go in Sheerness.'

'Ha Ha, very funny, you must be joking... it was a complete farce from start to finish,' responded DI Harman. 'Special Branch could not make a more calamitous job of bungling an operation from my view. Told us when to make a move, turns out most of the smugglers escaped the net before we could intervene. We captured and arrested three carloads of stragglers from the heist.'

'How are the prisoners you arrested from the boat earlier on the night?' Mattock enquired.

'What prisoners? They were taken by Special Branch less than two hours since,' DI Harman replied.

'Did you speak to them before they were taken away?' he said.

'Yes, name and from where they had come from, got no answer to these questions. Customs must have been expecting them. They were camped on our premises as we arrived back with those arrested in Sheerness at our headquarters in Maidstone. No sooner out of our vans, they were escorted into one provided by customs officials and transport away,' DI Harman replied.

Unsure what was happening Mattock asked D I Harman, 'Do you know to whom you spoke to in Special Branch?'

'Come to think of it, we just assumed they were Special Branch. Shown ID Cards, more shoved in the faces of our people. So, details of Special Branch not fully identified to the individual. No name given, but knew my name and that I was on the dockside at Sheerness. Said, they had been watching us, preparing for the boat's arrival at the dock.'

Mattock played on a hunch. 'Can you describe the Special Branch official who came to you?'

The description Harman provided matched the picture in Mattock's head.

From the fax sent by Mattock, he hoped that he had made the call correct. He awaited confirmation from DI Harman; asked Tatchell to put the photo through the police data bank to check that they had not been strung along. Within moments, a photo-fit came up on screen.

Mattock smiled as the picture of the man Harman described, was that of a man he had seen and been fully acquainted with in the last week or so. Mattock looked up at Helen and Dan Prescott standing before him, the realisation that he knew and could now establish a link between several elements that have thwart him and framed an end result in his head.

'DI Harman, if I send down a picture, a photo fit of someone. Would you be so kind as to confirm whether or not this is the same person you have just described to me?'

Mattock replaced the phone onto the receiver. 'Helen, go back to the interview room. I want Gary Parsons to tell us where he has been in the last twenty-four hours. Read him his rights as he has his brief already there. Officers from the Brighton and Hove Constabulary may be still in there questioning him. You can inform them I wish to see them back in my office forthwith before they leave back to their own patch. Catch up what they have ascertained from their interview.' Mattock walked away before Helen could respond. Helen noticed the smile still ingrained on Mattock's face as he left her still in the dark as to his thoughts.

Dan Prescott standing around in the foyer near the front desk. Assumed that Gary Parsons was the key to Mattock's change in outlook. Rather than be left standing around with nowhere to go, he followed Mattock to his office. DI Helen Smith, already going about and following her given requisite.

DC Tatchell, who was talking to other detectives in the detective's outer main room to Mattock's Office, looked up on seeing Mattock approach. The smile and the wave of his hand directing him to come into his office, he left the other detectives and followed Mattock.

Only when he sat down did Mattock notice Dan Prescott in his office. 'Mr Prescott, why are you here. You should not be here without my say so. However, as you are here you might as well stay. Tatchell, take this photo of Harry Tambling and fax a copy down to the Kent Police in Maidstone, address it to DI Ken Harman. Then we just wait for the phone to ring or a text message.' Mattock smiled again. Unaccustomed to Mattock's secretive ways of not conveying everything he heard to his fellow officers. Dan could not contain himself in wishing to find out what was going on in Mattock's mind and his upbeat mood.

'I noticed your infectious smile, of someone winning the lottery. Can you fill me in on what has just been said or not said that has you in a chirpy upbeat mood?' Dan asked.

'Not so hasty, Mr Prescott, all will be revealed in due course. Just need that confirmation from our friends in Kent. Do not wish to jump to conclusions just yet, but am hopeful,' was all Mattock would reveal and say.

The wait was longer than Mattock expected. For Dan the wait was an ordeal. The wait was never ending to the extreme. Mattock again revisited the notes on his wall chart. He hummed then sang quietly to himself a tune Dan did not recognise at first. Could see why Mattock took up the choice of being a police officer over that of a singer.

The office telephone rang, making Dan jump at the unexpected sound ringing out. Mattock made no reaction to the telephone ringtone. Calmly taking the phone off its cradle and placing it to his ear. Mattock listened then responded, 'Thank you, I will be in touch later if all goes well.' The infectious smile returned, as Mattock replaced the receiver back.

'Right, Mr Prescott, every piece of the jigsaw is coming together. The only missing link is Tom Brannon, why and who was his killer. I have my suspicions, but nothing concrete, nothing set in stone to point the finger yet,' Mattock said speaking to Dan Prescott.

Terri looked at Dan. 'I told him not to get involved.'

'Then why was I asked to help?'

'My opinion was that I never thought you would create the problems in the scheme of our plans made, one reason if had spoken to Tom myself before you saw him, then I could persuade Tom to leave well alone. Let you alone investigate his inquisitive notion to actively take action,' Terri said, musing aloud, 'that was my mistake, you are better that I gave you credit. Pity the boys never completed what they had to do. When they tied, and trussed you up, they should have killed you then.'

'Terri, you know, I should have known that your family are all the same. Think you are above the law. Give you a chance to stay this side of the law and you throw it right back.'

Dan walked away as the police took them away. He stopped and said, 'Am I right in thinking it was George who made them phone calls to Samantha, impersonating me. He was always good at mimicking others.'

Terri turned about and smiled, did not say another word, remained silent as two police officers dragged her away.

Dan watched, left with his own thoughts, knowing the answer to the question inside his head. For he, having kicked out Harry from the marital home. Was drawn into help provide cover for Harry when the heat turned towards him, enabling Harry into attempting to drag Dan into his scheming and pay the price of his civil liberty being taken away. Only they never considered Dan would help the police with their enquiries, knowing Mattock as the case went on exonerated Dan from any crimes committed, providing the ideal alibi. 'My opinion was that I never thought you would create the problems in the scheme of our plans made, one reason if I had spoken to Tom myself before you saw him, then I could persuade Tom to leave well alone. Let you alone investigate his inquisitive notion to actively take action,' Terri said, musing aloud, 'that was my mistake, you are better that I gave you credit. Pity the boys never completed what they had to do. When they tied, and trussed you up, they should have killed you then.'

Late afternoon arrived as Mattock suddenly noticed the light outside the police headquarters began to fade. The lights switched off in his office and only the light from the main detective room, two shadows formed on the wall, that of himself and Dan Prescott. Mattock was formulating his thoughts from the case notes on the wall-chart when DI Shepherd and DI Tanner from Brighton Police filed into the office door entrance adding their presence. Following behind DI Helen Smith. 'Helen, switch the lights on to allow us to see one another then. Please sit down, if you can find room. Room is slightly cramped. Helen, maybe you can remain standing and listen from the doorway. Now what can you tell me from your little chat with Gary Parsons?'

The former DI Shepherd spoke first: 'He is not giving out much information, denies knowing about the blood on the floor inside his kitchen. Says he rents out his home on occasion as a holiday let. What people do in his home he has no way of knowing.'

Mattock replied, 'Is that likely, when you searched his home, did you notice any photos or clothing appertaining to the people renting the property. Whether it was long or short term just for a month. A female occupant would more likely take some keepsake to remind her of someone or relations left back home while away. Same could apply to a couple.'

'That was our logic so we have spoken to one of our colleagues in Brighton and have asked that his home be rechecked out for clues. They will apply for a warrant first

274

thing, to check his property. As to whether Gary Parsons is stringing us along, depends on what answers unfold from the house search. Also, have some DNA taken around the kitchen, bathroom and other rooms. Ascertain whether they match up with any others on our data files,' DI Shepherd stated.

'If that is the case and he is stringing you along as you say, that would beg the question, why?' Mattock mused. 'He is just delaying the guilty verdict to his committing a felony. How long will it take to follow through with your DNA testing?'

Dan sat listening to the dialogue between the two, determining in which way the dialogue was going. The talk on Gary Parsons and blood found on his property; DNA could be linked to Harry Tambling's brother George, Gary's father. 'You are aware Harry and Terri have another brother. Gary is George Tambling's son. George spends a lot of time away, rarely seen locally. Not as close to Harry as is Terri. I heard, George was living abroad, had a property out in Spain. Could be the entire family are involved with your case in one way or another,' Dan said, interrupting Mattock and DI Shepherd.

Reflecting Dan's statement, Mattock nodded his acknowledgement before answering, 'Yes, I have been made aware of another brother recently. Your point is?'

'Just saying, George could be aiding and abetting Harry in some small way,' Dan answered.

DC Tatchell ambled into Mattock's office. His face had a smug look about it. He held a medical report in his hand which he pro-offered to Mattock. 'The blood found at Gary Parsons' home is a match to that of Jerome Williams, AB rhesus negative,' he stated.

As the blood group and its significance sank in, Mattock walked out of his office. 'Right, Helen, phone the desk, have Parsons brought up to the interview room now. Is his brief still on the premises, if not inform him? In the meantime, we need to have a chat with him about recent developments, just to clear up a few facts. Would one of you two officers wish to be present?'

Thirty minutes later Mattock confronted Gary Parsons and arrested him for the murder of Jerome Williams. Helen then read him his rights. With the facts stacked up against him, the evidence overwhelming. His brief stopped Gary Parsons from saying another word.

Gary Parsons was then taken back down to a cell, while Mattock and DI Shepherd held talks as to who would take the call on Parsons. DI Shepherd insisted Gary Parsons be taken down to Brighton as the crime took place in their manor. Mattock in turn stated that he was responsible for a possible murder on his patch. Could well be three in total.

DC Tatchell and DI Helen Smith left to track down George Tambling. Given no clue to his whereabouts, last known address had yet to be ascertained starting with The Waddon. They swooped to arrest Harry Tambling, seeking out his brother George's home address from Terri Chapman who withheld this information, her stating he was still living abroad. The search widened down to Brighton, along into East Sussex and Kent, bringing in the forces of both the Metropolitan Police and Brighton Constabulary together with the Kent Police Force.

Piecing together the information from DI Harman on the outcome of the drugs drop in Sheerness to the prisoners taken by Custom Officials at Maidstone Police Station. The Customs were called and asked for details as to the prisoners' place of confinement in Kent. The CCTV cameras on the dock of Sheerness taken for examination of evidence of all taking part in the Dockside arrest of others involved. Special Branch questioned about their lack of judgement in not actively playing apart in the arrest to the warehouse fiasco, wasting resources in not collecting vital police knowledge in what had been, a conducted police search, only days before to the warehouse several days earlier. The obvious reason possibly a cover up to why the drugs shipment did not arrive as expected at the warehouse in West Norwood, was corruption within the department.

News came in from Helen to Mattock confirming they had found a large quantity of drugs on the premises of a nearby building close to The Waddon. This information surprised Mattock at the thought Harry Tambling would actually keep the drugs on his own premises and thinking Harry foolish.

Special Branch finally brought about the arrest to members of the Hou-Lin Hoi family; swooped upon at the family residence, arrested for their involvement in the drugs. Accounting and verified with footage supplied by security cameras surveillance set up alongside the dockside at Sheerness.

These self-same cameras videoed the entire scene. It was thought that the CCTV cameras were switched off. Stupidity by the Hou-Lin Hoi family and Harry Tambling clearly seen orchestrating the transfer of drugs from the boat to the waiting vans.

It was when Mattock, taking a break from the events spinning around in his head, looked up at the photo of Martin Mandrell still attached to crime wall. His eyes wandered over to a Gary Parsons snapshot, then the adjoined note to a black person being an accomplice when seen driving away with the stolen car at the Aerodrome Hotel. Gary Parson clearly captured by his tattoo markings on the CCTV snapshot as the pair drove away from the hotel. Taking the photo down from the wall-chart Mattock took a closer look at the black person. The photo he previously looked at, told him nothing. However, other snapshot, taken seconds earlier gave Mattock a glimpse of the other person's face behind the hood. His mind racing on a hunch, he took down another photo of the deceased Jerome Williams, placed them both side by side. A smile of finding the matching profiles of the two pictures revealing the two men were the same person, this confirmed that Jerome was the other person seen driving away in the stolen car.

Helen found Mattock, sitting at his desk pleased as punch. A smile creased his face. 'Why are you looking so pleased with yourself?' she enquired.

Pointing to the photographs in front of him, 'We have a match, our black person on the CCTV who drove away in the stolen car with Gary Parsons. He has been looking down at us, right over our heads all the time from our photo crime wall-chart.' Mattock turned the photo around for Helen to confirm his evidence of Jerome's part played.

'All we need is evidence that either one committed the stabbing at the hotel and tie them both up with any phone records to receiving a call from Harry Tambling on the night Tom Brannon overheard Harry's fateful conversation to tie up another loose end in this case.'

DI Shepherd has called to confirm Gary Parsons as guilty. When no record of anyone renting his property in Hove from the estate agency he submitted to being his acting agency, when out of town. Arrested for the murder of Jerome Williams. DNA and fingerprints confirmed only the two sets of prints found at Gary's Home in Hove, only Gary Parsons and Jerome Williams used the premises in the last few months. With a third charge of attempting to murder Penny Conner, pending information from telephone records.

Harry Tambling seen socialising in the social bar of the sports club. Arrested and taken to Croydon Police Station in the early hours. As nothing could be found to pinpoint him to being anywhere near the crime scenes, witnesses providing an alibi on each occasion.

One by one, the Hou-Lin Hoi family were all interviewed and charged for smuggling drugs into the country illegally, running a drugs cartel in and around South London using Harry Tambling's contacts. Harry implicated by enforced involvement due to his involvement with a family member within the close Hou-Lin Hoi family.

The courts when they were found guilty and then brought to trial. The jury, at each trial judged all guilty for various crimes, for different reasons and sentenced accordingly.

DNA confirmed Hou-Lin Hoi's family, were at the scene of each crime. Harry Tambling implication in the death of Penny Connor aiding and abetting, providing information to her assailants, to cause harm emanating in her death. Telephone calls, narrowed down to the time. Harry had called between his call to Penny Connor while at the Wetherspoons pub in Cricklewood. The next call registered, sent to Gary Parsons. Later coincided with another returned call to Harry shortly after Penny Connor died in hospital. This registered two days after the first call, each to and from the same mobile contact number. Harry charged with manslaughter with intent to murder.

Gary Parsons also found guilty, implicated in the demise of Jerome Williams. Gary's DNA found on Jerome's clothing, also on the refuge bin where Jerome's body was dumped and that of Penny Connor, at the time of death. A member of the public taking a photo of herself whilst in hospital. The photo had a background picture showing Gary Parsons walking towards her in the same corridor of Penny Connor's Ward. Coincidence that he was in the same place as Penny Connor on two different locations, each when a criminal act of violence bestowed upon the deceased.

Samantha sat beside Dan on the garden bench, each holding a cup of tea between their hands.

'You think you know someone well, but you forget when your help asked for, your own involvement in looking after your own family relations, turns on its head. That family forgets that they were in the wrong when the husband hands out his own form of punishment. In this case, Harry lashed out at you. Terri should take her anger out on Harry's troubles being the focal point of his change of character.'

'What will you do now, Dan? Will you return State side?' she asked.

Dan smiled at the prospect. 'Not right now… maybe in a year's time.'

'And Shirley, you know she cares for you,' Sam enquired.

Dan stared off into the sky, then lowered his sight as if weighing up the option. 'Maybe.'

.

Lightning Source UK Ltd.
Milton Keynes UK
UKOW04f0308191017
311248UK00001B/48/P